The Nature of Grace

The Nature of Grace

Jane Ford

Writers Club Press
San Jose New York Lincoln Shanghai

The Nature of Grace

Writers Club Press
an imprint of iUniverse, Inc.

For information address:
iUniverse, Inc.
5220 S. 16th St., Suite 200
Lincoln, NE 68512
www.iuniverse.com

While mostly inspired by actual events, the characters are fictional and any resemblance to people living or dead is coincidental

ISBN: 0-595-20225-X

Printed in the United States of America

Dedication

To my mother, who encouraged me to use my head for something more than a hat rack, and to my husband, who has patiently waited for this moment more than 18 years, with much love.

And to Trinda, Susan, Carolyn and Cheryl, with love and gratitude, because it would never have seen the light of day without their friendship and support!

Prologue
1988

"Is that Rosemary over there with Harry?"

"Yes, it is…and that ridiculous-looking man seems to be with Rosemary."

"What's she doing here, anyway? I didn't think Grace was speaking to her."

Grace Lee shivered in the crisp, bright April sunshine and fleetingly wished that hats with thick, gauzy veils were stylish again. Maybe then she could concentrate on the beauty of the eulogy being spoken a few feet in front of her and not be so sensitive to the lively gossip whispered so loudly behind her.

Impulsively, she turned to the object of the gossip and smiled. The young woman for whom it was intended, however, was discreetly studying a long line of flower arrangements and didn't catch her eye.

But a tall man at the woman's side, the one they called ridiculous-looking, returned the smile as well as a flirtatious wink. Grace blushed hotly and turned around so suddenly her chair wobbled dangerously on the uneven cemetery ground.

"Shall we pray."

Damn...Oh God, I didn't really mean damn, here in front of all these preachers and educated people here to lay Dorothy to rest. But I didn't hear a single word, God, not one word.

Dorothy.

Grace gazed at the small gray coffin almost invisible beneath a vast spray of pink rosebuds and baby's-breath. How lovely this funeral is, she thought. She wondered if Dorothy knew how many people turned out. So many of her former students, her retired colleagues statewide, those of her friends still living...but so few church members.

The observation was so unbidden Grace had to stifle another gasp.

A satin streamer in one of the many flower arrangements flapped noisily in the rising breeze. Grace shuddered then snapped alert quite suddenly as she read the writing: *Daughters of the Confederacy.*

She almost laughed but turned the impulse into a cough. How Dorothy would rage if she saw it! It was obviously from someone who hadn't known her very well because it was much too heavy for her delicate taste.

She was a rebel herself, Grace thought, and Rosemary is like her, more like her than any of her own flesh and blood.

"Amen."

Grace kept her seat while people around her hastily stood and made their ways back to waiting cars. Her husband, Harry, would be champing at the bit to hurry away and beat the traffic but he would just have to wait.

The minister stopped to shake hands and say a few words to Dorothy's nephew. Grace took advantage of the moment to really look at him. In all the years she knew Dorothy she had never met this man. Was he the one Dorothy had so tartly christened Walter Mitty?

"It's a pity Miss Dorothy never married and had children of her own," the minister's accomplished voice intoned, the magnolias nearly bursting into bloom on the soft Mississippi drawl.

"Yes."

"Did you see *Good-bye, Mr. Chips*, son? When Mr. Chips died—"

"Chipp*ing*," Rosemary interrupted.

Grace bowed her head, trying to stifle her embarrassment.

"His name was Chipping."

The minister was only momentarily distracted but recovered himself sufficiently to turn away from her. He muttered to the nephew through clenched teeth, "I was only trying to say Miss Dorothy's students were her children."

Totally confused at the undertones of repressed hostility, the nephew could only stare at the minister and Rosemary without responding. He smiled nervously and hurried, with a great sigh of relief, Grace supposed, to his waiting limousine.

The minister glared fixedly at Rosemary for a long moment then turned on his heel and left the graveside, too.

"Are you ready, Mom?"

"No. Give me a few minutes."

Grace heard car doors slam, saw various people picking their ways through the cemetery headstones, locating dead friends and family members. She caught the faintest fragrance of the pink rosebuds.

Only at the very end a few hours of unmitigated agony, then over at last, a lifetime of brilliance and service.

Grace's eyes filled with tears.

No friend of her own generation had been so influential, so supportive...so loved! Her lips twitched into a smile at the unbidden thought, To think how she terrified and confused me before I really got to know her!

1
1968

It was hot, too hot for the second Tuesday in May and Grace mopped her damp brow with a tissue as she glanced nervously at the clock. Only ten, she noted with dismay. And we're in Kentucky, not even the deep south, she thought absently.

"I have an announcement that's sure to thrill you all," Frances Taylor said with an impish grin.

Grace pushed her dark bangs off her forehead, praying Frances would spare them a guessing game.

"Dorothy Blackwell will be joining our Circle once school's out."

The collective gasp wiped Frances's grin completely away. "Now girls," she started to chide as they started talking at once.

"She's always gone to evening Circle."

"She's retiring this year, isn't she?"

"Really? I thought she'd teach until they hauled her out feet first!"

"Why does she want to join *our* Circle?"

"Wouldn't she be happier in a group with other old ladies?"

Surprised at the bitterness, Grace bit her lip anxiously as the talking grew louder and more frenzied.

"I don't think I can stand being in the same Circle with her, Frances."

"You know how she waltzes in and takes over."

"Well, we're always complaining about how disorganized we are and how someone should step in and help us out." Grace was surprised to hear her own timid voice coming to the rescue.

"Oh, Grace, really!"

"Well, our girls loved her dearly when she was their Sunday School teacher," Grace continued. "And she was the only one to get the boys to pipe down in Bible School and learn something."

"That's all well and good for children, Grace. But we're grown women. Besides, I don't like those uppity ways of hers. She thinks she's better than any of us."

Grace blushed and narrowed her dark eyes. "She's a brilliant woman."

The tension broke as one of the women laughed. "You think so because she likes your Rosie!"

That's true, Grace admitted to herself. It had been a lively year when Rosemary was the star pupil in Miss Dorothy's Sunday School class. Undefeated, she glanced around at her friends. "How can any of you seriously think of asking her *not* to join our Circle? We're the Woman's Missionary Union and it isn't Christian-spirited to be talking about one of our own old ladies like this."

Frances Taylor sighed. "Christian-spirited or not, I bet we'll never be the same again once she joins us."

*   *   *

The Southern Baptist Church was the focus of Grace's life. She and her husband, Harry, were convinced of the importance of the church being the center of a Christian life but even more urgently, the church being the center of their daughter's life.

What a happy life it was! Harry was one of the best carpenters in town, a perfectionist with the reputation of an artist. His devotion to his family and his craft was matched only by his devotion to his Junior One Department at church. As superintendent, he was responsible for the teaching of fourth and fifth graders. He had made it the best attended class in the entire church and won the plaque for excellence for five consecutive years.

Harry believed two things influenced children: a clean, safe environment and being made secure enough to know they were loved. To that end, he had an arrangement with Old Henry, the church janitor, to have the entire department spotless. Harry took it upon himself to have a detailed system of follow-up on the children in his care. If they were sick, he and their teachers were responsible for sending postcards urging their recovery. If they were very ill, he expected the teachers to visit them at home or in the hospital.

When the children were well, he expected them to attend church regularly and learn what they were taught. He supervised his teachers with the air of a dictator, refusing to allow short-tempered adults the charge of young minds.

Grace was surprised he and Miss Dorothy got along so well. She gave him many ideas for his opening exercises and he dazzled her with his endless enthusiasm for challenging the children's intellects.

They had only one quarrel between them, a hilarious story that Harry told often. Like many women, Dorothy refused to reveal her birth date. Everyone knew she was born sometime in 1903 but Harry, organized in every detail, wanted more accurate records.

When she refused his request, he told her to her face that he would tell everyone her birthday was July Fourth, 1776.

The firestorm of a nuclear explosion could not have been as furious as Dorothy's reaction. She let him know in no uncertain terms her birth date was affixed to all her legal documents and for him to know so much about her personal business was totally unacceptable.

Harry was unmoved. Every July Fourth she received a birthday card from the Junior One Department until she resigned to join a class of women her own age.

He was in his element in the Junior One Department, the star of the show. Grace sometimes felt a stab of envy, knowing she was much too timid to feel in control of so many children.

Like all good Southern Baptist men, Harry never touched alcohol but Grace frequently caught him puffing a Lucky Strike. She always scolded him for the lapse. Rosemary was allergic to cigarette smoke and dust and pet hair and everything else under the sun. In the right mood, Harry scolded right back for her fondness of potato chips and cheese puffs.

And in the middle of their good-natured carping was Rosemary, their only child, born when Grace had nearly given up, at the age of thirty, the prospect of ever becoming a mother.

Grace was unusually tense when Rosemary went through Junior One. Competitive by nature, the child was her father's delight with her knowledge of Bible questions, surpassed only by a little boy in the race to recite all sixty-six books of the Bible.

Grace suspected everyone believed Harry coached her but he never did. His own sense of honor was much too important to him.

Besides, Rosemary loved to show off. She was the smartest child Grace had ever known, even if she was her own daughter. Except for math, the horrible new math, Rosemary was an excellent student in school, too. Thinking about her, Grace sat back with eyes half-closed and a smug little smile.

Gloating, Harry called it.

'Train up a child in the way he shall go, and when he is older he shall not depart from it.' Grace believed that as firmly as she believed John 3:16, confident she and Harry were doing all the right things now so Rosemary wouldn't be sidetracked later.

Older church members had college age children and those who failed to enroll their graduating seniors in the regional Baptist college had Grace's deepest sympathy. When Rosemary was born, Grace and Harry immediately decided the Baptist college was the only choice for her and saved methodically for that day.

She suffered a few anxious moments when she realized how much less expensive the local campus of the state university was but other people, important people in the church, assured her Rosemary would never come into contact with undesirable influences at the Baptist college. She wanted Rosemary to get a college education with the proper religious emphasis. Once she graduated, she would end up on a foreign mission field doing the best work of all.

But there was another side of Rosemary, however, that Grace disliked intensely. There was a fierce competitiveness driving her, she suspected, rather than a real love of God and the Baptist church. All too often, Rosemary would take it into her head that she knew more than her Sunday School teachers. When she arrogantly tossed her blonde curls and clenched her jaw, Harry's jaw, in stubborn defiance, Grace suffered a stab of apprehension she found difficult to dispel.

Good Christians were supposed to be submissive and meek. Especially Christian women.

Rosemary was entering an awkward adolescence. Her preoccupation with drawing annoyed both Harry and Grace but their quarrels usually blew over without any trouble. "You can't make a living drawing, miss," Harry informed her bluntly, frowning at her sketches.

"Why not?" Rosemary demanded.

"You can't major in art at the Baptist college," Grace reminded her. If her plans for Rosemary were only what other church women wanted for their daughters: husbands and babies, maybe the art would be satisfactory. Rosemary, however, had a higher mission to fulfill.

But now that Rosemary was twelve and less of a little girl, the storms didn't blow over with as little fuss. On the first day of summer vacation there was a new twist to Rosemary's argument. Grace was grilling cheese sandwiches to go with their tomato soup when Rosemary suddenly turned bright blue eyes upon her.

"Mom, there are some art lessons at the university this summer. Can I—I mean, may I take them?"

"No, you may not."

"Why?"

"Because they aren't fit to take."

"Why?"

Grace almost blurted out the stories she had heard about naked models but caught herself in time. She felt guilty for snapping. "Maybe you can find something to take at the Baptist College."

"I don't want to go there."

In her shock Grace almost scooped one of the sandwiches onto the floor. "What did you say?"

"I don't want to go there. It isn't a real college."

"What do you mean, not a real college?"

"I'm going to the university. It's a real college."

Grace scrambled to recover her wits. Rosemary had been a handful when she went through her twos. She and Harry had to learn the hard way to ignore her bluster and air of command for their own survival, if nothing else. Humor did the trick when Rosemary was two. Would it work at twelve?

"You do, do you? Well, since you've just completed the sixth grade, you're certainly in a position to decide." She laughed at her own offhand solution, feeling silly for allowing Rosemary to upset her. "Do you want Coke or Seven-up?"

But in her daughter's embarrassed face was the promise of something yet to come. Grace's spirits sank as she saw it because it had all the earmarks of rebellion.

It wouldn't be so bad, Grace decided, if Rosemary didn't have Harry's jaw to clench. She was her father all over again.

*　　　　　*　　　　　*

Frances Taylor was right, Grace decided. Shortly after Miss Dorothy joined their Circle things began to change. Tiny things at first but change, nevertheless.

Before Dorothy joined them the women wore casual outfits to their monthly meetings. They were, after all, gathered in each other's homes, not the church sanctuary.

Dorothy, however, arrived beautifully dressed and impeccably groomed. Grace could have sworn she listened to the programs without moving a muscle. She never leaned against the back of her chair. She never crossed her legs. Such presence and poise rubbed off on the others quickly but Grace was annoyed when she realized she would have to dress up for summer afternoon meetings.

With the retired English teacher a permanent fixture in their church lives, Grace and her friends moved cautiously for fear of provoking the wrath of an old-maid schoolteacher. After they completed their program one hot July day and refreshments were being served, conversation moved to the exciting focal point of their lives: the new church.

"I can't wait. Parking is getting to be such a problem."

"You wouldn't find that to be so if you were more punctual," Dorothy responded at once.

Grace bit her lip. It was starting already.

Another woman merrily took up the thread. "Why, Miss Dorothy, you know we've outgrown our old place."

"Oh yes, so I hear." She paused and politely sipped her lemonade. "But I would be a great deal relieved if all of you would simply admit we're leaving because we can't endure the thought of blacks coming to our church."

A sudden hush fell over the women.

"That isn't true," Grace said with a frown.

Dorothy turned bright hazel eyes on her and her small smile caused Grace to blush. "Tell me why you're so eager to leave, Grace."

"Lots of reasons. The university is swallowing up everything in its path...the area's getting bad...our kids aren't safe there anymore. God knows Old Henry can't protect them—" She stopped abruptly. Old Henry, the church custodian, was black; a huge benign presence so long associated with their church that new members wondered if he'd been set with the cornerstone. He had been utterly trusted as long as Grace could remember.

Lately, though, the men of the church had become concerned that Old Henry was too old to be saddled with such responsibility...or was it something else?

"Harry says the place is an accident waiting to happen," she concluded.

"I daresay," Dorothy agreed. "It's a firetrap without a doubt. It seems to be quite a coincidence, though, that we're rushing to build now with all the racial tension engulfing the country."

Grace twisted in her seat. There were always people who found the dark, uncomfortable side of every issue. Miss Dorothy was obviously one of them.

"By the way," Dorothy said, turning away from Grace to glance toward the Circle president, "I would like to request special prayers for the families of Martin Luther King, Junior and Robert Kennedy."

"Miss Dorothy, there haven't been many tears shed for either of those two around here," Frances Taylor said sternly.

"I didn't ask about your personal feelings, Frances," Dorothy replied tartly. "But surely we agree that it's a horror for men to be gunned down merely for their ideas. If there are tears they should be shed for the widows and children. Such young children! How would each of you feel if someone murdered your husband?"

Grace set down her plate, feeling numb and dizzy. She had been so uncomfortable the last few years and often wondered why she was so alone in feeling the way she did. She didn't understand the purpose of segregated education, thought it was ridiculous but hadn't the courage to say so.

There were so many things the civil rights activists said that she didn't understand. Could white people really be so cruel?

Absolutely, she knew. There was never anything uttered in her presence as cruel and inhuman as that collective sigh of relief from her church friends on April Fourth, 1968, thanking God "one trouble-making nigger is dead."

And here was Miss Dorothy, older than she was by a good twenty years, an old maid schoolteacher, descended from a long line of "good" Southerners, saying some of the things she would never dare. Grace's heart leaped with the knowledge she was no longer alone.

The closing prayer was one of the stiffest and most insincere Grace ever heard. The women were so distraught about Miss Dorothy's remarks there was none of their usual long leave taking.

"Grace."

She turned to find the petite schoolteacher at her side.

"May I impose on you for a ride home?"

"Why, yes, of course, you're on my way."

Inside the roomy car, Grace felt her confidence return. She frowned at her passenger as she turned the key in the ignition. "Did anyone ever tell you that you'd catch more flies with honey than vinegar?"

Dorothy laughed throatily, the bright sunlight glinting on silver combs holding her steel-gray hair away from her delicate, heart-shaped face. "My mother used to say that to me, Grace." She suddenly glanced down, realizing she was sitting on a paper bag. "Oh dear, what have I done?"

"Oh, that's okay, it's only a magazine for Rosie."

Without asking, Dorothy retrieved the bag and reached inside.

Grace unconsciously drove faster, her heart racing.

"Oh, Grace, it's one of those dreadful teenage things!"

"It's not dreadful. Just silly."

Dorothy paused. "Why give her sour milk, my dear, when you can give her cream?"

Tears stung Grace's eyes and she took the next corner on two wheels. "She has to have something in common with her friends."

Dorothy nodded and slipped the magazine back into the bag. "I suppose that's true. But keep an eye on her. Don't let her associate too much with children whose parents have no vision."

Grace stopped abruptly in front of Dorothy's house. "No vision?" she repeated blankly.

Dorothy opened the heavy car door and lightly stepped out. "Rosemary isn't like other girls, Grace. Don't you know that?" She closed the car door and waved. "I'll see you Sunday."

Grace smiled back and turned in the driveway. It wasn't one of those days she'd enjoy discussing with Harry, that much was certain.

2

Girls' Auxiliary was the training ground for future members of the Woman's Missionary Union. Junior GAs began in the fourth grade and with their monthly program guide *Tell*, that corresponded with Grace's *Royal Service*, learned about missions and missionaries.

More so than Sunday School or Training Union, Girls' Auxiliary provided a deeply intensive program of Southern Baptist doctrine and history that was rewarded in Forward Steps. It caught Rosemary's interest at once and she plunged into her manual with gusto.

There were four Forward Steps in Junior GAs: maiden, lady-in-waiting, princess and queen, with an optional queen-in-service step for the very determined girl who was able to complete two steps in one year. It had only been done once, twenty years ago. Rosemary immediately set her mind to becoming the second girl in the church to win queen-in-service.

The maiden step was easy enough, requiring basic scripture memorization and doctrinal issues. Rosemary completed it the summer of 1966 with two girls her age, Gretchen Finny and Jill Adams.

Lady-in-waiting was slightly more difficult, detailing the structures and purposes of the Foreign and Home Mission Boards and memorization of the Beatitudes. The Beatitudes were only difficult in remembering which one came before the other but Rosemary consistently omitted "Blessed are the meek" until Grace wondered if she confused "meek" with "weak."

The princess step, however, was nearly Rosemary's undoing. She had to learn the sixty-eight countries where Southern Baptists supported missionaries and point them out on a map. It was hard work for an eleven-year-old.

Trying to learn the countries in alphabetical order hadn't worked. Then Grace devised a system for Rosemary: start with North America, work down Central and South America, cross the Atlantic, pay particular attention to the Middle East, carefully backtrack through Africa, then skip to Asia.

It was a nerve-wracking experience and the reviewing council failed to pass her. Humiliated with her first rebuff from that august body of elderly WMU members, Rosemary assaulted the map again, determined her first failure would be her last.

She did well regarding the question "What Baptists Believe:" summarizing the Triune Godhead, salvation by grace through faith, inspiration of the Scriptures, Baptism and Lord's Supper being ordinances only and the separation of church and state. Her only sticking point was the Trinity. "I know it's the Father, Son and Holy Ghost, but it's hard to explain."

"Well," Grace said, eager to help, "your father is your grandmother's son, my husband and your father. One man in three roles. Could that help?"

It obviously had. The reviewing council failed her over the confusion of the sixty-eight countries, not doctrine.

She passed the reviewing council the second time and in the summer of 1967 credited two steps to her account, well on her way to the elusive queen-in-service. In her sixth-grade year Rosemary had started the queen step.

It was very difficult, Grace realized. Girls had to memorize the entire thirteenth chapter of First Corinthians as well as mastering the story of Queen Esther to the point of answering any trivial details the reviewing council might ask.

It was enough to put off the stoutest heart.

If the GA passed her reviewing council she received the privilege of wearing a long white dress for the August recognition ceremony. Grace had the sinking feeling the white dress, not the subject matter, was Rosemary's sole incentive for the queen step.

*   *   *

During the school year the girls met on Wednesday nights during Prayer Meeting but in summer they met on Thursday mornings in the church sanctuary, dedicating three hours a week to learning their Forward Steps. Some sat quietly with their King James Editions opened to required passages. Others recited to sympathetic ears.

Rosemary sat alone on a creaky wooden pew, her Bible open to the thirteenth chapter of First Corinthians. She'd had enough of Saint Paul for the moment and busied herself sketching Gretchen Finny.

There was very little in the old church that hinted at beauty with the exception of the stained-glass windows and the baptistery painting. The worn burgundy velvet curtains were open and the morning sunshine was bright enough to illuminate the painting without artificial lighting. The scene was tranquil in soft muted colors: a simple rolling meadow with a brook, grazing sheep and in the sky above, the faintest pastel mist of the Cross.

The stained-glass windows were delicately colored, too, giving the old sanctuary natural light even on the darkest days. New

Testament symbols: the Alpha, the Omega and the Dove shone brightly.

The light from the windows fell on a rather threadbare sanctuary. The carpet running down the center aisle was as dilapidated as the baptistery curtains, exposing between the pews scuffed and creaking wooden floors. The unpadded pews squeaked and groaned every time a person moved in them. The pew backs showed the artwork of petty vandals long since reformed and grown. The racks for hymnals and Lord's Supper glasses were loose.

But it was home to three hundred members of the congregation and was loved for all its squeaks and decay. No one suggested expensive repairs.

In eighteen months they would be in their new church.

"Rosie?"

Rosemary glanced up from her sketchpad to find Jill Adams scooting into the pew beside her. "Yep?"

"Will you listen to my Beatitudes?"

"Sure."

Jill handed her the Bible with the marked passage and looked at the baptistery wall. "We'll only have this year and next year here. I wonder if our new church will be as pretty."

Rosemary paused before answering. "I don't know. If it looks like this, sure. Our windows will make it home."

Jill smiled, sighed and took a deep breath. "Okay, here goes. 'And seeing the multitudes, He went up into a mountain…'"

*   *   *

The August recognition ceremony was lovely. Rosemary, in her long white dress, looked as smug and proud as if the GA crown she received for her hard work was a diamond tiara, not a simple green and gold, heavy-duty paper circlet. The GA octagon in front had *GA* printed on it. Very appropriate, Grace thought, for little girls.

At the reception Grace watched as Rosemary talked with other girls and overheard their conversation.

"Will you be doing queen-with-a-scepter next year, Rosie?"

"Nope. Next year I'll be a queen-in-service."

"No one does that," one of the older girls said haughtily.

Rosemary carefully tossed her curls, managing not to upset her crown. "That's because no one else did queen step with a year left in Junior GAs. But I will."

The older GA daintily sipped her fruit punch. "We'll see."

Rosemary caught the challenge at once and grinned. "Yes. You will."

*   *   *

Building a new church required more than a financial commitment from its members. Pressure was on to grow the congregation. Grace volunteered a day of her time to canvass the neighborhood around the new church.

The kids, restless before school started, joined their mothers for the day. Grace knew Rosemary's heart wasn't in it but today she would have to leave her friends at the public pool and learn that church work often involved a sacrifice of time.

"You don't know how nice it will be for these kids around the new church to feel welcome to join us," Grace said with gusto.

"I don't see why anyone has to be invited to go to church," Rosemary argued. "If they aren't totally blind they can see what's being built."

"It's a nice thing to do," Grace muttered through clenched teeth, rounding the corner on two wheels. She noticed Rosemary glowering at the construction site. "Now what's wrong?" she demanded.

"It's awful," Rosemary grimaced. "There aren't any trees."

"It used to be a corn field."

"Still looks like one, too."

"Rosemary," Grace warned.

"Look at the houses here, Mom. Everybody's place looks the same."

"How can you sit there and judge people by their houses?"

"I'm not judging anyone—"

"Yes, you are."

"No, I'm not. Look at the houses around our old church. The trees are tall, the flowers are gorgeous...there are porches with swings."

Unwillingly, Grace called to mind the stately old street that was still home to their church. Children's minds were so strange. Rosemary either didn't see or didn't care that those old homes were dangerously dilapidated, the original owners long dead, rooms rented piecemeal to characters growing more unsavory with each passing year.

"This place has no charm," Rosemary said matter-of-factly.

Grace laughed merrily.

Rosemary glared at her and held onto the dashboard as Grace bumped into the makeshift parking lot. "Mom, why are we always the first people to get anywhere?"

"Because it's rude to be late," Grace explained, bringing the car to a squeaking halt.

"It's so hot out here," Rosemary complained.

Grace jerked the key out of the ignition and turned to her daughter. "My little missy, I've had just about as much out of you as I'm going to take. If you don't straighten up right now you won't be going back to the pool this year."

Rosemary sucked in her lower lip and glared straight ahead.

I had the last word, Grace thought triumphantly. Then with a bit of fear hastily added to herself, at least for now!

*   *   *

Rosemary and Gretchen Finny, friends since they were on the cradle roll, worked as a team that day. Gretchen, like Rosemary, had grown up in the church and was in all the same programs. Grace was grateful for Gretchen and was glad they were close since Rosemary had no siblings.

Even now they got along well but Grace noticed how different they were and wondered if those differences would come between them later on. Gretchen loved to have fun and was beginning to notice the boys. Rosemary was content to curl up with art books and sketchpads and watch *Star Trek*. She's a loner, Grace realized dismally.

As the two girls delivered handbills door-to-door in the late August heat Grace caught sight of them frequently and wondered how they fared.

Returning volunteers had many comments. The church would need a large nursery because almost every family was a young one. A larger young adult classroom should be added to the building plans.

Grace smiled with pleasure. Young families were the lifeblood of a church.

Gretchen and Rosemary finally returned. Gretchen turned sad eyes on Grace. "There aren't many guys our age around here."

Behind her friend's back Rosemary rolled her eyes in mockery. Grace took the leftover handbills, boxed them and locked them in the trunk of her car. She noticed Rosemary standing alone in the lot, watching the construction. "What impressions did you get, miss?"

"They aren't Baptists, Mom."

"That's good."

"I meant you're going to have to get more teachers to tell these people what's what."

Grace fought to repress a grin.

"And Mom, we're going to have to be careful."

"Why?"

"A lot of these people will use us as baby-sitters."

"What makes you think so?"

"Oh, you should see how interested everyone is in Sunday School and stuff. For their kids."

"Are you sure?"

"You always told me church should be a family thing."

"Yes."

"Well, you're going to have to set some rules."

Grace stifled another laugh. "About who can come and who can't?"

Rosemary blushed. "Not exactly."

"Try not to worry, Rosie."

Rosemary only scowled.

"You and Gretchen did a good job today."

"Gretchen's looking for a boyfriend."

"Aren't you?"

"Nope. I want to be a great artist," Rosemary declared and turning into a child again, "and marry Leonard Nimoy."

"There's a difference in that line of argument, I take it?"

"Gretchen likes boys," Rosemary explained with a flourish. "I prefer men."

Grace could control her laughter no longer. That's one, she promised herself, I'll remember until my dying day. My daughter prefers men!

*   *   *

If Dorothy hadn't joined her Circle Grace supposed she would have considered nothing else the entire summer but the building of the new church. As it was, she found herself reading her newspaper from front to back, watching the evening news with much more care and listening to news commentaries on the radio.

It did much more than inform her, she soon realized. It was wonderful to share a conversation with someone as intelligent as Dorothy. The older woman's opinions were fascinating and although Grace was not as provocative, she found herself agreeing with Dorothy's position again and again.

Politics was as sacred a subject to the older woman as religion and Grace felt the thrill of power, as well as the fury of frustration, as the summer of 1968 unfolded in all its horror.

"Mom."

Grace blinked to clear her head, remembering Rosemary was reading an orientation guide for junior high school. "Mmm?"

"I don't want you coming to school with me on Tuesday."

Grace gasped and felt tears start at her eyes. "I always go with you to registration, Rosie."

Rosemary pointed to the paper. "I'll be in junior high, Mom. Besides, this thing says I'll only need two checks, one for my locker and one for a lab fee. So why should you go?"

Grace swallowed hard. "Well—"

"I need to get used to riding the bus."

"Yes," Grace agreed. Perhaps it wouldn't look good, she thought, if I insist on driving her as if I think she's too good to ride the bus with other kids. Six years ago I cried when she started to school and didn't seem at all upset to be separated from me. In another six she'll start to college...where do the years go?

"Mom, will Hubert Humphrey be the next President?" Rosemary suddenly asked.

"I hope so, honey. Why?"

"People say Democrats start wars."

Grace set down a glass of iced tea with such a bang the fluid spilled over her hand. "Rosemary, a lot of stupid people say a lot of stupid things."

It obviously hadn't answered the question.

"Congress declares war, Rosemary. Congress is made up of both Democrats and Republicans and I haven't noticed too many Republicans backing down from a fight these days."

Rosemary looked puzzled.

Grace shook her head. "You'll learn about it in civics."

"That's ninth grade," Rosemary informed her.

Grace smiled.

"So when people tell me Democrats start wars—"

"Just ignore them."

"But if they're lying—"

"They aren't always necessarily lying, Rosie."

Rosemary paused. "Tell me, Mom. Can you ignore them?"

Grace fought a guilty blush. "Not always," she confessed. "Rosemary, I want you to concentrate on doing well in school and in church. You don't have to grow up so quickly."

Rosemary shrugged and looked disgusted. "Oh, you mean boys."

Grace grinned. "Boys, too. But enjoy being a kid. There's plenty of time for everything else."

3

Rosemary eagerly started junior high school and Grace was relieved the transition from elementary school into such a different environment was an easy one. During the first week Rosemary complained about the lack of recess but stopped abruptly when the teenagers at church teased her.

In the meantime Grace found herself looking forward to the monthly Circle Meetings and other church functions in which Dorothy participated. She felt a little guilty about enjoying Dorothy's company so much. Mission work and church education were once her driving forces and though they were still important, Dorothy had so many interesting things to say she forgot about them. The older woman seemed interested in Grace's opinions, as well.

After their Circle Meeting the two women went to lunch. Grace laughed as she told Dorothy about Rosemary's comments on the people around the new church.

Dorothy sat very quietly before responding. "In a way, she's right, Grace."

"What do you mean?"

"Think about it, dear. Some of these people have had only limited exposure to church. Those of us brought up in a church atmosphere are grounded in Bible, in doctrine...can you imagine how bewildered they'll be when they realize we expect them to know what *we're* talking about?"

"Isn't that what adult education is all about?"

"Some of these people will only have been to Christmas and Easter services. We expect more of a commitment. It's going to be very hard for them to understand why."

"If lots of them come we aren't prepared, are we?"

"No, indeed. You can't exactly reward an adult with a piece of candy for knowing the weekly Bible verse."

Grace chuckled. "Rosemary was depressed. She thinks the entire situation is hopeless."

"She isn't happy about the move to the suburbs, is she?"

"No. She told me the new site has no charm."

Dorothy grinned. "When we moved to our present location I thought it was highly unattractive, too. Tell her so."

"Oh, were you part of the first church?"

"Yes, my mother carried me there as a baby. Now that was a church with a great deal of charm." Dorothy paused a moment and sighed. "Tell Rosemary it's far better to leave a church willingly than to be burned out like we were back in '26. A church fire is the worst fire."

Grace honored her silence a long moment then gently pressed ahead. "You've seen so many changes. And so many preachers."

The usual spark of fire again brightened Dorothy's eyes. "Oh yes," she replied, "and if I live a few more years, I daresay I'll see more. Tell me, is there any truth to the rumor Brother Bradshaw will leave by the end of the year?"

Dorothy's hostility toward their minister momentarily shocked Grace. "I don't know."

"I'm so weary of ignorance in the pulpit. I'd have moved my letter long ago but I refuse to be chased off by such a fool."

"He's a good man," Grace offered in his defense.

Dorothy tossed her head haughtily. "Being good isn't enough. These are difficult days, Grace. We need an intelligent man with a cool head to see us through."

Yes, Grace found herself agreeing, there were too many Sundays when Brother Bradshaw used a membership drive as a sermon topic. It seemed the contest wasn't so much about saving souls as competing with their sister churches.

He got so worked up! It wasn't proper for Southern Baptists to rant and rave. That sort of behavior was for lesser Baptists and Pentecostals.

"What do you think of the organizational changes scheduled for next year?" Dorothy suddenly asked. "Have you seen what they plan to do to WMU?"

"No, but I've seen what they plan for Girls' Auxiliary."

"You don't sound optimistic."

Grace twisted in her chair. "Rosemary will hate it. Since there won't be any more Forward Steps, I doubt she'll go. I'm beginning to think the only reason she went in the first place was to lord it over Gretchen and Jill."

"Grace!"

"If she did it for love of the Lord would she be so interested in competition?"

"She prefers a classroom. Instead of pushing her to be like Gretchen and Jill, maybe you should encourage the part of her that loves to study. She would make a wonderful teacher, you know."

"I want Rosemary to go the mission field."

Dorothy raised one delicate brow and measured Grace carefully with her hazel eyes. "*You* want?"

"Or nursing."

"I can't imagine her as a nurse," Dorothy said coldly.

"Why not? She's smart enough—"

"Of course she is. But if nursing or the mission field were on her mind, Grace, I think she would have said something by now."

Grace breathed quickly; embarrassed Dorothy seemed to be more in tune with Rosemary than she was.

Dorothy smiled suddenly. "Is she enjoying youth choir?"

Grace snapped herself back to attention. "Oh yes, she loves the choir even though she can't sing a note. She and Gretchen and Jill feel very grown-up."

Dorothy laughed. "What do they think of all those older boys?"

"So far, Rosemary isn't interested. She told me Gretchen likes boys but she prefers men."

Dorothy's laughter, turning quickly from delight to tearful guffawing, brought disapproving glares from restaurant patrons. Grace smiled, too, glad she'd struck such a chord.

"Prefers men," Dorothy repeated and collected herself. "Has her art class started yet?"

"No, next quarter."

Dorothy collected her bill. "If you and Harry have no objections I'd like to loan Rosemary a few of my books. They're photographic collections of ancient art."

"Ancient...all those headless naked things?"

"Why, Grace Lee, I daresay your daughter has seen very much the same thing at the public pool this summer," Dorothy scolded. "I didn't think you were such a prude, my dear."

Grace's face went scarlet. "I—I—"

"Talk it over with Harry and decide," Dorothy suggested calmly but Grace noticed her smile was about to turn into another burst of laughter.

*   *   *

Grace forgot momentarily about the art books. The Democratic Convention in Chicago consumed her attention. The riots, the divisiveness—dear God, where would it end?

"I'm voting for Nixon," Harry declared furiously.

Grace gasped.

"I am, I swear to God. Another Democrat will be the end of us. We need the law on those damned draft-dodging kids."

"The law? Or the army?"

"Whatever it takes."

"On our own kids, Harry? Is that what you're saying to me?"

"All that long hair and filth—"

Grace pulled herself up to her full height. "Jesus Christ didn't wear a pinstripe suit, you know."

Harry's mouth flew open.

Grace pressed her advantage. "And let me tell you something else, Harry Lee. If Rosemary were a boy I'd take her to Canada myself before I'd send her to Vietnam!"

Harry recovered himself somewhat. "Have you said this to any of our friends?"

"No, but if they push me I will. So there."

"My God—"

"I won't listen to anymore," she cried, feeling she would never have had the nerve to speak out if it weren't for Dorothy's influence.

She shivered in the late summer heat. It wasn't good to feel so cut off from things she'd once believed.

              *   *   *

The most frightening aspect of the political turmoil was Grace's feeling of isolation. Time and again she wondered why Harry didn't see and feel the same things she did. Besides the frustration there began to grow, deep inside, a small bubble of discontent. She grew more uncomfortable with her old friends and their ideas and was embarrassed she was ever as naive as she was now convinced they were.

The dissatisfaction grew deeper. For years her political thinking was shaped by her religious convictions. She was fervently patriotic and an old Democrat. Her parents worshipped Franklin Roosevelt. Grace believed the victory of the Second World War was not only a military masterpiece but the product of Divine Will, as well.

In the wake of the victory the establishment of Israel was, for a Southern Baptist, the proudest moment of American foreign policy. Baptist youth were raised on the admonition that to mistreat the Jews was to thwart God; therefore it was the duty of all Christians to support Israel. To do otherwise was unthinkable. How could Christians, real Christians, stand in the way of God's chosen people?

Naively, Grace assumed anti-Semitism would never again rear its ugly head. Didn't the world know by now that any people who oppressed the Jews were themselves ingloriously conquered?

It was quite another thing, however, to raise her voice to complain about her community's treatment of its black citizens. Why did Harry, upon his discharge from the army, enjoy so many benefits black veterans did not? Why were the terms of their mortgage explicit in forbidding blacks to live in their neighborhood?

For a little while she succeeded in stifling her conscience. Marriage, a home and finally Rosemary herself filled Grace's every waking minute. She threw herself into her role of homemaker, mother and church-worker with delirious abandon.

The Woman's Missionary Union was her favorite church activity. She loved the stories of missionaries who risked life and limb to go abroad for Christ. Her heart ached for those without Jesus.

She never tired of the stories, never failed in her prayers and gave God the use of Rosemary for His instrument.

She had no such tolerance for Home Missions. Southern Baptists didn't preach a social gospel and the home missionaries, as much as she respected their dedication, smacked of the Salvation Army to her and she didn't approve. Christianity that had to be bribed with food and financial assistance was suspect. She saw no reason to change her mind about people who rejected God and were perfectly free to worship.

But there were others in the world, especially the poor Russians, who were forbidden to worship and Grace wept for them. Communism was the work of anti-Christ. No freedom at all. There was something breathtakingly exotic about the thought of living someplace where it was forbidden to worship.

The few foreign missionaries Grace met patiently explained it wasn't only in Russia that such awful things went on. Spain and Brazil rigidly controlled Protestant missionaries and their activities. Some of the horror stories enforced what she'd been raised on: the Catholic Church was a greater instrument for evil than for good.

She believed that, without question, until John Kennedy ran for President. Not so much Kennedy himself but his mother broke the first barrier, causing Grace to think about Catholics in a truly objective light. What a fine woman Rose Kennedy was!

When it came time to vote, Grace found herself supporting Rose Kennedy's son with a zeal that surprised her. When Kennedy won, Grace looked back on the experience with amazement. How had she found the nerve to vote against the Baptist church?

She never regretted it.

*   *   *

It seemed she would have to find the same sort of nerve again because things were changing. There was no trick left to keep the outside world from knocking on her front door. Try as she did, she could no longer ignore the troubles.

Her fury with Harry dissipated slowly. She was certain something was going on she didn't know, or Harry, either, for that matter but the college students knew. They needed baths very badly but they were brave and they knew something Grace did not.

Her thoughts cycled to the blacks and the Civil Rights Movement. Grace decided, long ago, that young black veterans who came home in 1945 should have had everything Harry did: the same housing opportunities, the same educational opportunities for their children she and Harry had for Rosemary. All the kids should have gone to the same schools and the same swimming pools together. They were never going to be one nation until the segregation stopped.

She was furtively pleased with her expanding conscience and looked forward to telling Dorothy about it. Before she had the chance, however, God decided to test her new mind-frame. She again knew the twisting in the wind that came of a growing conscience housed in timid flesh.

The university's fall semester started in late August. Along with many other college students seeking their old church as a home-away-from-home came Will Cummins.

Will was the first black to set foot in their church besides Old Henry. And somehow Old Henry didn't seem to count.

Grace could almost see the lines of support and opposition forming before her very eyes. The adults held their tongues and refused to smile with the exception of a very few...but the kids!

Those college age didn't seem to notice Will was black or if they did, ignored the fact. Younger teenagers wavered momentarily, awaiting their parents' permission to be friendly. If not forbidden to associate with him, they plunged ahead fearlessly.

Rosemary, along with Gretchen and Jill, accepted Will as another college guy. But the reason for Rosemary's total acceptance slipped before long.

"Mom, you should see how he draws. He's an absolutely perfect artist! He's fascinated with the painting in the baptistery and said Mr. Todd was a genius. What do you think of that?"

Grace smiled wanly, glad Rosemary felt the way she did but fearful, too.

One Sunday morning as Grace walked through the church basement on her way to class, she heard the four-year-old beginners loudly lisping *Jesus Loves the Little Children.* The words flooded back to her: "Red and yellow, black and white, they are precious in His sight, Jesus loves the little children of the world."

The four-year-old beginners, Grace was certain, were far closer to the truth than the adults.

* * *

While Grace tensely watched events unfold around her, Rosemary received Dorothy's art books and began an obsession with painting. "Mom, if you and Daddy haven't already planned my Christmas stuff all I want is a set of oils."

"Well, we'll see. How will your grades look by then?"

"I bet I get an A in everything but math and home ec."

"What's the matter with home ec?"

"It's stupid."

It was Rosemary's catch phrase lately. It annoyed Grace when she first heard it and now—"Well, you'll be the stupid one, little miss, if you don't master those skills. One day you'll be living on your own doing your own cooking and sewing."

"How am I supposed to cook when you won't let anyone in the kitchen?"

Grace sighed and counted to ten. Rosemary certainly had her there. She had a routine in her home, abhorred disorder and the thought of a child in her kitchen was more than she could bear. "Rosie, if you can read, you can cook," she declared, turning to the stove and stirring her green beans.

Rosemary became engrossed in the art book again. "I should really do something nice for Miss Dorothy for letting me borrow these," she said impulsively.

Grace turned around with a smile.

"I'd like to paint a picture for her, Mom. Do you think we could get that old picture of the first church from the preacher's office?"

Grace stared at her, amazed at the detail of her plan.

"I'll have to do it in colored pencils, of course."

"Oh yes, of course," Grace agreed, trying not to laugh at Rosemary's serious tone.

"Would Daddy make me a picture frame?"

"If you ask I'm sure he'll be glad to." Grace covered the beans and joined Rosemary at the kitchen table. "What do you think of the books?"

"They're great!" Rosemary turned to a color plate of Renaissance sculpture. "How did those guys ever hack this stuff out of solid marble, Mom?"

Grace took the book from her, gazing at the extraordinary work. "Talent."

"I wonder if I'll ever be able to do anything like that."

Grace glanced up. "You're still determined about the art, aren't you?"

"Yes, *ma'am*."

The added ma'am was emphasis enough.

"You don't have to worry, Mom. Career education is ninth grade."

"Oh." Grace stood and gathered the books. "It's time for you to set the table."

Rosemary made a face.

Grace sighed. It obviously didn't matter if career education was a ninth grade subject. Rosemary seemed so determined. Maybe by 1974 the Baptist College would have something for her.

*   *   *

"I hear Rosemary created quite a stir last Sunday, Grace."

"What was she up to? She tore through the hall looking like Harry in a rage."

"I can't begin to tell you how embarrassed I was, Grace. I had family in for the weekend. How was I supposed to tell them it was *your* daughter who actually grabbed a member of the building committee by the tie?"

"I never thought I'd hear a child of yours speak so sharply to an adult."

Grace sank deeper into her chair, her head spinning, her heart racing. It was here, at last, what she'd dreaded since opening prayer. The last amen had scarcely bounced off the ceiling when they turned on her.

All day Sunday and yesterday, too, her phone rang off the hook. How such news made the rounds so quickly she never knew but she was sure she'd heard from every member in the church. They demanded answers and she stammered and tried to soothe them but today—

—Today she'd expected a reprieve. It was Circle Meeting, after all. How could she go over it another time?

Dorothy's piping voice rose above the din. "Rosemary and her friends had just discovered we won't be taking along our beautiful stained-glass windows to the new church."

"Windows? All that hullabaloo about windows?"

"Wait," another voice said. "Weren't those windows made special for us, hand made or something, by one of the charter members?"

"Yes, that's right," Dorothy replied.

"I didn't know our windows were anything special."

"Why didn't someone tell us?"

"We *should* take them to the new church."

"Yes, I can't imagine sitting anyplace but by the Omega window."

"Is that what that thing is? It always looked like a horseshoe to me—"

"Good heavens, whoever heard of such a thing? The Alpha and the Horseshoe?"

Nervous laughter rose thinly but Grace, weak from the scolding and apprehension, felt sick. She glanced at Dorothy.

"It's too late, I fear," the older woman said softly. "The art department at the university purchased them. We'll have new ones. Something very modern, I'm told."

The silence fell heavily. Grace felt a stir of anger. "That's what Rosie was so upset about," she explained. "She went about it all wrong and is being punished for being so obnoxious but she was furious because the windows were sold right out from under us—"

"Which they were!" someone interrupted.

"That's why she acted so bad...ly," she concluded, remembering her adverb.

"What else is the building committee doing we don't know about?"

While Dorothy updated them, Grace rested her head and closed her eyes. It was over. Thank God for her today, she thought with relief. She not only helped me explain about Rosemary but turned the tide in her favor, too. They're alike, those two. I wonder if Dorothy was much like Rosie when she was twelve?

Had that dignified, sophisticated old woman ever been a child?

Grace rubbed her throbbing head. It was all so complicated. She expected the usual struggle with a growing daughter: boys and clothes and telephone time. It didn't seem to be shaping up that way at all.

Nothing, as a matter of fact, was going the way Grace thought God should arrange things. She was so shocked when Richard Nixon won the election, although Dorothy was the only other person she knew, beside herself, who voted for Hubert Humphrey.

Why didn't other people see what she and Dorothy saw?

*   *   *

Rosemary completed the colored pencil work shortly before Thanksgiving and Harry made a red cherry frame for it. The two of them decided to invest in a piece of non-glare glass and only the very best of picture-hanging materials.

"I can't decide how to sign it," Rosemary announced, looking at her work for the hundredth time.

Harry grinned over her head. He'd watched the project with interest, recognizing his daughter's artistry as his own talent in another medium. It flattered him to be consulted on the project.

But he'd earlier said to Grace, "She's looked at the picture of the Leaning Tower of Pisa too long. The poor old church kind of leans—"

"Harry Lee, that picture is very good!"

"Yes, it's good…it just…leans."

After that, Grace could scarcely look at the picture without wanting to laugh, too.

Now it was complete save the signature. "How about a pretty little rosebud, baby?" Harry suggested.

Rosemary took the grin off his face with a scorching glare. "I am *not* a rosebud or even a rose. I'm Rosemary," she coolly declared.

"How about some classy initials? R.S.L. would look nice," Grace offered.

"Everybody does that," Rosemary sighed.

"Oh," Grace replied, almost as shaken as Harry.

"Mom, let me see your cookbook for a minute. Please."

Grace reached for the heavy volume. "What are you looking for?"

"I want to see the part on herbs."

"That's pronounced 'erbs, dear," Grace corrected.

Rosemary opened the cookbook to a color plate and smiled. "That's it. A leaf of rosemary. I'll use that." She started a practice sketch on a note-pad.

Harry smiled again, his faith restored. "This is a first. In a few more years we'll see that sprig of rosemary everywhere."

"Very funny," Rosemary muttered to herself. "You'll feel kind of silly when it *does* show up in great museums, won't you, Daddy?"

Harry laughed, not catching the challenge but Grace had a sick feeling it would probably happen. It would be her luck to send her daughter to the fleshpots of Paris for art rather than a foreign mission field where she belonged.

*   *   *

Harry never received the week off between Christmas and New Year's Day so the Lees stayed home over the holidays. Grace loved Christmas dearly but wasn't especially taken with New Year's Eve.

It was their tradition to celebrate quietly with friends, sharing each other's leftovers, talking until a few minutes past midnight to wish everyone a Happy New Year then race home quickly, ahead of the drunks.

New Year's Day, in Grace's opinion, was the biggest waste of a holiday on the calendar. Every year Rosemary frantically attacked her homework, having ignored it until the last minute and Harry napped all day.

It left Grace with all the tidying and putting away of the Christmas gifts. What a forlorn chore!

She sat down in her rocker and examined the colorful chaos in front of her. No one ever made a mistake buying books for her. Gothic novels, historical fiction, crime dramas, biographies of movie stars, she loved them all and her family readily indulged her tastes. But she'd recently caught Rosemary thumbing through some of her books and wondered if it were time to start censoring the reading material. It seemed so hypocritical but there were certain subjects unfit for a child. Unfit for her, too, probably, as she remembered defying her own mother and reading *Forever Amber*.

The newest member of Rosemary's Barbie family caught her attention and she relived the horrible moment when Rosemary opened the package. Harry was mercifully distracted opening his own gift and was spared the lightning-quick expression of shock and indignity that she would receive a doll in her first year of junior high school.

It was the last doll, Grace realized, tears welling in her eyes. This year the inexpensive set of oils won the day and poor Barbie spent the entire holiday perched rather miserably on the drab gray tie Harry's colleagues had given him.

Soon there would be Christmas presents from boys under the tree and clothes and jewelry and perfume.

"Mom?"

Grace whisked her tears away and glanced up to find Rosemary watching her. "Yes?"

"Will you hand me the doll?"

"Are you going to play with it, after all?"

"No, I'm going to use her as my model."

Model...the art again!

"All artists have models, Mom."

"You'll need to put those oils up soon, Rosemary. They smell up everything and I'm getting a headache."

"But, Mom—"

"You heard me. Is your homework finished?"

"Yes."

"Good. Take your things. After supper we'll strip the tree."

"Let's leave it up until the weekend."

"No. I want everything done so we can be back in our routine tomorrow."

"We should leave the tree up until Epiphany."

"...Until what?"

"Twelfth Day."

"It won't last eleven more days."

"Not January Twelfth. The twelfth day after Christmas. January Sixth."

Grace frowned at her.

"When the Wise Men found the Baby Jesus."

"What Catholic stuff have you been reading?"

"Not Catholic...well, sort of, I guess...it's from an Episcopalian."

"What Episcopalian?"

"Melanie said her family always leaves the tree up until Epiphany."

"Who's Melanie?"

"A girl on my bus stop. She's in eighth grade. All advanced classes, too, even math."

Grace rocked in her chair, moistening her lips. A new friendship. That was why she and Gretchen were drifting apart. It was because of this other child, this Episcopalian child. "Why don't you invite her home after school, Rosie? The two of you can play—"

Lord, there it was again, that look of righteous indignation!

"—Watch television, I mean."

"I'll ask her when she gets back."

"She's not here?"

"Her grandparents live way down south."

"Oh."

"Well, can we leave the tree up?"

"Until the weekend," Grace bargained.

Rosemary smiled and scooped up the Barbie doll. "G'night, Mom."

*   *   *

It was amazing how quickly Rosemary was changing, all due to Melanie's influence, no doubt. Grace had no idea what to expect when Melanie visited and was somewhat taken aback by the tall girl who strolled in the door behind her daughter.

Melanie's background disturbed Grace in a way she found difficult to explain. Rosemary raved about the marvelous collection of books in her house and complained it was in a constant state of disarray. She keenly noted Episcopalians were very different from Southern Baptists but, Grace grieved, wasn't as shocked as she should have been.

Grace found herself almost in tears when she finally unburdened herself to Dorothy. "I really want her to stop seeing that little girl. But she's such a nice little girl."

"Don't interfere, Grace," Dorothy warned.

"All that talk about Epiphany."

"Rosemary should have a working knowledge of other denominations. Knowing the history of Christianity and its fine points is a good thing."

"She's too young—"

"No," Dorothy declared emphatically, "she is not. The sooner she's exposed to differences, the sooner she'll reconcile them."

"What if she doesn't?"

Dorothy smiled. "Well, I wouldn't want an automaton for a daughter. There should be differences in your thinking, Grace. It's only natural."

Grace clenched her teeth. "I don't want any differences."

To her surprise Dorothy laughed at her. "I'm sure you don't. But it will happen whether you like it or not."

"Rosemary's not thirteen yet and I already hate the teenage years."

Dorothy paused a moment before continuing. "As a high school teacher, I saw such different sides of children. I like them as they start to mature and think. I could see the adults they would become. Is that what's bothering you, Grace? Are you suddenly aware Rosemary is growing up?"

"Oh, I don't know. She's beginning to ask questions I don't have answers for. I don't like that."

"If she asks a question and you don't know the answer, tell her so."

"How can I? She'll think I'm stupid!"

Dorothy blinked in surprise. "Stupid? There is a world of difference between stupid and ignorant, my dear. No one knows everything."

"It isn't easy to admit that to a child, that I don't know the answers, I mean."

"Find answers together," Dorothy suggested. "I think you'd both enjoy that. Such a project would bind you not only as mother and daughter but as two women pursuing similar interests."

Grace could only stare blankly. It was impossible to think of Rosemary on the threshold of womanhood.

"Find a common interest, Grace. It may mean all the difference in the long years ahead."

"I'll think about it."

"You could start by reading something about Epiphany." Dorothy went into another peal of laughter at the sight of Grace's grimacing face.

*   *   *

Melanie and Rosemary were inseparable. It finally dawned on Grace that Melanie shared Rosemary's passion for art. They loved the wretched serial, *Dark Shadows*, and raced home every day after school to watch it. They discussed every detail carefully and offered their own ideas about characters and story lines.

It was hero-worship on Rosemary's part, Grace decided. Melanie came from a very educated family. Her father was a professor at the university and represented a world of culture Grace resented since it seemed to have turned Rosemary's head so completely.

Melanie was many things Rosemary was not. She was tall and thin, graceful and dainty and cultivated an aura of mystery. In

very little time she would turn heads with something more allur-
ing than beauty.

And she could sing. "An absolutely gorgeous voice," Rosemary
said. She tried every trick up her sleeve to get Melanie to join her
youth choir but Melanie always politely refused.

"You should be more concerned about her religion," Grace
chided. "You know it's nothing but ritual."

Rosemary frowned. "We've talked about it, Mom. You know
what she told me?"

Grace clenched her teeth, bracing herself against the heresy she
knew she was going to hear. "What?"

"If it was as obvious as I claimed, every smart person in the
world would believe the same thing."

Grace felt her breath exhale in tiny uncomfortable bursts. Oh
God, she thought, that makes so much sense I have no idea what
to say.

Rosemary, unaware of her mother's distress, plunged ahead,
"So we've agreed to disagree about religion. There are things she
likes about Baptists and things I like about Episcopalians. That's a
good trade-off."

"Trade-off?" Grace's head began to pound. "Religion is not
about trading off, Rosemary—"

"Of course it is," Rosemary insisted, paying no attention to the
fire in her mother's eyes. "How do you think Europeans ever
stopped killing each other if it hadn't been a trade-off?"

"This isn't Europe—"

"No, we have separation of church and state to protect everybody here. But in Europe they were happy to kill each other over
religion."

"Are you learning this in school?"

"Nope. Melanie's father teaches the Reformation."

"And what do you know about the Reformation?"

Rosemary tossed her head. "Not much. Yet."

4

To the women in Grace's Circle there was only one topic of conversation during the spring. What in the world were the preacher and the deacons thinking in allowing that young black man to keep coming to their church?

The subject hovered ominously over the horizon of every church function. It was all Grace could do to keep her mind on her church work. She noted most people had an off-on switch regarding the propriety of discussing the subject. She had a difficult time deciding whether or not they rushed through church business so they could have more time to gossip. Was her imagination running away with her?

It was Annie Armstrong Home Mission Week. A few of the women volunteered to give the annual lesson to the girls about the Cooperative Program, the only centrally controlled organization in the Southern Baptist Convention. A fraction of each church's budget went to this program, funding various mission efforts within the United States and abroad. At this particular time of year the Girls' Auxiliary would be reminded how home mission dollars were spent.

The Circle lesson was very effective but the refreshments had scarcely started around when the subject of Will came up. Again.

"As though he's rubbing it in."

"First Street Baptist has always been the Negro church. Why doesn't he go there?"

Dorothy, settling deeper into her comfortable armchair, sighed deeply. "He came on a general campus invitation. I thought we were supposed to welcome *all* college students."

"Miss Dorothy, they have their own churches—"

"When Dr. and Mrs. Wang were here from China none of you suggested them finding a Chinese Baptist church. And that was, my word, how many years ago?"

"That was different."

"How so? They weren't lily-white," Dorothy reminded them.

"Dr. Wang was a college professor."

"They were persecuted in China."

Dorothy smiled. "Will Cummins strikes me as a very fine, very talented young man. I have no idea why all of you are so upset. It's ridiculous."

Lorene Wright fell into her trap. "My daughter is the same age he is, Miss Dorothy. I don't want him getting ideas."

Grace watched as the others nodded.

"All right, Lorene," Dorothy continued, "for the sake of argument let's say Will brings along a nice black girl he plans to marry. Would that ease your mind?"

Lorene visibly relaxed and Grace feared for her, recognizing one of Dorothy's sweet-but-lethal games to expose hypocrisy. "Of course. Who would object to any nice young couple?"

"Now cast your mind forward a few years. Let's say this nice young couple marries and has children. Your daughter will eventually marry and have children of her own. Would you object to black and white children sharing the same church nursery?"

"No," Lorene said so weakly that Grace knew she lied.

"When they go through Sunbeams and Bible school, Sunday School and Training Union together and are ready to select their own mates, how will you have the nerve to tell them they're equal enough in God's eyes to be fellow-Christians but not equal enough in *yours* to marry?"

The silence was deafening. Grace wondered if anyone heard her heart thudding. She swallowed hard to dissolve the enormous lump in her throat, to no avail.

Lorene obviously felt no such twinge. "You've proved my point exactly, Miss Dorothy. Open the door just a crack and our world is gone forever."

Dorothy started to speak but catching sight of so many disapproving faces around her, closed her mouth and sighed deeply. She almost seemed contrite. "Since I never had a child, ladies, I don't see why this young man threatens you so personally. I will add, though, if it were the world it ought to be, you'd find Will Cummins as fine a match for your daughters as any white man."

Lorene's glare didn't diminish. "Well, it isn't a perfect world. This is the only one there is. The government may make me send my children to school with them but it cannot make me socialize with them or worship with them. If moves aren't made to get him out we plan to move our membership."

Grace bit her lip. It's Annie Armstrong Home Mission Week, she remembered. We're supposed to be concentrating our energies on spring mission projects, not talking like this.

Annie Armstrong fought valiantly to bring a message of hope to her own people. What had that strong-willed woman thought of the segregated Christianity of the nineteenth century? Would she, as well as those other old warriors of the Baptist faith, be shocked to learn so little had changed?

How could the Southern Baptist spirit of inclusiveness condone what was *still* going on? There's a showdown coming, Grace suspected, right in the middle of my own church. If church members, especially wealthy church members like the Wrights, were threatening to leave then Will Cummins was as good as gone.

"Grace, will you lead us in prayer?" Frances Taylor asked.

Grace shook her head. "I can't," she muttered. "Not today."

They were strangers to her, these women who prayed so demurely. All except Dorothy. She glanced up and found Dorothy also observing the women.

It was the first time she'd ever looked defeated.

    *   *   *

Will was, as Rosemary claimed, enchanted with the painting on the baptistery wall. He spoke with the elderly church deacon, David Todd, who'd drawn the beautiful scene in 1926. He took dozens of photographs.

Between choir and Training Union he spent his time in the sanctuary sketching the scene. Grace suspected the growing number of novice artists trickling in to draw, too, had been harangued by Rosemary.

"The lighting in this sanctuary is just terrible," Will muttered. "But that's a masterpiece if ever I saw one." He rose from the pew and slipped his wire-framed glasses further down on his nose, squinting at a detail.

Rosemary, practicing her hand-to-eye coordination on the figures of the sheep, sighed deeply. "I'll never get these right. Everything goes downhill."

"Feel the points of your page with your wrist, Rosie, without taking your eyes off the painting," he reminded her.

Gretchen Finny tossed her long blonde hair out of her face. "Mr. Todd says he's too old to paint a picture for our new church, Will. Why don't you do it?"

"That's a great idea," Rosemary chimed in. "Mr. Todd told us you're a very great artist."

Will laughed. "That's very flattering, girls, but your building committee has already decided on the artwork for your new baptistery."

"What is it?" Rosemary asked.

"A gold-leaf cross," Will replied.

"A cross?" Rosemary repeated numbly, then frowning deeply, "That's it? A plain old cross?"

Will glanced up from his sketchpad toward her and raised one brow. "That isn't very enlightened of you, Rosemary. The victory of an empty cross is the very essence of Protestant Christianity."

Rosemary blushed beneath the gentle rebuke.

Gretchen and Jill compared their sketches. Jill innocently added, "But it won't be the same."

Will smiled. "Nothing stays the same, girls." He sat down again and Gretchen, curious about what claimed so much concentration, leaned over his sketchpad.

It happened in a split-second. Even Rosemary couldn't remember the details.

One of the deacons softly entered the sanctuary. Mistaking Gretchen's curiosity for a caress or worse, he made his way to her in few enough strides to take her completely by surprise. He yanked her up by the hair and Gretchen, shocked and terrified, spilled everything on her lap and screamed.

Rosemary bent down for Gretchen's sketchpad and colored pencils. The deacon dragged Gretchen off the pew and as she stumbled into the aisle, the heel of her shoe caught Rosemary full in the face.

Will and Jill fought the deacon valiantly, Will demanding he release Gretchen at once, Jill trying to loose the deacon's maddened death-grip on Gretchen's hair.

The screams and hysteria brought church members streaming into the sanctuary. Jill, shoved out of the way, caught sight of Rosemary standing with a bleeding mouth and hurried to her.

Pale with fear and pain, Rosemary tried in vain to staunch the bloodflow with her dress-tail. Jill pulled her into the aisle. "Hurry," she urged, pulling her into the ladies' room.

No one followed them. The scene unfolding in the sanctuary was much too lurid, far too exciting. Jill motioned for Rosemary to sit down on the toilet seat and she soaked paper towels on cold water, making a compress.

When the bleeding eased, she left to find Grace.

When Grace reached her daughter, she was too shocked to scold. "Let me see," she said quietly, pulling the paper towels from Rosemary's lip.

"It wasn't Gretchen's fault—" Rosemary started to say.

"I know," Grace soothed, blanching at the sight of the deep cut. "That's going to need stitches, Rosemary. Come now, we have to go."

Rosemary stood weakly and Grace wondered if she'd faint. Her daughter paused at the door and looked back at Jill. "You have to tell them what really happened in there."

Jill's eyes flashed angrily. "Don't worry about it. I will!"

*   *   *

It did no good. Whatever explanations were made went either unheeded or unwanted. The more people it involved the more bitter the episode became.

It was hatefully, racially motivated.

The teenagers and children lined up behind Will without hesitation. The adults who supported him were so few they were easily shouted down and words were tossed in both camps that would never be forgiven or forgotten.

The young people would forget, the church hierarchy said. One day they would understand why the deacon was so upset and not be so harsh in their judgment.

At the next Circle Meeting the women in WMU learned David Todd, the artist of the baptistery, had sent all his original sketches and notes on the painting to Will. The gesture in itself was worth a thousand words.

We are all, Grace decided, guilty of driving Will away. It's all because of this notion of white womanhood under siege, too. How stupid, how completely stupid it is!

The Wrights and their cohorts got what they wanted. The point of segregation had been won with the abject humiliation of a fine young man.

*   *   *

The summer finally arrived and Rosemary's friendship with Melanie intensified. Occasionally, Grace ventured to suggest Rosemary include Gretchen in her plans but soon realized Gretchen, too, had her own friends outside the church.

In spite of Dorothy's warnings Grace never gave her wholehearted approval to Melanie. The girl simply came from a background she found unsuitable and that was that.

Rosemary, however, stubbornly held her ground, refusing to allow her mother to choose her school friends. Since the neighborhoods adjoined, the two girls were within bicycling distance of each other and practically lived at each other's houses.

They went swimming together, playing all day in the water and the sunshine, breaking only for lunch and their serials. After dinner they went back to the pool until it closed. On rainy days they stayed indoors and practiced their drawing skills. For a brief moment they flirted with the idea of becoming astronauts as they watched Neil Armstrong and Buzz Aldrin walk on the moon.

Grace nearly despaired.

Then, at last, her salvation appeared.

Finally, after months and months of rumors, Brother Bradshaw, their preacher, handed in his resignation. The congregation, he reportedly said, was stubborn and didn't share his vision of making theirs the largest church in the association. The congregation, for its part, was unhappy about the episode with Will Cummins and made it known that if more aggressive action had originated from the pulpit when the problem first came up, the horrible scene with Gretchen would never have happened.

There were no tears shed on Brother Bradshaw's last Sunday. Everyone looked forward to hiring a new preacher and hoped the pulpit committee would find the perfect man.

The new preacher was younger than any the pulpit committee ever hired and his daughter was Rosemary's age. Grace sighed with relief at the news. Not only would she prefer Rosemary to cultivate friends within the church but being part of the inner circle around the preacher's daughter...well, that would be perfect!

Rosemary glanced up from her drawing tablet as Grace told her about the new preacher. "They'll be arriving soon and I want you to be especially nice to her."

Rosemary ignored her.

"It wouldn't hurt you to invite her over for a day," Grace found herself scolding.

Rosemary turned again to her drawing.

In spite of the fact there was no argument Grace found herself feeling defeated. Again.

*   *   *

Everyone in the church was crazy about the new preacher and his family. He brought youth and a breath of spring air to their congregation. It was well over a generation since a preacher arrived with a young family.

To her credit, Rosemary behaved when she first met Pamela although the possibility of sharing any common ground was shattered within minutes. "What step are you working on?" Rosemary asked, meaning the GA Forward Steps.

"Lady-in-waiting," Pamela confessed dismally.

"Lady-in-waiting, only up to lady-in-waiting, that *I* did two years ago!" Rosemary exclaimed haughtily to her mother, her blue eyes flashing. "She ought to be ashamed of herself."

Grace frowned. "Not everyone does queen-in-service, Rosie. You know that."

"I don't expect it from just anybody. She's the preacher's daughter. She should be doing queen-in-service with me and doing it better, too."

It was obvious Pamela had other things on her mind. Almost thirteen, she was a beautiful girl with luxurious chestnut-brown hair and large brown eyes.

"All she thinks about is a boyfriend," Rosemary sniffed.

"So does Gretchen and you don't mistreat her," Grace reminded her.

Rosemary blushed.

She expects so much out of people, Grace realized. After the July WMU Meeting, Grace confided as much to Dorothy. "I think I've got the makings of a snob on my hands," she said quietly.

"Because she was surprised about the preacher's daughter?"

"It seems to be a pattern with her."

"You have no idea where she got her ideas?"

"No. Harry and I try to get along with everyone—"

Dorothy grinned. "Be honest with yourself, Grace. You've encouraged her every step of the way to excel in everything she does. Her achievements have been the key to your approval. Why should you be surprised when she turns that demand on others?"

"I only told her I wanted her to do the very best she could do—"

"She expects that out of other people, too."

"I'll have to tell her it isn't right."

"Why not?"

"What I expect of her is what I should expect as a good mother. You can't sit in judgment like that on your friends—"

"I'm not so sure of that one, Grace," Dorothy interrupted. "Would a good friend let another good friend slide through life?"

"That's not what I mean."

Dorothy smiled. "You must point out to Rosemary to be more tolerant in her opinions toward others. And Grace, I think you'd better let go of any hopes of Rosemary being a best friend to Pamela. They're too different."

Grace sighed deeply. "That's what I was afraid of. I keep having this dream about Rosemary coming home and telling me she wants to be an Episcopalian."

Dorothy laughed. "Would she be so involved this summer with her Forward Steps if that were the case?"

Grace met her gaze and repressed another sigh. It was too cold a fear believing Rosemary was working on queen-in-service as some sort of trophy.

She's only been a teenager a few weeks and this horrible time will be on me until she's in college, Grace thought. *I'll never live through it.*

*　　　　*　　　　*

Rosemary pulled the curlers from her hair, shaking her blonde mane free. She started brushing her hair slowly and gently.

"Put some elbow grease into that, miss," Grace advised, "or we'll be here all night." She reached for the brush but Rosemary pulled away.

"Don't," she warned, "you try to pull it out by the roots."

Grace sighed and then decided to change the subject. She smiled at her. "You did it, you know! Queen-in-service!"

It was a tremendous accomplishment. The reviewing council offered to take Rosemary to tea but Grace thought that was going too far. Rosemary's ego was unmanageable enough.

"Tonight'll show them," her daughter gloated.

Grace's smile faded. "Sometimes I think you did this step just to show off," she admitted.

Rosemary shrugged. "That's what Melanie said but I don't care. I just wish there were going to be Forward Steps next year so I could have gotten that scepter and green cape."

Loot, Harry called it.

Grace helped her into her long, white dress. "Your father wants to take some pictures." She held Rosemary's white gloves while her daughter bobby-pinned on the GA crown. It had gotten bent in storage and the large octagon showed a rather unmendable crease.

"Mom, what do I get for this step?"

"I don't know," Grace admitted, "but it'll be something nice, I'm sure."

*   *   *

When Rosemary entered the church there was something of a hush. Everyone knew, after all, it was 1949 when the only other queen-in-service was recognized in the congregation. Grace glanced at her daughter and confirmed her fear of the gloating.

Harry wasn't much better. He and Grace made their way into the sanctuary and while the polite chatting went on, Grace overheard him. "It's been twenty years since anyone else did what my daughter's done."

Oh God, they're two peas in a pod, Grace thought, her face flushing. He doesn't seem to suspect she might not have the purest of motives at work, probably wouldn't care if he did suspect.

She glanced around the congregation and saw Dorothy smiling at her. She smiled back and Dorothy flashed her a very improper, white-gloved vee-for-victory.

Three peas in a pod.

It was a full agenda. There were six little girls who'd completed their maiden steps that summer, three ladies-in-waiting, one princess, two queens, and Rosemary. Then there were the older girls in Intermediate GAs: one queen-with-a-scepter and one queen regent, the ones who would receive the scepter and the cape Rosemary so desperately wanted.

At the beginning of October, the new fiscal year, there would be no more GAs as they knew them. Never again would an August Prayer Meeting turn into a coronation ceremony, with the girls of the church in short pastel or long white dresses.

Acteens would replace Intermediate GAs. It wouldn't be as rigorous, as achievement-oriented. "Sounds like acne," Rosemary said angrily, hating the changes before she was even aware of them.

Knowing the changes, Grace hated them. How many other girls besides strident Rosemary would be put off? Would Baptists lose the interest of younger girls, too?

She suddenly had a sinking feeling. If girls lost interest in mission work at this stage would they value WMU when they were grown?

*   *   *

The maidens, ladies-in-waiting, princess and queens seemed to take forever. When the music for Rosemary finally began and she came into view, Grace looked at her long and hard.

She wasn't a bit nervous. In fact, she grinned from ear to ear. Earlier, one poor little girl had almost fainted with fright. How could Rosemary be so cool?

The president of WMU introduced Rosemary and her rare accomplishment and Grace saw nods of approval in the congregation. The question was put to Rosemary and she answered, like Harry, by casting her gaze across the congregation, as though speaking casually to certain individuals.

Nauseating, Grace thought. She was the star of the show, just like Harry.

Rosemary grinned again when she finished, knowing her answer was perfect, knowing she had the congregation in the palm of her gloved hand.

The WMU president took Rosemary's crown and everyone watched interestedly. Very carefully, the woman put on a sticker reading *In Service* below the octagon-shaped emblem.

Grace caught sight of Rosemary's face. Her daughter might just as well have cried out, "A sticker? All this work and I get only a *sticker* on my crown?"

Smile, Grace willed her, don't look like a pole-axed calf, for God's sake!

Rosemary took back the crown and gave the WMU president a look of shock the woman wouldn't likely forget anytime soon.

Harry nudged her. "A sticker? All that work and all she gets is a sticker?" he cried, not bothering to lower his voice.

Grace shuddered. They were two peas in a pod, that's all there was to it.

5

Rosemary started back to school and life fell into its autumn routine. Grace noticed Melanie beginning to pull away a bit. She was a ninth-grader, after all, officially in high school and her exalted status seemed to separate her from Rosemary.

Rosemary found the reality of the situation difficult to accept. Grace tried to explain that sometimes a year's difference in age was very critical. Nevertheless, Rosemary was desolate.

As Melanie's circle of friends changed, Rosemary, Gretchen and Jill seemed to find their way back to each other. It didn't take Grace long to learn the reason why.

Pamela, the preacher's daughter, had taken an instant dislike to Rosemary. Although Jill and Gretchen were more eager to be friends than haughty Rosemary, Pamela found their company too immature for her sophisticated taste.

The older children in the church were more to her liking. It flattered her that they were so attentive and the boys fighting for her favor went straight to her head.

Jill seemed not to notice but Gretchen was grief-stricken because she wasn't part of Pamela's circle. Rosemary seemed to enjoy her black-sheep status. "The princess and her creep-brigade," she christened them and Grace shivered under the hostility of her tone.

It would have killed me to be excluded from the preacher's daughter's set, she thought. Is Rosemary simply pretending she doesn't care? She can't be that thick-skinned!

Growing up was hard but hard things didn't end with growing up, Grace found. The organizational changes in the church scheduled for October upset everyone. In the wake of the announcements Harry and Grace overlooked one critical issue: the power plays.

They knew all departments were to be re-structured and assumed Harry would be in charge of one of the children's departments, probably fourth to sixth grades. It was a bolt from the blue and Grace actually felt her fingers and toes go numb with the shock of the news.

Harry would not be a superintendent of *any* department. A relative newcomer was awarded Harry's favorite age group.

The look on his face didn't invite comment but Grace plunged ahead anyway. "You'll just have to tell someone you thought—"

"I'm not telling anyone anything."

"Harry, you've given too much to back down now—"

"I'm not backing down from anything," he declared. "Don't you have any pride? They don't want me anymore."

They'd forgotten completely about Rosemary sitting at the dining table with them. She chased her peas around the plate with her fork. "I think we should go to another church," she put in.

Grace blinked, suddenly remembering her there, witnessing it all. "We can't go to another—"

Rosemary glanced up and Grace saw the same barely contained rage in her face as in Harry's. "Why not? That would fix them, wouldn't it, Daddy?"

Harry didn't meet her eyes.

Grace's heart hammered in her ears. "I—I c-can't go to another church! Why, it's home. They're family—"

"Some family," Rosemary snorted, "stabbing Daddy in the back like this."

"Be quiet, miss," Harry said forcefully. "Your mother won't go, so we can't go."

Rosemary blushed beneath his rebuke but her antipathy seemed directed completely toward her mother. She glared at her for a long moment then resumed the struggle for the peas.

*   *   *

"I'm tempted to call that fool of a preacher and give him a piece of my mind he won't soon forget," Dorothy said over the phone to Grace. "How dare he and that band of idiots? Harry Lee made that Junior Department what it is!"

"Oh Dorothy, don't," Grace begged. "It's been awful. Rosemary's tried everything to get us to leave."

There was a long pause. "Well, Grace, I'll miss you very much—"

"I can't leave."

"You should think about that."

"How can I? Everything I am is defined by the church."

"Really?" Dorothy needled. "Well, miss, I think your first loyalty should be to your husband. He's been badly treated in this matter."

"I'd die if I had to go—"

"What are you so tied to, Grace? You sound neurotic."

That was it. Grace set the receiver down quietly but hung up on her, anyway.

The phone rang again. "I'm sorry, Grace," Dorothy apologized. "I was quite rude. Will you forgive me?"

Grace shook in her shoes. "I—I don't think it has anything to do with forgiveness—"

"You sound so confused—"

"I am. I still can't believe they would do this to Harry."

"Believe it, my dear and don't be so trusting. When a church is made up of people it's susceptible to all the political back-stabbing of any other business."

"Business?"

"Yes, of course. Now that you're aware of it, don't be so gullible."

Is that what I am? Grace wondered.

"If you and Harry decide to move your letters, Grace, let me know. I may just join you!"

"Thank you," Grace said quietly and they said their good-byes.

It was horrible. How could this happen to Harry? But she simply couldn't leave. Her heartsblood seemed mixed with the mortar in the bricks and she suspected she would begin to die if she had to go.

There was obviously a groundswell of protest on Harry's behalf, however, because shortly before promotion day in October he was offered the superintendency of fourth to sixth grades. He shook his head and said, "Nope," eloquently omitting any sign of a thank you.

Grace finally found a moment alone to sob her heart out. It was no way to begin the new church year.

*   *   *

She tried to soothe herself by taking more interest in the new church. Like the rest of the congregation she was worried because they were moving into an unfinished building. Everything had fallen so far behind and gone so far over the budget!

She and her WMU group took an unofficial tour during their November meeting and Grace's heart sank. The unfinished sanctuary was large enough to accommodate their expected growth but the classrooms were hardly bigger than the ones they were leaving. She shivered in the damp cold.

"It looks like a tobacco barn," Dorothy said grimly, standing in the sanctuary perilously close to a wobbly scaffold. "I cannot imagine how this place will be habitable by January First."

"Well, we aren't going to occupy the sanctuary until spring," Grace reminded her.

"Look," Dorothy pointed upward toward the balcony where workmen were hanging the new chandeliers. One was uncovered and they looked closely at it.

"The decoration looks like broken glass," Grace noted.

"That, my dear, is supposed to match our new windows," Dorothy sighed. "What a travesty! Rosemary will be quite beside herself, I fear. You must prepare her for the shock."

"Well, the windows come in later this week. Maybe they won't be so...modern."

"Ugly," Dorothy corrected.

Grace turned and glanced at the front of the church. "They've marked the new choir loft," she noted with a smile. "That ought to hold all those kids."

"Yes, there are quite a lot of them, aren't there?"

"They sound so good! I've heard the choir director wants to take them on tour this summer," Grace said happily.

"That ought to be interesting. I wonder who they'll find to chaperon so many?"

Grace's face fell. "Was that a hint?"

Dorothy laughed. "Maybe I'll volunteer."

Grace gasped. "I didn't think you cared very much for that age group."

"What a brazen assumption! I taught high school for more than forty years, remember. Besides, being a chaperon might be fun. Also, I must remember to attend the business meeting to suggest we invest in a church bus. I think the numbers of that youth choir would support my argument."

Grace smiled. "That's a good idea but I still can't imagine you on a church bus with fifty teenagers."

Dorothy laughed. "I'm ready for lunch, Grace, are you?"

They picked their way carefully out of the construction site. Grace turned to look at it once more. She wanted to feel proud but didn't.

She had to put a good face on it for Harry and Rosemary. These days, those two needed no encouragement to be negative.

*　　　*　　　*

New Year's Eve was the date the church members were scheduled to move their belongings from the old location to the new. The church staff decided to treat the event like a party.

They didn't seem to notice that not everyone was delirious with joyful anticipation. Grace fought depressing thoughts and a headache all day.

Rosemary and Gretchen gazed forlornly out the living room window, watching the cold rain fall in unrelenting sheets. "Mom," Rosemary asked, "how in the world are we going to move everything without getting soaked?"

Grace sighed and wondered if the two girls were as depressed as she was. Her headache was definitely getting worse. "We'll have lots of plastic, Rosemary. Everything will be fine."

"Dad's already been out to the new church today," Gretchen said. "The lights in the parking lot still aren't on and there's only plywood planking by the doors. He said it'll be the cause of at least two broken necks tonight."

Hadn't anything gone right? Only the church basement was completely finished, four months behind schedule. Grace suddenly remembered that the old church was far from safe, too. "You two stay off the fourth floor tonight, do you hear?"

Rosemary scowled. "We volunteered to help move the old Junior One Department, Mom, so you don't have to worry."

"There isn't a lot left except chairs and song-books," Gretchen tearfully reminded her.

Grace quietly sat down in her rocker. "What's the matter with you two? You look as though you're going to a funeral."

"We are," Rosemary muttered.

"How can you be so ungrateful? You're going to be in a brand new church home. We'll be in that beautiful new sanctuary by spring."

Gretchen blushed and looked away but Rosemary's eyes flashed defiance. "It will never be home to me. It will never be beautiful, either. Everything about it is cheap and ugly."

"That isn't reason enough to hate it, miss."

"Why are we moving anyway? No one wanted to go!"

Grace rubbed her head. "We don't consult thirteen-year-old children about things like this, Rosie."

"Then why don't you all change all the rules so we won't be church members until we're twenty-one?" Rosemary snapped back.

Gretchen glanced up, desperately uncomfortable, and Rosemary stilled her tongue.

The clock started chiming and Grace rose. "Get your coats, girls. It's time to go."

        *   *   *

Rosemary, Gretchen and Jill disappeared with a few other adults to the third floor of the old Junior One Department and

Grace went with a few women into the library. Her spirits lifted somewhat.

"We'll have a window to display new books," the church librarian said, "and we'll be right across from the sanctuary to attract new readers."

Grace removed several volumes from a shelf and started upending them into boxes. Already she could hear the squeaking of folding wooden chairs and the clanging of metal ones. A muffled dragging sound distracted her from the conversation around her.

"They're moving pianos," someone said.

The noise started at once. Teenagers bounced down the stairs to stack chairs against the wall for loading onto trucks, stronger adults shifted boxes of church literature and song-books while other volunteers dragged along the odds-and-ends of teaching aids: maps and easels and pointers and posters. All collected inside the door.

Two old pianos had to come from the upper floors and it wasn't until the six men moving them were poised at the head of the stairs that they realized, possibly for the first time, how steep was the pitch of those creaky old stairs. How innocent they'd looked until now!

Distracted by the clamor around her, Grace overturned a card file and five hundred three-by-five index cards scattered across the littered library floor. For a split second she could only stare at the mess then, humiliated and shaky, dropped to her knees.

"You won't have time to alphabetize them," the librarian snapped.

"I hadn't planned on it," Grace said without thinking and noted the disapproval all around her. She stuffed a stack into the file.

Choking, she suddenly realized she'd started to cry. She finally managed to get the cards back in the box. She pulled herself up and left the room.

She found herself running toward the old sanctuary. In spite of her tears she was shocked to see it so bereft. Of course, all the Christmas decorations were gone but this…no flags, no hymnals, and no instruments. The greenery was gone from around the baptistery.

And there, standing in the dry baptistery well, was Rosemary drinking in that lovely scene for the last time. Grace stopped dead in her tracks, afraid of disturbing so private a moment.

It was good-bye, she knew, when Rosemary stepped forward and kissed the wall. Using the exit into the old Junior Department, she was gone herself.

*   *   *

The three girls volunteered to ride out on the first truck. Grace caught sight of them as they waved.

The chattering hadn't diminished in her absence but she hadn't the heart to join in.

"Where's Miss Dorothy tonight?" someone asked her.

"With the other old ladies at the new church," she replied. "They have sandwiches, coffee and hot chocolate waiting for us."

"The men are certainly going to need it. They've just discovered four more old pianos in the basement that have to go, too."

"Those old things! Why should we bother? They aren't fit for anything!"

"Yes, but my children learned their first songs on one of those old monsters. I can't imagine them being anyplace but in the Beginner and Primary Departments."

Grace laughed suddenly. It was, after all, better to laugh than to cry.

Rosemary was right. It *was* a funeral.

* * *

She stepped gingerly across the plywood planking with a box of books in her arms. Bright fluorescent light poured from the new church. It was a cold blue light, as cold as the rain.

It was cold inside, too. The new floors were muddy and strewn with boxes. Grace set hers down and moved aside to let other people past.

She heard Rosemary and Gretchen and found them in the new library. Gretchen, sitting on a table, was in tears. Rosemary, hovering nearby, looked like a thundercloud.

"What's the matter?" Grace demanded.

Rosemary glanced up and Grace noted the clenched jaw, Harry's jaw, and the thin-set lips.

"Answer me, Rosie."

"It's okay, Mom—"

"They wouldn't sit with us," Gretchen confessed miserably and broke into fresh sobs.

"Stop crying, Gretchen. Don't give them the satisfaction of seeing you like this," Rosemary ordered.

Grace frowned. "Who wouldn't sit with you?"

"The princess," Rosemary snapped, "and her little creep-brigade."

How it annoyed Grace when Rosemary referred to the preacher's daughter in such language! "And just what did you say to her?" Grace cried.

Gretchen sprang to Rosemary's defense. "She didn't say anything."

Grace caught a twitch in Rosemary's eyelid and Gretchen looked away too quickly to be honest. "Are you sure?"

"Well..." Gretchen hesitated.

"After they said they didn't want us sitting with them I told them to go to the opposite of heaven," Rosemary said.

"You said hell? You said hell in this brand new church—"

"No, I said opposite of heaven. Didn't I, Gretchen?"

"Yes, she did, Mrs. Lee. She never said hell."

"You'd better be telling me the truth, miss." Grace turned on her heel and left for the basement.

How quickly they rushed to tattle on Rosemary! Six of them, talking all at once, saying essentially the same thing: Rosemary Lee told the preacher's daughter and her friends to go to hell.

Grace raised her hands to her temples, closed her eyes and wished for one desperate moment that she were dead.

"I think you children would do better if you told the truth," came a high-pitched, stern voice from behind them. Grace opened her eyes to find Dorothy and four other older women standing behind the tellers of the tale.

"Well, she didn't exactly say hell."

Dorothy nodded. "That's right. Also, the remark was not unprovoked, was it?" She smiled menacingly at the preacher's daughter, as though she dared the girl to contradict her.

Embarrassed, the group dispersed.

"You have a headache, Grace," Dorothy said, leading her away to sit down.

"Yes, it's been building up all day."

"Why did you come out tonight?"

"I had to."

"No, you didn't. We can manage, Grace, without you being here," she scolded then relenting, "let me get you some tea."

Grace rubbed the back of her head. Why did Rosemary seem to enjoy a fight? It was as though she liked causing a scene.

Dorothy returned and set a mug full of steaming cinnamon tea on the table. "Don't make more of this than there is, Grace."

"I can't help it. Rosemary seems to enjoy being rude."

"Really? I think she gave them exactly what they deserved." Dorothy turned to glance at the preacher's daughter. "I see trouble ahead for that pretty little miss. For her favor the children of this church will stand on their heads. Except Rosemary. You should be glad of that."

"I don't like Rosemary's mean streak."

"You don't think what she and Gretchen suffered was a mean-spirited attack?"

"I—I don't know."

"It was brilliant," Dorothy whispered, stifling a peal of laughter. "'Go to the opposite of heaven.' She didn't even have to stop to think! It was wonderful! I wish I could still think that quickly!"

"Don't you?"

"Oh, not anymore, Grace." Dorothy paused. "Rosemary will never be anyone's doormat. Tonight was proof."

"Tonight," Grace sighed, rubbing her head again, "has been the opposite of heaven all the way around."

*   *   *

In March, all eighth graders were required to attend sex education classes. Grace received an information packet well in advance and noted she and Harry were invited to attend a question and answer session for parents.

She was impressed with the program and said as much to Dorothy at Circle Meeting. "I expect the teachers to teach the mechanics and I'll teach the morals," she said.

"Well, my kids aren't taking it," an eavesdropper commented. "I see no reason to stir up a lot of questions in a child's mind. My son is still such a little boy."

Dorothy glanced up and frowned deeply. "Do you think forbidding your children to take the class will prevent their curiosity about sex?"

"That's not the job of school teachers," came the haughty reply.

"Of course it is," Grace argued. "It's biology."

Dorothy nodded. "Your children will either receive the facts from you and their teachers or nonsense from their friends. That's hardly a choice, I should think."

The other woman frowned. "What nonsense?"

Dorothy tossed her head. "A girl can't get pregnant the first time she has sex. A boy will become a monster of some sort if he masturbates. That sort of foolishness." She didn't seem to realize that almost everyone, even Grace, choked on the refreshments when she mentioned the word 'masturbate.' She glared at them. "For heaven's sake, what's the matter with all of you? Don't you see if you talk about sex openly with your children that you'll take the mystery out of it? If they know the facts they're more unlikely to make mistakes."

Grace regained her composure. "It isn't easy to talk to children about sex. When they turn those big eyes on you and ask some questions you feel well...naked."

Her peers nodded vigorously.

Dorothy shook her head. "I should think given their backgrounds, when you speak of sex being an expression of married love, everything should fall into place."

Frances Taylor breathed a bit easier. "An expression of married love. I like that, Miss Dorothy."

"Well, Frances, I'm glad I could help."

Grace smiled. "For one thing, although we haven't said so, I think our children realize we live that example."

"That's important, I agree," Dorothy nodded, "but it doesn't hurt to reinforce the message with words."

*　　　*　　　*

Grace was proud of the way she handled Rosemary's sex education class. Rosemary discussed the films with her and confessed she was relieved the question and answer sessions were divided between boys and girls.

"But there are a couple of things I didn't get," she confessed.

"Which couple of things?" Grace pressed.

"A bunch of us don't understand masturbation and orgasm. The teacher tried to explain it but I really don't think she knows, either," Rosemary said, completely unaware that her mother's heart had nearly stopped beating.

Grace wondered how she herself would have handled the question from forty or more teenage girls. What could she say?

The truth about masturbation would mean a sordid digression onto the subject of boys that Grace preferred to ignore. So she considered how to answer about orgasm. "Orgasm is the climax of sex," she said cryptically.

"What does that mean?"

"A big thrill of pleasure."

Rosemary frowned. "Like what?"

Oh God, Grace thought, will this never end? She cleared her throat. "Like nothing else."

"Why?"

It was as bad as having a three-year-old around again. "When your body has finished developing, it will respond differently. It isn't supposed to respond to sex when you're a little girl but it will when you're a married woman."

"Oh." Rosemary looked away and digested the explanation in silence. She shook her head and looked solemnly at Grace. "I can't imagine it in the first place, much less liking it."

At that, Grace laughed. "Oh, but you will! You're supposed to like it with your husband."

Rosemary smiled. "That's what the teachers say, too."

Grace watched her as she put her schoolwork away. That ended rather well, even if she *had* dodged the question of masturbation.

　　　　　*　　　　　　　　*　　　　　　　　*

People came in droves to the new church. Just as Rosemary predicted, there were many children who attended without their parents. There were young families, too, and the church nursery swelled.

It was hard to cram everyone into fellowship hall for the morning worship service. Until the new sanctuary was finished they would be packed as tightly as sardines into it and Grace was miserable.

Rosemary's eighth grade Sunday School class grew, too. The new girls didn't quite know what to make of the two camps represented within the four walls: the preacher's daughter quietly sitting through the lessons while strident Rosemary took the lead in discussions.

In that setting, Rosemary's group looked more inviting but once Sunday School was over and the new girls saw what influence Pamela commanded over the boys, the choice grew clearer.

There were new adult members, too. Before, when new members joined the church, they were usually established Southern Baptists but these new people—how uneducated they were!

Besides their enthusiasm, they had no idea at all what separated a Baptist from a Methodist or a Catholic and, more tellingly, no idea what separated a Southern Baptist from other Baptists.

To the few members who thought like Grace, it was very upsetting. How in the world could a lifetime of doctrine be concentrated into a few lessons in order to educate them?

The preacher didn't think a special study course was the answer. It was enough for him that they attended.

"They bring such fat offerings," Dorothy said cynically, "and they're white-collar employees. I can't believe we have such a shallow little fool in our pulpit."

Grace cringed at her words. How annoying Dorothy could be when she was depressed or angry, just looking for trouble!

One Sunday night as Grace policed the hallways searching for Training Union truants, she found two girls from Rosemary's class standing outside the building. She opened the doors, prepared to deliver her direst blood-and-thunder speech, when she noticed they were crying. All her anger melted. "What's wrong, girls?"

They blushed, obviously uncomfortable. One said quietly, "We've called my mom to come after us."

"Why? Are you sick?"

"No, just poor," the other muttered.

Grace stepped closer, unsure she heard correctly. "Poor?"

"We can't help it if we don't have a new dress every week and live in a mansion like *they* do—"

"Who—" Grace paused. "Did someone say something to you, girls?"

"They asked me why I wear the same dress every week and told both of us we aren't supposed to wear black shoes after Easter."

Grace didn't know what to say. She had a vague recollection that one of the girls had only a mother raising her. Illegitimate, people whispered. Her eyes went over the simple little cotton dress the girl always wore. It was faded and mended, but clean as could be and starched stiff as iron.

Her eyes darted down to the offending shoes of both girls: black patent leather, not to be worn after Easter. Grace remembered her own rigid dress code. Spring clothes and white shoes were put on at Easter, even if it was snowing, to be worn through Labor Day weekend. Then out with the wool and the plaids and the black shoes, even if it was over eighty sweltering degrees through most of September.

How stupid it was! Two little girls sacrificed on the altar of vanity and superficiality.

One of the mothers came after them and Grace hoped she said something soothing and added that she wished they would come back in for Training Union. They were gone suddenly, lost to her and lost to the church, as well.

White flight, Grace decided, meant abandonment in more than terms of race. Didn't anyone believe what she'd been taught? Poverty had nothing to do with respectability. There was trash in every color and in every income stratum. Church members who were ashamed of their poorer brothers and sisters said a lot about their own respectability.

"A shallow little fool in the pulpit," Dorothy had said of their young minister and his influence over their changing church. She hadn't been wrong, after all.

*   *   *

What a beautiful day it was! The sky was clear blue without a trace of a cloud and there was a slight chill beneath the breeze. It was a perfect Mother's Day, a perfect day to dedicate their new church.

Grace refused to take another look at their sanctuary until that day. After Sunday School the doors were opened and the congregation streamed in.

The windows weren't too bad but it was still awfully dark inside on such a sunny day, she decided. The matching chandeliers were on to help illuminate the interior.

Padded pews, what luxury! But she winced when she saw the carpet. Of course, it was all the rage, that yellow-green color but it seemed strange, nevertheless.

The organ and the piano had been painted white. When the choir entered Grace shuddered. They wore yellow stoles on new robes the same sickening color as the carpet.

She forced herself to look up and as she did so, found herself waiting to be half-blinded by the sunlight streaming through the old church window. She realized suddenly that no one would ever be blinded by the meager light from the new one.

The service was lovely but it wasn't what Grace expected. The usual Mother's Day observances were made: giving a flower to the woman present with the most children, the oldest mother present and so on. The congregation dutifully sang *Faith of Our Mothers* but the usual thrill of a special Sunday didn't effect Grace that day.

It just wasn't the same as the old church.

6

The congregation enthusiastically approved of Dorothy's suggestion to buy a church bus. An appropriate committee was formed to have one in operating condition by the time the kids went on choir tour in July.

Before the youth choir could go on tour, however, they had to have uniforms. Rosemary came home with an unusually sour face. "We're going to look so stupid."

"Why is that?" Grace asked.

"Pink and burgundy uniforms, Mom. The guys, too. I can't believe they'll wear pink shirts."

"I heard your dresses are going to be long."

"Yeah, that's true. I think everyone's tired of looking at the princess's underwear."

"Rosemary—"

"It's true!" She laughed suddenly. "Daddy says her hair is twice as long as her skirt!"

Grace glared at her. Why did Rosemary find everything he said so amusing?

"We ladies are going to have little burgundy chokers, too," Rosemary went on melodramatically. "In fact we're going to look so angelic we might just float up to heaven whole!"

They left for a week-long choir tour early on a Monday morning. They met in the church parking lot with one piece of luggage each. True to her promise, Dorothy volunteered to chaperon. Grace almost laughed at the prim little woman talking so earnestly to one of the tall college boys. How did she manage to look so cool and comfortable in July?

As the kids' names were called they were assigned roommates. Grace heard a new name called to be Rosemary's: Laura. Rosemary moved forward to join the new girl with more than a little trepidation but the new girl smiled and started talking to Rosemary eagerly.

Why had the choir director separated Rosemary and Gretchen, Grace wondered. Was Rosemary being punished for something? Her big mouth, probably. Just like Harry.

The ancient bus wheezed to a stop in front of the group and the boys started loading luggage. Grace caught her breath. Even with the new paint job, it was an old, old bus. Could anything so old be safe enough?

No one seemed to notice her anxiety. Off they went in the summer heat, fifty-seven rambunctious teenagers and six adult chaperons. Grace wondered if Dorothy would regret her decision by lunch. She waved until she could no longer see them.

*　　　　　*　　　　　*

I always wanted Rosemary to draw her circle of friends from church but this wasn't what I expected, Grace thought dismally as she watched Rosemary and her new best friend, Laura, head for the balcony for Sunday worship service. I wanted Gretchen to always be her best friend.

She looked around the filling sanctuary to find Gretchen negotiating a seat with the preacher's daughter's set. Gretchen desperately wanted to be Pamela's friend but that silly girl only wanted to associate with kids two or three years older.

Grace gulped and sighed. Adolescence was a terrible time of life and it seemed these days poor little Gretchen was getting it right in the teeth. Why didn't she try to get closer to Rosemary and Laura, she wondered.

Grace had no idea what drew Rosemary to Laura until she discovered another budding artist at work. Laura was more interested in sculpture, Rosemary informed her, and anything three-dimensional. Art. Again.

She had the sickening feeling they went to the balcony for privacy to pass notes rather than listen to the sermon. For a moment she flirted with the idea of forcing Rosemary to sit with Harry and herself but abandoned it immediately. Such a move would invite certain disaster.

As the choir entered and silence fell over the congregation Grace wondered when Rosemary would make a friend she approved of. Melanie's faith was a problem but thank God Melanie outgrew Rosemary before any real problems developed.

She had a deeper feeling of dread about Laura. Their personalities were different as night and day. Laura was soft-spoken, gentle and sweet but she and Rosemary were definitely on the same wavelength.

The child had not been brought up in a Southern Baptist home and it showed. Grace overheard her mention the hypocrisy of the deacons smoking in the parking lot before church began, just after they'd told the youth group never to pollute their bodies that were the temples of God.

It was an eye-opener for Rosemary who obviously viewed the smoking men as part of the scenery until that time. Laura was disrespectful of the long prayers of one of the deacons, adding that if she were the head operator in heaven she'd disconnect that particular call after the first five minutes.

Rosemary dissolved in laughter.

The newer young members weren't as aware as their better-grounded-in-Bible classmates that to say, "Oh God," or simply "God" in an off-hand manner was as bad as swearing itself. When Laura was told this a second time by older members of the youth group, her large brown eyes flashed with a rare fire and she shrugged, saying, "I'm sure God knows the intent of what I say."

Rosemary hovered in the background with a threatening face the others knew all too well, supporting her. Laura's lack of submission and Rosemary's championing of her set them apart from their peers and Grace was worried.

She would have had ammunition if she'd caught Rosemary excluding anyone who wanted to be friends but she and Laura seemed to welcome any and all. On that level the old *Star Trek* reruns drew many of them loosely together but always at the core were Rosemary and Laura. Starting to the ninth grade in separate schools only made them more inseparable at church.

As with Melanie, Grace kept her mouth shut, allowing Rosemary the privileges of associating with her but with strings attached. Grades were all-important.

She didn't have any grounds to set limits on the friendship yet. With the exception of first year algebra all of Rosemary's grades were A's.

Guiltily, Grace knew she was looking for an excuse to break up the friendship. She glanced again at the pew where Pamela sat, "holding court," as Rosemary called it. I won't have Rosemary crawling to her like Gretchen, she thought. It was so hard being a mother in such a day and age!

*   *   *

"Why isn't Daddy's name on this list?" Rosemary asked, look-ing at the church newsletter.

Grace hadn't read it yet, so she frowned. "What list?"

"For new deacons."

Grace set aside her mending and looked deeply into Rosemary's angry eyes. "His name has never been on the list, Rosemary. Why is it coming to your attention today?"

Rosemary blushed and threw the newsletter down. "I wish I could take the credit for noticing it, Mom, but it was Laura."

"Laura?"

"She asked me why Daddy isn't a deacon and I had to sputter around and say I didn't know. I had to admit that nobody ever asked him. The only reason I could think of why is that Daddy doesn't have a college degree."

"That isn't necessary."

"Then maybe she's right," Rosemary said quietly.

"About what?"

"Laura said maybe my big mouth was sinking Daddy's chances." Rosemary looked up at her mother and Grace could see her fighting back tears. "Is that so?"

"She said that?"

"No, not that way. She said because I didn't sit back and let the princess's gang run all over me that maybe some of them have poi-soned Daddy's chances—"

"Your father never wanted to be a deacon."

"Why not?"

"Well," Grace paused, trying to think of anything, anything, to stop Rosemary's fit of rage.

"You never asked him, did you?" Rosemary accused.

Grace could only stare.

"Don't you think he ever deserved it, Mom?" Rosemary cried. "All he's done for that bunch of assholes."

"Rosemary!" Grace shouted, "I can't believe you said—"

"Assholes," Rosemary repeated, lifting her chin defiantly.

"Go to your room right now," Grace said sternly, "and you have no telephone privileges for a week, do you understand?"

Rosemary left the room in a huff and Grace tried to calm her racing heart. Her eye rested on the discarded church newsletter. Why, yes, why hadn't Harry ever been asked to be a deacon?

          *   *   *

"She called them assholes and I grounded her for a week," Grace said over her sandwich as she and Dorothy ate lunch after their Circle Meeting.

Dorothy nibbled on her own sandwich then daintily wiped her mouth on a paper napkin. "If I were you I'd be much more concerned about her feelings of the rejection of her father."

Grace frowned. "I *am* concerned about it. To be honest, I never thought seriously about Harry being a deacon. Rosemary wouldn't have, either, if her new friend had kept out of it."

"I'm sure this girl can't understand why a fine man like Harry isn't a deacon."

"She made Rosemary think it might be her fault."

"I don't think it's true in Harry's case," Dorothy said gently, "but you'd be a fool, Grace, if you didn't believe it's one of the pettiest processes we have. A man often has to be a flatterer and a follower to be welcome into that select group."

Grace held her breath in suspense. This was *not* what she wanted to hear. She exhaled slowly. "I can't believe men like David Todd—"

"I said often, Grace, not always." Dorothy frowned slightly. "I must admit, though, Harry would be a good deacon in the old-fashioned definition of the office. He's organized and methodical and fair-minded. It's probably his fair-mindedness and his big mouth that have kept him out of the ranks so far, you know."

"Big mouth?"

Dorothy smiled. "Oh yes, dear. Rosemary comes by it quite honestly."

Grace paused for a long moment. "Rosemary is beginning to resent the church hierarchy, Dorothy. It makes me so nervous. She's liable to say anything to anyone when she's angry."

"Calling them assholes, you mean?"

"She's swearing behind my back, I know she is," Grace said quietly. "I overheard her saying 'shit' on the phone the other night."

Dorothy shrugged. "I find it very amusing that it's perfectly all right to urinate and defecate but quite socially unacceptable to piss and shit. The sophisticated Greco-Roman versus the vulgar Anglo-Saxon, I call it."

Grace nearly spit out her bite of sandwich as she heard those words come out of Dorothy's mouth. She looked up to find the older woman barely repressing a shout of laughter. "You said that," she muttered with her mouth full, "just to shock me!"

"But about Harry," Dorothy continued, "I think it's time for you to tell Rosemary exactly what I told you."

"That Harry keeps his trap open—"

Dorothy shook her head. "He isn't a flatterer and a follower."

"Then she'll turn those cold blue eyes of hers on me and demand to know why that sort of behavior is tolerated in a church."

Dorothy nodded. "It's a very good question, don't you think?"

Grace sighed. "I don't have an answer."

"The only thing to say is that a church is made up of imperfect people who make, at times, very bad decisions. This is one of them."

Grace paused. "She's going to find it difficult to accept, you know."

"So do I, dear," Dorothy said energetically, "so do I! Part of growing up is accepting the fact some very bad decisions are out of our hands. When she's older, maybe she'll be in a position to change a few of those things."

*　　　*　　　*

Grace repeated Dorothy's words to Rosemary who nodded her head vigorously. Grace thought she'd scored a major victory until Rosemary declared, "When I grow up I'll be a deacon and I'll get the ball rolling to really change things."

"You can't be a deacon, Rosemary."

"Why? Because I'm a girl?"

"Yes."

Rosemary narrowed her eyes, bit on her lip a moment then shot back, "You know, Mom, I think that's just about the stupidest thing I've ever heard." She turned on her heel and left the room.

Grace sat down to ward off a dizzy spell. I should have seen that one coming, she thought. She's reading women's lib stuff in the school library, sure as the world, or associating with non-Baptists. I wonder if Laura's family used to be part of churches that ordained women as deacons. Or maybe even as preachers. God, Oh God, what's next?

*　　　*　　　*

Rosemary and Laura saw each other as often as possible and the ranks of their group swelled. After Christmas another family joined the church and tall, tall Christine was quickly adopted into the inner circle.

When school started after the Christmas holidays Rosemary invited a school friend, Angela, to church. When yet another family joined the church and Lisa's phone calls became as plentiful as the others', Grace realized seven of them ran around together all the time. They comprised the entire 1956 age group in Sunday School with the exception of Pamela who coolly maintained her distance.

They were on the phone constantly. How in the world could Rosemary have anything left to say when she saw four of them at school every day?

They were, on the whole, a very unusual group. Angela and Lisa were interested in science and medicine, Rosemary and Laura in art, Christine, the flautist, wanted a career with a major orchestra, Jill wanted to be an ace newspaper reporter, and Gretchen, enjoying her Spanish class, wanted to teach foreign languages.

The ninth grade Sunday School class was nearly full to overflowing. The teacher seemed a little lost at times with eight or more giggling girls in her charge but she was as enthralled with them as they were with her.

More specifically the girls were enthralled with their teacher's son, Eric, who was a year older than they were. Tall, blond and dreamy-eyed, he even charmed the uncharmable Rosemary.

In spite of their mutual crush none of them challenged each other for his affection and Grace bemusedly wondered whom Eric would eventually choose. She started to ask Rosemary about it once but was put off because "it's time for *Star Trek*."

Eric's charm was obviously not up to Leonard Nimoy's.

Grace never knew exactly who gave up on Eric first or if it really mattered. And so the school year rolled by.

They looked forward to their summer vacation and Rosemary marked one week in July for Ridgecrest, the Southern Baptist retreat nestled in the mist-enshrouded mountains of North

Carolina. "Foreign Mission Week, Mom," she smiled, reading the bulletin. "It'll be good to hear this stuff again."

"Well, you could get all your friends together for a chapter of Acteens," Grace reminded her.

"Acteens are useless without Forward Steps," Rosemary shot right back.

Grace gave up. "Who are you going to room with?"

"Jill, Lisa and Laura."

"What about Gretchen?"

"She's going, too."

"Why aren't you rooming with her?"

"Laura and I are staying together."

That was obviously the end of that conversation.

Harry warmed to the idea. "An entire week to ourselves, Gracie," he grinned. "I think it sounds great."

"Harry Lee, I can't believe you're so anxious to get rid of her!"

"The phone will be quiet and I won't have to listen to seven of them at one time." He paused and repeated, "The phone will be quiet."

Grace couldn't help but grin.

Early on a hot Monday morning in July Grace helped Rosemary load her things onto the rickety old church bus. She watched somewhat forlornly as the overflowing vehicle pulled away from the church parking lot and headed towards North Carolina.

She remembered all the exciting plans she and Harry made and her twinge of dismay turned into delight. "Ah, just listen to the quiet," Harry said later that evening. "I can't believe silence sounds so good!"

Grace couldn't, either.

"I forget how old she was when she started to talk," Harry continued, "but I don't think there's been a moment when she hasn't rattled about something."

Grace laughed.

"I hope she marries and has a baby who talks to her from the minute it wakes up in the morning until it finally collapses at night," he went on.

"What's all this about, Harry? If she were shy I bet you'd be singing a different tune."

"I'm just grateful for this week."

So am I, Grace thought a little guiltily. She's getting so willful I need a break to regroup.

She wondered how the kids were getting along at Ridgecrest then, remembering her promise to Harry, stopped talking about her. It was time to enjoy their week alone.

                    *   *   *

Rosemary returned with a duffel bag full of ruined laundry and a sketchbook full of drawings of people and places at Ridgecrest. "It was wonderful, Mom. You should have seen the displays from the missionaries in Japan."

It went right over Grace's head as she finally identified the problem with the laundry. Mildew! "What in the world have you done to your clothes?"

"It rained every day. I got caught in it lots of times and my clothes never got dry," Rosemary explained, tossing the sketchbook onto the table. "The food was awful. I'm so glad to be home!"

"What happened to your umbrella?"

"I didn't have one."

"Yes, you did."

"Nope."

"I know I packed—" Grace paused and looked at her. If she kept complaining about the laundry she might lose Rosemary's positive response to Ridgecrest. "I'm glad you had a good time," she managed to say. "Did the other girls enjoy the missionaries?"

"I think I'm the only person who went to classes," Rosemary confided. "It's strange down there, Mom. There's a tunnel under the highway and everybody goes there to make out."

Make out…neck…Grace's fingers and toes went numb.

"They spent much more time there than in classes. The local boys cruise the area trying to pick up girls. It looked like something out of the 1950s."

"Did you—"

Rosemary made a face. "Hardly. Laura and I had better things to do. She's gotten some great ideas for a sculpture, Mom. She loved the stuff some of the missionaries had."

Grace glanced at the sketchbook. "You filled that up mighty quick. Should you have taken a camera instead?"

"It rained so hard I don't think I'd've had enough light. Besides, I'm not too good with a camera and I don't want to spend that kind of money."

"Oh," Grace replied. Then she smiled. "Your schedule got here," she announced, remembering that Rosemary would start senior high school in only a few weeks.

"Did you look at it?"

"Was I supposed to?"

"Who did they assign me for geometry?"

"It only lists a room number."

"I will *die* if I get that old hag. She fails everybody and I don't think I can stand it."

"Rosie, won't you need some grasp of geometry for art? I mean, a lot of art is like architecture, isn't it?"

Rosemary's face went pale. "I might do all right if I get someone besides old Witch-Hazel."

"That's a mean thing to say."

She refused to be chastised. "Didn't you call your librarian Puss Irving?"

Grace blushed hotly. How could Rosemary remember the most embarrassing things? "We didn't mean what you trashy kids mean today."

Rosemary chuckled. "Nobody said you did."

I walked right into that one, Grace decided. She looked back at the clothes. "Is everyone else's stuff as bad as yours?"

"Yep. The girls on the other side of the building had mold in their underwear."

"We'll have to think of something before next year."

"I won't be going next year, Mom."

"Why not?"

"I heard the adults talking. They plan to schedule us for music week and I'm not interested in that. There's no interest in missions anymore. We were the only teenagers there and no one was really interested but me." She paused. "Was it like this before re-organization?"

Grace shook her head. Only a few years ago churches raced to schedule their young people for foreign mission week because the demand was so high the facilities were booked in a matter of days.

"It looks like they screwed up, doesn't it?" Rosemary asked point-blank. "I bet they wish they'd left everything alone."

Grace couldn't say anything. She didn't think there were any regrets. Missions had lost all their former emphasis in the re-organization. She had no idea what supplanted it.

7

Music programs. That was what supplanted it.

It finally dawned on Grace as she watched the youth choir file into the choir loft, all the kids fresh-faced and cute in their crisp uniforms. There were too many of them, some people complained, but their vast number provided an absolutely glorious sound unequaled in the rest of the association. So many of them were musical they were able to perform very difficult works.

Grace smiled at Rosemary on the first row, wedged between the strong altos of Laura and Gretchen so her cheerful monotone wouldn't stray too far across the congregation. The other girls had such pretty voices. Why did Rosemary sound like a crow?

It didn't seem to bother her friends. There were, after all, a lot of other kids who couldn't carry a tune in a bucket.

Could that youth choir sing! Why did the invocation sound so much prettier when they sang it? Was it because of the sheer number of them or were those young voices simply easier to bear than the ones of the adult choir?

They stood for the first hymn and Grace was proud Rosemary never once looked at her hymnal. She knew the words for all three verses even if she couldn't sing.

The congregation and the choir sat down. During the obligatory announcements and welcome to the visitors, the girls'
ensemble made its way quietly onto the podium. Grace smiled as
she recognized faces. Three of those "little girls" had started to
college a couple of weeks ago, to the Baptist College where she
wanted Rosemary to go.

Grace shifted in the pew and nudged Harry to keep him awake.
Rosemary had mentioned how good the girls were.

One of the girls stepped forward to introduce the song. It was
standard procedure because the choir director had little patience
for shyness but there was something odd today. The girl's face was
radiant and her smile, as Harry would say, was just a little bit too
toothy for sincerity. Grace twisted in her seat.

"Praise God we've come together in His Spirit on another Holy
Sabbath day," she said.

Rosemary snapped to immediate attention and Grace knew
exactly what she was thinking. The Sabbath was Saturday and
Rosemary expected the announcer to know it.

Grace squeezed her eyes shut for a moment, hoping Rosemary
would have recovered her composure by the time she dared peek
again at the girls. When the song title was mentioned Grace felt it
was safe to open her eyes.

To her astonishment the girl lifted her hands, smiling toward
heaven, ending with, "Praise His Holy Name."

Rosemary was staring, open-mouthed, at the spectacle before
her. Is she so unpoised, Grace wondered wildly and nearly died in
the pew as Laura leaned toward her daughter and obviously whispered to her to close her mouth. She could almost hear
Rosemary's jaw clamp shut as she automatically did as Laura said.

Rosemary recovered somewhat and her wild eyes found her
mother's. Grace gulped and frowned, not knowing what to do.

The song was indeed beautiful but the three girls who'd just started to the Baptist College seemed most affected by the music. It was as though they were three different girls, not the self-contained young Baptists they were three months ago.

Was something going on at the Baptist College?

*   *   *

"You aren't mad at me, are you, Mom?" Rosemary asked after church as they drove home.

"No, honey, I'm not mad at you. I just wish you hadn't looked so shocked."

"But I was shocked!"

So was I, Grace thought to herself.

"They've gone crazy on that college campus, Mom," Rosemary hastened to tell her. "You should have heard the nonsense they spouted! I don't know what's going on there but it sure isn't academic."

"Oh Rosie, you always overreact."

"Maybe so, Mom." She paused and looked out the window. "They aren't real Baptists anymore, Mom. I know the things they say aren't so."

Harry ventured to look back at her in the rear-view mirror of the car but Grace turned around to face her. "What do you mean?"

Rosemary shrugged. "I remember in Daddy's junior department, when we studied Genesis, Daddy said the six days of creation weren't six days like ours. They could have been six million billion years for all we know."

Grace nodded, wondering with a knot of fear what her daughter was getting at.

"Now we're supposed to believe they were six real days," Rosemary finished.

"Oh, that's ridiculous," Grace snorted. "Who ever heard tell of such a thing?"

"Mom, what's all that pre-millennium and post-millennium stuff?" she asked point-blank.

Grace's eyes widened. "What?"

"We're going to be studying it in Training Union. One of the deacons is going to bring in a tape for us tonight and told us to bring a friend or two if we wanted."

Harry chuckled. "Are you going to ask anyone?"

Rosemary grinned. "All my friends will be there."

Grace, however, couldn't shake a sense of foreboding about Rosemary's question. Her own memory was sharp and she was certain she'd never heard the terms Rosemary mentioned.

That night the combined junior and senior high departments were played a tape depicting events on earth immediately after the rapture. Grace's curiosity was roused by Rosemary's questions on pre-millennium and post-millennium so she attended hoping to get some answers.

The tape played on suspense, she noted with her heart hammering. It also played on fear and not small fear, either, but paralyzing, mind-numbing fear.

What would you do if you were left behind at the rapture, knowing all you had to look forward to was the very worst of hellfire? Were you saved? Were you *sure* you were saved?

Grace suddenly remembered the teenagers sitting in the darkened room with her. She could hear many of them weeping softly. Others trembled in their seats. Not one was unaffected.

That couldn't possibly be what Christianity meant! Where was the dignity, the common sense in such a definition?

This isn't the way it's supposed to be, a small voice of reason said to her. The choice for Christianity should be a dignified one of wanting to live a better life, not the humiliating crawling of the spiritually terrified. Fearing God meant healthy respect not literally being so afraid you were sick.

She knew, though, come the invitation hymn at the end of evening worship, a flood of teenagers would go to the front of the church. In fear.

I don't want anyone in fear, Grace thought, and I bet Jesus doesn't, either!

What would she say to Rosemary about the tape? Funny, I never thought I'd have to tell her the stuff she hears in my own church isn't right. This just can't be happening in a Southern Baptist church!

*   *   *

Grace's curiosity turned into apprehension about what was going on in the senior high school department. Every week Rosemary came home with odd questions Grace couldn't answer. When Grace brought up the problem with Dorothy the older woman frowned.

"This is going on in *our* church?" Dorothy asked. "We used to look down our noses at Nazarenes and Pentecostals who believed those sorts of things."

"What am I supposed to tell Rosemary?"

"Certainly not to swallow that nonsense hook, line and sinker. I think it's only a passing phase, Grace. There seems to be a backlash at work now."

"Backlashes undo things."

"Not necessarily. A religion must tolerate debate in order to survive."

"Well, I don't know about that, Dorothy. The Catholics don't seem to tolerate a lot of debate."

"Nonsense. Vatican Two has had a most liberalizing effect on Catholics. The door has been opened and will never close again."

"Mmm," Grace mumbled.

"We could use some debate ourselves."

"Rosemary doesn't seem to think that's the case."

"Why not?"

"Well, she claims this new way of thinking tolerates no other opinion. She called her Training Union director a Gestapo man. I didn't like that."

"No, I can see that," Dorothy agreed. "Well, Grace, let's hope we get an intellectual here for fall revival. It should give her a rest from her soap box."

Grace smiled. "Harry said if she'd been born in the last century she'd have been another Carrie Nation."

Dorothy laughed. "I can see that, too. Don't give her an ax and send her to Training Union, Grace. She might turn out to be another Lizzie Borden instead."

It was Grace's turn to chuckle and she suddenly realized she hadn't laughed in a long, long time.

*   *   *

The guest for fall revival wasn't the intellectual Dorothy prayed for. He was unlike anything their church had ever known before: a screamer, Rosemary called him, obsessed with the sins of teenagers.

They were treated to one of the most graphic sermons Grace ever heard, all about what happened when weak parents allowed their children to go to dances.

Grace squirmed in her seat. The ban on dancing was nothing new, really. When she was a child it had seemed to her that the church hierarchy frowned on any extracurricular activity because decent people simply didn't do those things. But as times changed no one gave a second thought to high schoolers attending properly chaperoned dances.

Now this lunatic raved about how girls incited boys to lust when they danced. If anything bad happened to girls it was no more than they deserved for being promiscuous.

Grace's eyes bugged. Promiscuous? At a high school dance? Who did this nut think he was, anyway?

In spite of the hysterics he was charismatic. By the time he finished the teenagers in the congregation looked as though they'd endured a torture test.

Grace glanced around the sanctuary, her eyes finally resting on her daughter. No tears or remorse there, Grace noted with relief.

Later in the week the guest speaker brought up the topic of the teenagers' friends. He began by reminding them how much they valued their friends, would do anything for them. He promptly informed them that if their friends died without Jesus it was their fault. Not only the ones who didn't attend church but the ones who attended the *wrong* church.

The wrong church was any but the Baptist one. Of course, Grace remembered, that's what our foreign missionaries preach, too, but they can't be as horrible about it as he is, though, can they?

She couldn't bring herself to believe they could but a sliver of doubt nagged her. If non-Baptists were capable of salvation, might there be a wider world beyond Christianity itself? If so, would it reduce the scope of evangelism?

Thinking like this pushes me into the realm of United Methodists and Presbyterians with all their talk of one central truth through many expressions, she thought with a shudder. But am I slipping in my faith? Or growing?

*   *   *

Kevin, one of Laura's classmates, came to church. Grace wasn't surprised because Laura was the cutest of the seven girls and sure to have a boyfriend before the rest of them.

When it finally dawned on Grace he was there for Rosemary her heart nearly stopped. Were there signs she hadn't noticed?

"It's going absolutely nowhere," Dorothy laughed.

"Why?"

"They sat in front of me on Sunday morning, Grace. I don't think Rosemary was doing it for my benefit but she wouldn't even let him hold her hand."

Nor did she let him put his arm around her, either, Grace noticed. She didn't understand Rosemary's coldness. He was a darling boy with brown-blond curls, merry hazel eyes and a grin to charm the birds out of the trees.

Fifteen and too young to drive, he rode to see her on his bicycle, most often with a box of chocolates tucked under his arm. What a sweetheart, Grace thought warmly.

He shared Rosemary's passion for drawing and was better at it, too. Occasionally he brought over stacks of used computer paper his father brought from work and the two of them practiced their art.

They went to a few movies together but mostly Kevin was content to curl up on the living room floor and draw with Rosemary.

Harry shook his head. "I don't even think it's puppy-love," he said dryly. "They're only one jump above coloring books."

Grace thought seriously about speaking to Rosemary about her cool, reserved behavior but realized her daughter wasn't so cool and reserved when Kevin kept his mind off necking and talked to her. It finally occurred to her that Kevin was only another friend, much like Laura and Christine.

When Grace found out he was a Catholic she was so relieved they were just friends she nearly fainted. When she recovered she wondered why Rosemary hadn't done anything to convert him.

She overheard them talking about confession. "It's very private," Kevin assured her, "and in the last few years, you don't get off with a few Our Fathers or some Hail Marys. You really have to be sorry to get absolution."

"Well, I don't like that part," Rosemary returned, "but I do think people need to talk to someone when they carry big secrets. Someone who can't tell."

"That's the psychological factor," Kevin explained.

Grace tiptoed away, almost in tears. Somehow it all went back to Melanie and Epiphany. Why did Rosemary have to be so curious about things she should leave alone?

*   *   *

There were dozens of small gifts for Rosemary under the Christmas tree that year. She herself worked hard for her friends, painting pictures of their favorite *Star Trek* characters and making stuffed animals for them.

It took tremendous effort for Rosemary to share her crush on Leonard Nimoy with Christine. The finished portrait of Spock, Grace had to admit, showed much promise. Of course, the Vulcan ears were a bit on the large side but all in all, Rosemary's work was coming along nicely.

Grace found it hard to believe fifteen-year-old girls enjoyed making stuffed animals but it seemed to be all the rage. She noticed Rosemary planned her list early, set aside free time without being asked and only asked Grace to help when she came across a sewing instruction she didn't understand.

She practically went through an entire roll of tape when she wrapped her gifts and Grace couldn't resist teasing her. "Little wild with that tape, aren't you, missy?"

"I can't help it. Nothing wants to stay put. Don't they look as good as the packages that come from gift wrap at the department stores?"

"No," Grace said honestly. "You're very artistic, Rosemary, but gift wrapping...maybe you just need practice."

Rosemary made a stuffed animal for Kevin, a beleaguered calico frog filled with dried navy beans "so he can sit up and look adorable," she explained, playing with it before she wrapped it. "I just love this thing. He looks like he has the weight of the world on his frog shoulders."

"Like Kevin?"

"I don't think anything gets Kevin down for long."

"What is he giving you?"

Rosemary smiled but didn't blush. "I have no idea."

"Should I prepare your father for anything?"

"Like what?"

"What are they called? Identification bracelets. Will the two of you be going steady?"

Rosemary met her eyes. "I like things just the way they are."

"And how's that?"

Rosemary smiled, tormenting her mother. "The way they are."

*   *   *

Christine made stuffed animals for Christmas, too. After the Lees opened their gifts Grace inspected the varicolored fluff balls in the box. "They don't have faces," she noted.

Rosemary rolled her eyes. "They're tribbles, Mom. From *Star Trek*." She picked up a white one and tossed it to her mother. "Only these are guaranteed not to multiply on us!"

How could Rosemary and her friends be so grown-up one minute and the next enjoy stuffed animals like children? It was very confusing.

Grace set the tribble down and smiled at Kevin's gift, a lovely gold pin with Rosemary's name engraved on it. "That's a classic, Rosemary. It's mature enough for you to wear the rest of your life."

Rosemary smiled. "I know."

Harry glared in their direction. "Chocolates every time he comes over, now this pin. I wonder what he has in mind," he said darkly.

Rosemary started to argue but Grace shook her head. Fathers were never quite prepared for their daughters' boyfriends, no matter how innocent they were. Harry, Grace noticed, had been pouting ever since Rosemary opened the gift.

Didn't he know that as long as Rosemary and her friends were content to play with stuffed animals he had nothing to worry about? Yet it had to be hard to share that pedestal with a mere boy.

8

It's election year again, Grace thought dismally. We're no closer to the end of the mess in Vietnam, no closer to achieving racial harmony than we were in 1968. The college kids get more daring. People say they'll provoke a violent situation yet. Look how many adults support shooting them for demonstrating.

Although Rosemary saw Kevin only occasionally Grace worried about the threat of boys. When girls started noticing boys it was a bad day for mothers.

In Rosemary's group, only Angela had a boyfriend and Grace wondered if Rosemary's disapproval was genuine concern or jealousy. It would kill me if Rosemary were serious about a boy at fifteen, she decided.

An undying passion for a boy was impossible as long as Rosemary, Laura and Christine continued to live in each other's pockets. They were so artsy. Grace didn't know if their aspirations to sophistication were products of real taste or egos spinning out of control but it continued to set them apart from the other girls. The three of them wanted more, much more than the husbands and children the other girls dreamed of.

Grace had to admit Laura showed tremendous talent with her sculpture. When Christine visited the soft sound of her flute in gentle studies or fiery exercises convinced Grace she was on the path to success, too.

They were not the sort of girls that teenage sexpots were made of.

However, they would turn sixteen that year and most women at church said turning sixteen created monsters out of their darling daughters. Falling grades and the threat of unsuitable boys consumed parents' every waking moment.

Rosemary had been monstrous in a different way, of course, since she was twelve. Grace was more than willing to take the intellectual rebel over the sexpot.

Rosemary liked to do some of the things her friends enjoyed. She seemed to take pleasure in the shock on her mother's face when she spent her monthly allowance on a haircut.

"Your hair, Rosie! Your beautiful hair!" Grace cried, aghast the nearly waist-long blonde hair was cut in varying layers, neither short nor long.

"It's a shag," Rosemary explained.

"A what?"

"The name of my haircut. Laura had hers cut in a gypsy."

"Laura, too?"

"All of us, Mom! You should have seen those beauticians' faces when the seven of us marched in for haircuts!"

Grace tried to imagine it and wondered if the haircuts looked as similar as the long, center-parted tresses the seven of them wore. Had worn, she corrected herself. She tried to smile. "Were there any regrets?"

Rosemary sighed. "I don't think so. I wouldn't trade my new freedom for anything!"

"Rosemary, your hair is so straight. I never noticed how much so until now."

"I love it. I feel like Jo in *Little Women* when she sold her hair. I know exactly what she meant by feeling free and light. I wish I'd done it sooner."

"What do you plan to do with it, to dress it up, I mean?" Grace asked, fingering the short layers brushing Rosemary's collar.

"Wash it and forget it. Angela suggested we all get together for a curler-burning party."

"Well, I'd wait on that if I were you. You might change your mind."

Rosemary fluffed her hair with her fingers. "Me? I doubt it!"

Grace looked carefully at the new Rosemary with the shag. She doubted it, too.

*   *   *

Grace's secular reading material had definitely taken a turn for the lurid. So Dorothy said when her sharp eyes caught sight of Mario Puzo's *The Godfather* not-too-deftly hidden under Grace's *Royal Service*.

Grace blushed up to the roots of her hair and bit her tongue to keep from saying it was none of Dorothy's business what she chose to read. She tried to say something soothing but had the distinct impression she'd shocked the old schoolteacher.

Well, she thought to herself later, so what? The book was *so* good! Grace had loved stories about gangsters since she was a child hearing about the real thing. And the Italian Mafia! How poignant, how sad!

How erotic! She blushed deeply when she read the graphic sex scenes in the book but the violence, for some odd reason, didn't bother her at all.

She'd told no one about buying the book except Harry who thought that it was hilarious. She hid it carefully before Rosemary came home from school, wondering what a hypocrite she was for reading something she thought was inappropriate for her sixteen-year-old daughter.

The movie was playing nearby and she intended to see it. She gasped when she learned the rating was an R and supposedly unfit for any good Christian to see. For a very short moment, she wavered.

My book with my money, the movie with my money, too, so who cares and whose business is it, she thought. She practiced her defense over and over until she was sure no critical tongues would shake her resolve.

"I'm going to see *The Godfather* Tuesday night," she announced to Harry and Rosemary one evening, "so you two make some plans."

"I want to see it, too," Rosemary said.

Grace nearly stopped breathing. Composing herself, she shook her head. "You're too young. You have to be eighteen."

"That's X," Rosemary corrected. "I can go to an R if you or Daddy go with me."

"X, R, whatever, I don't care. You're not seeing it," Grace snapped.

"If it's so bad why are you going to see it, O Pillar of the Baptist Church?"

Grace bit her lip and counted to ten. "I don't recall having to ask your permission to see a movie, miss. I make the decisions around here."

Rosemary sat back in her chair and glared at her.

The first battle, the worst battle, was over.

⋆ ⋆ ⋆

Tuesday night came quickly and Grace left for the mall cinema
an hour before show time so she could be first in line so no one
would see her.

Damn this guilt-complex, she thought angrily. If I were really as
justified as I thought, I wouldn't be going so early.

She parked under a light on the opposite side of the mall from
the cinema. No one must ever suspect she was there to see *The
Godfather.*

The mall was crowded with spring sales shoppers. How many
other people had the same idea she did? The first two days the
movie line trailed halfway up the mall and the local news team
interviewed people waiting to buy tickets.

Thank God I waited until some of the excitement died down! If
a news crew got my face on camera, well, they'd throw me out of
the church!

The teenager at the ticket counter looked surprised when Grace
handed over her money. "You have forty-five minutes before the
next show," he reminded her.

"That's okay," Grace said gently.

"Four dollars, please."

She'd been warned about the expense but still thought it was a
fine day when a two-hour movie cost four dollars. Moving into
the lobby, she sat down on a padded bench and eyed the concession stand hungrily. There was nothing like the smell of buttered
popcorn.

That popcorn would really be good, she thought. I was too
nervous to eat much dinner and look at that perfect, tantalizing
stuff! Maybe I shouldn't have anything to eat, though. The movie
is going to be very violent and the sight of all that blood might
make me sick.

"Well, hello there, Grace!"

Grace's heart nearly stopped. She hadn't the strength to turn her head but from the corner of her eye watched as her preacher strolled toward her from the opposite end of the concession stand.

He was smiling. Was it a natural, friendly smile or the nervous one of another guilty party caught in the act? Grace felt her throat constrict and a sudden dew of perspiration dampen her brow and palms.

"Getting here early to get a good seat?" he inquired pleasantly.

"Wh—what are y-you doing here?" Grace managed to utter, finding it difficult to breathe.

"A bunch of us are here to determine how morally corrupt this film really is," he chuckled. "Obviously, you don't think it is."

Oh yes, I do! Grace wanted to say but the words wouldn't come. It's not right that he's here, she thought. This is no place for the clergy.

The still small voice she'd wrestled with for weeks piped up, Not right for him but right for you?

Her appetite for the popcorn disappeared. She held her ticket limply in her hand, watching the minister as he bought a large popcorn and a box of chocolates.

He smiled at her again as he returned to his friends and Grace smiled back wanly. God, what a night this was turning out to be!

*   *   *

She rushed out into the parking lot, hoping she had the presence of mind to recognize her car when she came to it.

The film essentially ended for her when Sonny and Lucy had a quickie in the bedroom during Connie's wedding reception. It was right there on the big screen for the entire world to see! How in the world did they have the nerve to depict such trash on motion picture screens across the country? It was one thing to put graphic sex in a book but quite another to put in on the screen. In her heart of hearts she truly believed movie makers wouldn't do such things.

God, how awful! How awful! She jumped into her car and raced home, wondering how she would explain her state of nerves to Harry but Harry had already gone to bed.

Rosemary was busy at the kitchen table doing her geometry homework and glanced up briefly when Grace came in. She still looks insulted, Grace noted, and quickly felt deep relief she hadn't allowed herself to be talked into taking her to see the film.

"What's the matter, Mom? You look like you've seen a ghost."

"The preacher saw me at the movie," Grace blurted out. She was immediately furious with herself because she'd had no intention of telling anyone, especially Rosemary.

"Was he taking names of bad church members or something?" Rosemary teased.

"No," Grace explained, taking off her coat, "he was there to see the movie. Just as cool and calm as though it was *Bambi.*"

Rosemary laughed and Grace glared at her. "What's the problem, Mom? Did he intimidate you?"

"A little, maybe. I just wish I hadn't gone."

"Why?"

"It was filthy."

"You thought that R was for religious?"

"It isn't funny," Grace muttered, blushing deeply.

"If it was so bad why didn't you walk out?"

"I paid four dollars—"

"And you were going to get your full four dollars' worth of smut? Is that it?" Rosemary giggled.

"That's enough out of you!" Grace cried. "I will never, never go to another movie rated R, do you hear me? I'd better not ever catch you at one, either, miss."

Rosemary stifled her laughter but couldn't control the sparkle in her eyes. "What are you afraid I might see, Mom?"

"You just make sure you steer clear of them."

Rosemary turned back to her geometry. "This is one of the dumbest, best things you've ever done. I can't wait to tell everybody you thought the R was for religious."

Grace went to her and shook her shoulder. "You'd better keep your mouth shut! It's nobody's business!"

"If the preacher saw you there, Mom, don't you think half the church already knows by now?"

God, God, oh God, how true! Grace released her and sat down heavily. "My life is over," she murmured.

"Well, your double-life at any rate," Rosemary smiled. "Cheer up now. You can re-dedicate your life Sunday morning and everyone will forgive you."

Grace frowned. That *was* an option...she glanced up again at Rosemary and saw her stifling another bout of laughter.

Rosemary would never apologize if she'd gone and been caught. Neither would Dorothy, she suspected.

By God, she thought, finding strength, I won't, either. The people it concerns will know I went and made a total jackass of myself. No one else needs an explanation.

She felt the corners of her mouth twitch upward. "R for religious. That's pretty good, Rosie, if I do say so myself."

*   *   *

How could a student make straight As in every other subject and fail geometry? Grace stared at Rosemary's report card for the umpteenth time, not understanding such a total lack of mathematical ability.

Artists were supposed to do well in geometry. So what happened to Rosemary? Grace couldn't bring herself to cheer the other grades because she was so depressed over the big bold F staring at her from the list.

Rosemary herself was so relieved to be out of the horrible class that she offered no apologies for the grade. Grace glanced at the other subjects: English, Physical Education, Biology and Latin. The Latin, of course, was Dorothy's influence and Grace somehow expected it to be a struggle but Rosemary grasped the language with ease and swore she'd take it every year she was in high school.

The problems with geometry hadn't stopped Harry from tossing her a driver's manual and insisting she pass her written test on her sixteenth birthday. "No one else is driving," she pointed out.

"If you don't learn to drive by Labor Day," Harry said sternly, "you'll make your own arrangements for transportation. Your mother will not be a chauffeur after that, do you understand?"

Rosemary swallowed the threat in silence and learned enough to pass the written test on her birthday.

What hypocrites parents are, Grace thought, watching Harry dig out the previously unused seat belts so Rosemary could buckle up. He hates the things but wouldn't hesitate to punish her for not wearing one.

Grace didn't quite know what to make of his methods, either. Instead of taking Rosemary to a deserted stretch of country road he found a quieter section of interstate and switched places with Rosemary. "Learn to drive while the traffic moves beside you rather than toward you," he said to her.

Grace braced herself every time she got into the car. Thank God they had automatic transmission. She could imagine Rosemary sliding all the way down a hill if she had to stop at a red light.

Her skills were amazingly good. She still complained, of course, and Grace cringed as she wondered what her daughter called other drivers when she wasn't there to hear her.

Harry was pleased in every respect except her attempts at parallel parking.

"For crying out loud, Dad," she argued, "you don't do that anywhere in town anymore! When will I ever have to do this?"

"You have to do it to get your license."

Every night he took her downtown to practice. He wanted the car parked correctly in less than five minutes.

"I'll never get it right," Rosemary predicted.

On the hot August day she took her test Grace wondered if Harry would have allowed her to schedule the test if he didn't think she could pass it. The state trooper assigned to Rosemary was the great ogre with the reputation of failing most of the sixteen-year-olds who crossed his path. Grace saw Rosemary's face fall and hoped the experience wouldn't be too traumatic.

At the end of the test Rosemary turned the corner, her face shining with joy and Grace knew she'd passed.

"The parallel parking went all right?" Harry asked.

"Honestly, Dad, I don't think he even noticed it took me an eternity. His first grandson was born last night and that's all he could talk about. He'll probably pass everyone today," she laughed.

Harry paused and gave her a measuring gaze. "Well, since you're now an officially licensed driver you can take yourself to choir practice tonight."

"Alone?"

"What's the matter? Are you afraid of the dark?"

"Doesn't get dark until after nine," Rosemary shot right back. "I mean may I take Laura?"

Grace smiled, understanding at last. "If her parents don't mind."

Rosemary grinned. "A licensed driver at last!"

"Well," Grace reminded her, "the privilege of driving depends on grades, you know."

"And staying out of trouble," Harry added.

"I'm not interested in trouble," Rosemary said off-handedly. "I simply want to roll into that parking lot tonight, just a tiny bit late, so they'll all know I did it and on the first try, too!"

So, Grace sighed, it *had* been a competition after all! "Why do you always have to be first, Rosemary?"

"I wasn't first," Rosemary corrected. "Lisa got her license right after school was out. I could have killed her."

Grace laughed. That was why she hadn't fought Harry about all the time practicing! Her vanity had been touched. It was good to see her slightly humbled but knew that wouldn't last very long.

          *   *   *

Because she'd failed geometry Rosemary had to take second year algebra. Unhappy at the prospect of seeing her overall grade point average slip because of the detested math, she didn't seem eager to start back to school. "It's funny," she said sarcastically, "that kids get doctors' excuses to get out of taking gym class but I can't get a doctor's excuse to get out of this stupid math stuff!"

"Think of the other classes you have. You love Latin," Grace tried to soothe.

"I like everything on the schedule except the algebra. I absolutely *have* to pass this. I can't stand it another year!"

"Don't you have to have math in college?"

Rosemary's face blanched. "I sure hope not. When will I ever have this monkey off my back, Mom?"

"Don't you have to be better at math to be a really good artist?"

Grace meant the remark with no hostility but saw from the expression on Rosemary's face it was taken as an insult, like most things these days.

Why did Rosemary assume Grace always meant the worst? It seemed to be a problem with most sixteen-year-olds and their mothers. They were so much closer to friends, so much more liable to be influenced by the wrong things.

Grace stayed vigilant looking for the danger signals.

The group of girls took a particular interest in the Olympics that year, rather, a particular interest in Mark Spitz. Laura had the hardest crush and Rosemary immediately decided to paint a picture of him, scandalizing Grace by threatening to capture him in the nude. She only backed down when she realized her artistic attempt might not be so favorably accepted by Laura's parents.

Their innocent delight in the games was horribly disrupted when, on that horrible September Fifth, the Israeli athletes were murdered. It was probably, Grace realized, the same kind of shock her own generation weathered when Pearl Harbor was bombed.

"Why, Mom, why?" Rosemary asked, totally thunder-struck. "I don't understand what the journalists are saying. Who are the Palestinians and what does it mean, a separate Palestine?"

Grace paused. There would be sermons a-plenty reminding all good Baptists Israel would continue to be persecuted even after statehood but that didn't answer Rosemary's question.

"They're a group of people living in Israel."

"Are they Arabs?"

"They're Moslems."

"Yes, but if they're living in Israel, aren't they Israelis?"

"I don't think their government works like ours, Rosie."

Rosemary frowned. "How does it work?"

"I don't think those people are citizens."

The struggle was apparent on Rosemary's face, the disapproval unmistakable. "They live in Israel but they aren't citizens," she repeated. "Why not?"

"Because their government doesn't work that way."

In spite of everything she'd ever heard in Sunday School, every sermon reinforcing Genesis, chapter twelve, about God's curse on people who mistreated Jews and His blessing on those who helped the Jews, she looked her mother straight in the eye and said, "That's not right."

Grace felt the same way, too, sort of…but a good Baptist couldn't take anyone else's side. It was against the faith. The Jews were God's chosen people and they were right. Always.

Or at least they were until Rosemary planted the suspicion of doubt in her mother's mind.

9

In spite of the preacher's daughter's set being the most desirable clique at church, Rosemary's was by far the most powerful. She and her friends had adult approval because she was the voice of Biblical expertise. The girls were nice and weren't considered hot as mustard-pots.

For a long time the two camps coexisted somewhat peacefully. Then, almost without warning, they were in open conflict.

Grace casually glanced up at the kitchen clock as the phone rang promptly at three-fifty. That would be Laura calling before she dropped her schoolbooks. She barely heard Rosemary's gusty hello but knew, without another word, that something was wrong.

She tiptoed into the hallway and found Rosemary, shocked and pale, listening. Finally, she broke in, "He *will* pay you back for it, too. You wait and see. Hold on. Let me see if Mom will let me come over." She paused and looked up at Grace.

"What's going on?" Grace demanded.

"I'll call you back," Rosemary said hurriedly, hanging up the phone. She exhaled deeply to calm what Grace knew to be a rising temper. Grace motioned her into the kitchen.

"What is it?"

"That idiot choir director marked up Laura's music!"

"What music?"

"Don't you remember, Mom? She and Angela came back from Ridgecrest with copies of a musical. They loaned him their copies so he could look at them and see if we could sing some of the songs. He gave them back last night after Prayer Meeting all marked up!"

"Why would he do that?"

"I have no idea. That's what I get for not being at Prayer Meeting last night. If I'd gone we'd have straightened this mess out right then and there!"

Grace looked into Rosemary's furious face and was fleetingly glad she hadn't gone last night. No telling what would have erupted.

"May I go over to Laura's for awhile?" Rosemary asked suddenly.

"After we eat, maybe. You're too upset to drive right now and I don't trust you when you act like this."

"Don't—trust me? What's that supposed to mean?"

"I know the church is only a couple of miles from Laura's house. I can see you storming over there and having a show-down."

Rosemary sucked on her lower lip a moment, then said, "What if I promise I won't go storming over to the church?"

The promise should have allayed Grace's fears but there was something else in Rosemary's eyes, something deep and cunning. She had the feeling she would regret it but couldn't help saying, "Okay, after we eat."

*   *   *

How Grace wished she'd said no! She realized, too late, if she'd wanted Rosemary not to meddle in the problem she should have forbidden any and all contact with the choir director. Rosemary wasted no time telephoning him at home giving him a piece of her mind he wouldn't soon forget. His temper was roused, too, and within five minutes the two of them were at war.

That was on Thursday night. Now on Sunday, the whole congregation knew about it. Rather, they knew what their gossiping sources told them.

Grace could have strangled Rosemary without an iota of remorse. Nothing was solved by her action. The choir director refused point-blank to reimburse the two girls, claiming they'd given him the music. Rosemary called him a liar and conditions deteriorated from bad to worse.

It was the best scandal to hit the church in years. Who would win the battle of wills and how much unchristian behavior would the congregation witness before the little drama concluded? From shadowed classrooms Grace eavesdropped on pieces of conversations and decided the whispered excitement in some people's voices was the same sort of titillation she knew when she went to see *The Godfather.*

In the wake of the conflict Angela and Laura left the youth group and the church. Rosemary's group suffered a fatal rupture in numbers and in reputation and the preacher's daughter's set was ready.

It was high time to call Rosemary Lee to account for her arrogant, high-handed treatment of them. Minor members of Rosemary's group, seeing the handwriting on the wall, put some distance between Rosemary and themselves.

Church occasions became battlegrounds. Rosemary took on her rivals at a moment's notice for what she considered a lapse in theology but beneath the excuse of dogma, they were fighting about Angela, Laura and the choir director.

"Rosemary, it's a fact people in church will treat you worse than people of the world," Grace tried to soothe.

Rosemary raised horrified eyes to her. "Why?"

Grace opened her mouth but no words came out.

"It doesn't say much about people in church," Rosemary concluded, then begged, "Please, Mom, let's go someplace where people never abandoned their mission programs, someplace that might let me sit in on WMU if I went at night—"

"No!" Grace shouted. "We are never leaving our church, do you understand?"

Rosemary bit down on her lip.

Grace shook with fury. "You started this mess, you'll see it through. If the other kids mistreat you it's no more than you deserve!"

The look on her daughter's face was such Grace thought maybe, finally, she'd gotten through to her at last but the astonishment vanished quickly. "I am *not* going back to choir now that Angela and Laura are gone," she said firmly.

"Yes, you are—"

"Oh no, I'm not," Rosemary said lethally. "And if you try to make me I'll run away."

Grace could barely hear her for the thudding of her heart. The cold hand of reason stilled her tongue. Rosemary couldn't possibly be as street-wise as she pretended to be but could Grace take the risk? "All right," she heard herself saying quietly, "you don't have to go back to choir."

Rosemary nodded once but didn't say thank you. Grace trembled as she watched her leave the room. God, if we were Catholics I'd slap her in convent-school so fast it would make her head swim, she thought furiously.

The local Catholic high school had a sterling reputation for academics, turning out more national merit scholars than the public schools each year. It was a model for straightening out Catholics' problem children.

Grace shuddered, unable to contemplate taking so drastic a step at this stage. It hadn't gone too far yet. Every bit of Rosemary's questioning went back to contact with Melanie the Episcopalian. Just think what the Catholics would do to her!

*　　　*　　　*

Grace began to dread Sundays. What new argument would Rosemary start this week? Did she explode just for the love of the fireworks or was there something truly insidious in the way the lessons were taught?

If she only had more tact! That was Harry in her plunging in where angels feared to tread, without a backward glance at the destruction her sharp tongue caused. Where did she think her carping and teasing were getting her? If anything else, her peers hated her all the more.

Grace was tempted to confront Rosemary's teacher about the literal interpretation of the Bible but couldn't do it. It was one thing to take up for Rosemary at school when a point of fact was involved. Stirring up a hornet's nest over a matter of faith didn't seem appropriate.

Christine remained involved in church and loyal to Rosemary. Grace smiled at the disparity of the two: Christine tall and gentle, like a human willow-tree, trying to wave a breeze over Rosemary the human battering ram.

Grace prayed earnestly for some of Christine's temperament to rub off on Rosemary. She couldn't understand why Christine dealt more stoically with situations than Rosemary.

"If I could figure out what's going on, maybe I could get to the bottom of it," Grace told Dorothy after the June Circle Meeting.

"It's very simple what's at the bottom of it," Dorothy sniffed with a superior air. "We have Sunday School teachers who don't know what they're doing and teenagers who haven't the backbone to challenge them as Rosemary does. The children think she's showing off and it certainly doesn't endear her to her elders, as you can well imagine."

"I'm sure it wasn't this way when I was growing up. I never remember my teachers being as ignorant as Rosemary claims hers are."

Dorothy leveled her bright eyes on her. "They weren't, my dear. When you grew up there was a great deal of consideration of teachers for young people. The criteria are changing. We have a group of people in charge now who have a different agenda."

"Agenda?"

"Look at the emphasis. Our young preacher wants a young church. To this end, he overlooks all the experience and wisdom of his older church members and promotes these new people—people who probably have no idea what makes a Southern Baptist different from any other Baptist—into positions of leadership."

"Rosemary says they're not real Baptists."

"Well, not real Southern Baptists."

"What should we do?"

Dorothy shrugged. "Do? I don't know what there is to do, Grace. Don't worry. Maybe it'll blow over."

"Yes, I hope so," Grace sighed, "but what am I supposed to do with Rosemary in the meantime?"

*   *   *

The kids always looked exhausted on the last Sunday night before summer vacation. It was as though the weight of the entire school year fell on them in the last week of school and all of them seemed ready to drop.

Exhaustion wasn't good for Rosemary, either. She was worried about her final grade for algebra and her nerves were raw.

Senior high Training Union had been a fiasco for quite sometime with Rosemary leading the opposition single-handedly. Grace tried to stay out of the fray. Rosemary seemed so adept at confusing the issue to gain points for herself she didn't dare trust her.

Grace offered to help the church secretary complete some records and took a stack of paperwork downstairs to mail to the Sunday School superintendents. Her foot hadn't touched the last stair when she heard the din in the senior high department.

She nearly dropped the records as she heard Rosemary's furious voice challenge someone. "It's nothing but poetry, you idiot, how can you be so stupid?"

"Song of Solomon is the inspired Word of God and foreshadows Christ's love for the church," argued the director of her age group.

"Right. Seems like Christ has a pretty racy attitude towards his church, huh?" Rosemary taunted viciously.

Grace heard the collective gasps of other teenagers and several of them started talking at once.

"Oh come on, you know I'm right! When we learned the books of the Bible back in the fourth grade, we had a little foldout brochure that listed the categories. Song of Solomon falls right in there with Job, Psalms, Proverbs and Ecclesiastes in poetry! You remember it, I know you do!"

What is happening, Grace wondered frantically. What did the director mean by foreshadowing some relationship between

Christ and the church? If that were so, Song of Solomon would have been designated prophecy, not poetry.

"I think we should build a circle of prayer around you, Rosemary," the director said. "You have closed your heart to the truth and are acting like one of Satan's own the way you speak to me and your friends."

"They're no friends of mine!" she heard Rosemary cry and suddenly there she was, storming out of the department doorway, almost crashing into her mother.

Grace could only look at her with stricken eyes, taking in the fury that commanded her.

Rosemary took a long breath and said quietly, "You may make me go to services on Sunday morning but I am *never* coming back on a Sunday night!"

Grace tried to catch her dress-tail as she fled up the stairs but wasn't fast enough. What in God's Name was she going to do with her?

*   *   *

Rosemary and Christine were the only two teenagers in church instead of Ridgecrest. Grace hoped Rosemary would change her mind at the last minute but it didn't happen.

The two girls went to the balcony and Grace took her own seat with trepidation. Rosemary wore her don't-tread-on-me look and Christine looked especially curious. What were those two up to?

She glanced absently at the empty pew where Pamela and her friends usually sat. All of them were gone today, learning interesting material and having fun in North Carolina. All except Rosemary and Christine.

The service ran a little over and Grace's stomach was growling loudly when the last amen bounced off the ceiling. Rosemary was late getting to the car and Harry was furious because the traffic was horrible. "You're going to start getting out here when we do or I'll go off and leave you next time," he threatened.

Grace glanced toward the back seat to see Rosemary's reddened face. She started to face Harry but turned around again, noting it wasn't embarrassment coloring her daughter's cheeks. "What's the matter?" she demanded, seeing the sparks in Rosemary's eyes.

"Nothing."

"Did you and Christine have a fight?"

Rosemary turned shocked eyes on her. "What? No, nothing like that."

"Then what?"

"Nothing, I told you."

Grace wasn't convinced.

The phone was ringing off the hook as they entered the house. Even before she answered it, Grace knew it had to do with Rosemary.

"Grace, this is David Todd."

The grand old man of the church! Grace smiled. "Hello, Mr. Todd—"

"Grace, before you hear it from anyone else, I thought I should tell you Rosie exchanged a few heated words with Jim Walters after church."

The new deacon, the ex-Marine, the one Harry detested so thoroughly. "What did she say?"

"She and her friend whispered together all through the sermon and afterwards, Jim turned to Rosemary and offered to help her with any doctrinal questions she had. They were obviously talking about different beliefs in other churches.

"Now, Grace, while I don't approve of children talking through service, I must admit their whispering wasn't disturbing. The balcony was practically empty, anyway, since all the kids are at Ridgecrest."

"That's no excuse," Grace muttered through clenched teeth.

"Maybe so," David Todd sighed, "but Jim was very high-handed with her. If I weren't so crippled up with this knee, I would have gotten to them sooner but I couldn't."

"What did she do?"

"She told him she'd forgotten more about doctrine than he would ever know and while that's probably true, Grace—Grace—"

"I'll kill her," Grace breathed softly.

"Of course you won't," David Todd rebuked, "but I'm afraid Jim is hopping mad and plans to have it out with you and Harry before the day is over."

"Oh God," Grace murmured, "what am I going to do with her?"

"We're going to help Rosemary with her temper, Grace, that's what we're going to do. She's growing up and has to learn there are diplomatic ways to get her point across."

"She had no business talking in the first place!"

"Were you stock-still and absolutely silent in church when you were her age?"

Grace blushed to the roots of her hair, remembering how she once loved to whisper and giggle, too, but when she was called down she took her punishment and never, never talked back to an adult, especially an ex-Marine.

"Thank you for calling me, Mr. Todd," she said gently, "good-bye now."

She hung up the phone and walked upstairs to Rosemary's bedroom. How quickly her daughter had shed her Sunday finery for her jeans and tee shirt!

"I heard what you did today," she said quietly.

Folding her pantyhose, Rosemary scarcely missed a beat. "I imagined that's what the phone call was about. Well, what does the creep want? A signed confession of horrible guilt before he asks the other deacons to burn me at the stake or will they dig up that old threat of yore and church me?"

Grace took a step closer to her. "I ought to slap your teeth down your throat."

Rosemary tossed her pantyhose on the bed and shrugged.

"It was Mr. Todd."

That took the color out of her face, Grace noted. She's always loved David Todd and in her tantrum probably didn't notice he'd been a witness to every bit of it.

"He said he wanted to tell me about it before Jim Walters did."

Rosemary sat down in her rocker and looked away. "I didn't know Mr. Todd was there."

Grace paused and tried to calm her racing heart. "That's the only thing you're worried about, isn't it?"

"Yep," Rosemary confessed. "Why, are you expecting me to be sorry for what I said to that jack-ass?"

Grace felt her blood rise to the challenge. "By the time I finish with you, little miss, you're going to be very sorry, do you hear me?"

Rosemary shrugged again. "I'm only sorry Mr. Todd heard me. I'm not one bit sorry for anything else. He made Christine cry, Mom."

"She wouldn't have had to cry if the two of you had kept your mouths shut."

Rosemary glared at her. "Of all the places in the balcony to sit, he could have been away from us but no, he sat down right in front of us."

"I guess we'll get a call this afternoon from Mr. Walters. You're going to apologize to him, too."

Rosemary stopped rocking and lifted her chin. "Like hell I am."

Grace closed her eyes, hearing her heart thudding in her ears. "Well, if you don't, you won't see any of your friends or be in touch with them."

Rosemary looked as though she'd been struck. Grace hoped it would break her but the stunned look was gone quickly, replaced by another shrug. She knew she wouldn't apologize that day.

✶   ✶   ✶

Grace fully expected Rosemary to relent within the week and apologize to Jim Walters. It didn't happen in a week or even two, or in a month, either.

By the end of July Grace realized it wouldn't happen at all, no matter how dire the punishment. She set harsh rules anyway, hoping they would work: no dates or phone calls, not even letters. She expected the telephone-addicted Rosemary to crumble at the penalty.

Dorothy cornered Grace at the August Circle Meeting. "I have an idea I want to discuss with you, Grace."

"About getting Rosemary to apologize?"

"Are you two still fighting?"

"She hasn't apologized yet so she's still grounded."

"How long do you intend to do this, Grace? I can tell you right now that Rosemary will never apologize to that man."

Grace caught her breath then cleared her throat. "Oh, yes she will. If I have to punish her this entire school year—"

"What a deep resentment you're creating," Dorothy interrupted. "Is it worth it?"

How can she overlook Rosemary's behavior, Grace wondered. Surely she didn't approve!

"I'm going to be teaching a new Sunday School class the first week in October," Dorothy announced, changing the subject abruptly.

Grace smiled. "Back to the fourth graders?"

"God in heaven, no!" Dorothy cried before remembering herself. "It will be an ungraded, non-promoting class. I plan to start with Genesis and move right through to Revelation, no matter how long it takes."

"And you want me to join?"

"No, I want Rosemary to join."

That's an unexpected dip into ice water, Grace thought angrily. "Rosemary is fine where she is."

"No, she is not," Dorothy retorted, fire in her eyes. "If you force her to go to Sunday School with those girls who hate her, she'll leave the church when she's eighteen, Grace. I can see it coming."

"Wh—what do you mean?"

"You're driving her away yourself. Your authority looks to me like coercion. If you don't start dealing with her differently, she's going to leave us."

Grace's knees began to shake. Could it be true?

"Let her come to my class next church year, Grace," Dorothy said softly. "You won't regret it. I promise."

"She should be with girls her own age."

Dorothy laughed.

Grace wasn't convinced. "She'll never learn to get along if she runs away."

"Runs away? Rosemary Lee will never run away from anything!" Dorothy said haughtily. "It's too late for her to forgive her peers, Grace. You must accept the fact and go on."

"How can it ever be too late to forgive?"

"Oh, it's decidedly unchristian, I know. Those deeply spiritual types who'd have us believe such things are generally superficial and always tedious," she went on, forgetting for a moment Grace fell into that camp. Awareness suddenly dawned on the old lady and she blushed. "...Almost always, that is."

"But still generally superficial?" Grace demanded.

"Well," Dorothy hesitated, "perhaps I should have said naive. It's more appropriate."

You haughty old bat, Grace thought furiously.

"Tell Rosemary about the class," Dorothy suggested.

Grace nodded. It was worth a try if, indeed, the stakes were as high as Dorothy claimed.

*   *   *

This is the first day of Rosemary's last year in high school, Grace thought sadly as she waved her off. Next year she'll have university classes.

Since Dorothy's warning Grace had surrendered her siege and allowed Rosemary to see her friends. Earthshaking changes had occurred with a few of them.

Laura was in love. Sickeningly, truly in love, Rosemary reported, shocked at what happened. Angela's relationship, too, intensified with the boy Rosemary called "the creep" and Rosemary was disappointed Angela hadn't yet seen through him.

"Maybe you'll meet some nice boy in school this year," Grace soothed.

Rosemary shook her head. "I don't want that to happen yet. I have more to do than worry about some male's ego."

The school year promised to be a successful one. There was no more math, Rosemary noted, so she set a goal of straight A's for herself.

When the new church year started Grace realized it would be a good one, too. Rosemary didn't even say good-bye to the girls her age on the last Sunday before promotion day. Grace decided to overlook it in light of the fact she was actually excited about Dorothy's new class.

Grace wasn't quite so happy. Most of the women in it were as old as Dorothy or only slightly younger. Rosemary was the only one under fifty. For some strange reason the older women took a great liking to Rosemary. Many remembered her from GAs and were delighted having a young person around. It was only a matter of weeks before Christine, too, jumped ship and joined Rosemary. So the class formed with several older women and two teenaged girls.

*   *   *

True to her word, Rosemary dropped out of every activity except Sunday School and morning worship and Grace finally decided it was just as well. It was wonderful to see her tension and fury dissipate.

With more tranquillity in her spiritual life, Rosemary concentrated on her senior year and brought home report card after report card full of A's. It was a delicious victory.

Before the holidays the preacher announced he was leaving to start a ministry in a new church. Like so many of his predecessors he received the call from the Lord.

"Received the promise of a larger salary," Dorothy commented as she and Grace went to their favorite restaurant after their Circle Meeting. "I wish once, only once before I die, I'd hear one of them get up in the pulpit and tell us exactly why he's leaving."

"Why are you so upset? I didn't think you could stand him," Grace frowned as they took their seats.

"I can't but I really shouldn't be surprised, should I? Oh well, the more things change, the more they stay the same."

Grace perused the menu. "How's Rosie doing in your class?"

"Wonderfully, of course. They all love her as much as I do. You know what I find hilarious, Grace?"

Grace pointed out the chicken salad on the menu to the patient waitress. "What?"

"She isn't afraid to take me on when she thinks I'm wrong." Dorothy gave her order to the waitress and handed her the menu.

Grace looked at Dorothy closely to see if she was angry with Rosemary. Her heart skipped a beat. "What do you mean?"

"Last Sunday she called my bluff about a point in Genesis and took me completely by surprise. Before I could gather my wits and give her my glare of authority, she'd turned to Esther Stock and said, 'Isn't that so?' Poor Esther! She'd been daydreaming, I think. When Rosie and I explained the problem, I'll be confounded if Esther didn't grin at me and say she agreed with Rosemary." Dorothy laughed heartily.

"Was she obnoxious to you?"

"Obnoxious?" Dorothy stopped smiling and took a sip of water. "Grace, why do you think Rosemary's difference of opinion means she's obnoxious?"

"She isn't supposed to disagree with her Sunday School teachers."

"Why on earth not? She's entitled to her opinions if she can prove them. At least, I think so."

"Oh."

"Didn't any of your teachers ever say anything you disagreed with?"

"Yes, but—"

"You didn't say anything, did you?"

"Not until I was a grown woman."

"Have you forgotten how old your daughter will be this spring?"

Grace swallowed hard and blushed, wondering if the waitress setting her food in front of her heard any of their conversation. "No, I haven't forgotten. It's very scary, thinking she's getting ready to graduate from high school. She wants Harry to take her downtown on her birthday so she can register to vote. I can't believe it. In the fall she'll start to college!"

"Has she taken her entrance exams yet?"

"This Saturday. She's been making a list of all the places she wants to send her scores."

"Which colleges?" Dorothy tried to ask absently, cutting her hot roast beef sandwich into small pieces.

Grace shot her a knowing glance, realizing she was making sure the choices were indeed Rosemary's and not her mother's. "The local university, Smith and Vassar, Ohio State and Vanderbilt. And the Baptist college, of course."

Dorothy chuckled. "Wouldn't you love for her to go to Smith or Vassar?"

"No, I would not. Up east, I couldn't keep an eye on her."

Dorothy's mirth vanished and she pondered Grace's statement a long time before speaking. "You're going to have to relax your strangle-hold on her one of these days, you know."

Grace nodded but kept silent.

"If she wins a full scholarship, you won't have the financial card to play. She could go away to school whether you like it or not."

Grace frowned. "Are you encouraging her to go away to school?"

"No but if she wanted to I *would* indeed help her."

Grace's eyes widened.

"I say this," Dorothy continued, "because I don't think you and Rosemary are good for each other these days. Of course, things are better now that she's in my class but I have the strangest feeling Rosemary's problems with church aren't over yet. Do you ever feel that way?"

Grace could only stare at her. No, she thought, I guess I was stupid enough to think the problems were over.

*   *   *

On the day school was out for the Christmas holidays, Rosemary came home with a look of stunned disbelief on her face. Grace frowned. "What's the matter?"

"Gretchen's engaged," Rosemary replied softly. "Really engaged, a diamond ring and everything."

Grace smiled. "These things happen, Rosie."

"Gretchen's barely seventeen. She isn't old enough to get married."

"A lot of my friends got married when they graduated from high school—" and Grace broke off, seeing Rosemary flinch.

"She doesn't want to wait until graduation, Mom. She and this nut want to get married in the spring."

Grace sat down. Gretchen's parents would surely go crazy with this turn of events. "She *has* to graduate, Rosemary."

"I think so, too, and get at least two years of college behind her but Gretchen doesn't want to go to college now."

"Because she's getting married?"

"I can't tell. We've grown apart. She's much friendlier with Angela than she is with me. They have all those Spanish classes together."

"I thought she wanted to teach Spanish."

Rosemary sighed. "So did I." She paused a long moment. "Sometimes, Mom, I think we had better sense when we were ten years old and thought boys had cooties. At least we didn't get talked into bad decisions back then."

"Do you think those boys you've been dating have cooties?"

"No," Rosemary blushed and grinned, "but they sure can mess up things all the way around. I wouldn't be surprised if Laura gets married after graduation, too."

Was it envy, Grace wondered. Two friends serious enough to think about marriage could cause other friends to be jealous. "So what else did Gretchen say?"

"She asked me to be a bridesmaid."

"Did you say yes?"

"Yeah, after I recovered from the shock."

"Well, it looks like your summer is going to be eventful, doesn't it?"

Rosemary cast her a sidelong glance. "A damned sight better than last year, that's for sure."

10

"When I heard what my kids went to see I was ready to kill them. I've never heard of anything so silly," Lorene Wright said to Frances Taylor during the monthly Circle Meeting.

"A lot of kids were scared to death. I've heard church attendance is up almost every place as a result," Frances replied.

"What are you ladies talking about?" Dorothy asked sweetly, eavesdropping on the whispered conversation beside her.

Grace bit her lip and sank deeper in her chair. *She* knew what Frances and Lorene were talking about, what everyone was talking about. Dorothy, the old vixen, probably knew it, too, but loved playing games.

"It's that awful movie, Miss Dorothy: *The Exorcist.*"

Dorothy maintained the innocent look on her face but as she turned to Grace, her hazel eyes sparkled with mischief. "Exorcist, exorcism...goodness me, that's what Catholics do when a house is haunted."

"Or when someone is demon-possessed," another woman added.

Dorothy smiled at Grace. "Have you seen this film, Grace?"

"Of course not," Grace snapped.

"Why not?"

"Because it's rated R," Lorene hastily explained.

Dorothy threw her a wicked smirk and Grace's face went scarlet. Would she and Rosemary never let her live down *The Godfather* incident?

"Now really, ladies, where's the harm in a film like this?" Dorothy continued.

"It's terrifying the children."

"If it's rated R there shouldn't be any children on the premises," Dorothy reminded them.

"I mean our children. Older children."

"They'll do stupid things, you know, before they turn thirty," Dorothy replied.

"People ask me the funniest questions about this movie. Has anyone asked you about it, Grace?" Lorene asked.

"No."

"They ask me if this stuff really happens."

"What stuff?" Dorothy queried.

"Demon-possession. I don't have a nice little pat answer for people who remind me Jesus cast out the devils into the swineherd," Lorene said.

"Into the swine," Dorothy corrected. "What would be the point of exorcising demons from one person and sending them to another?"

"Miss Dorothy, you always think you know all the answers," Frances began.

Grace's eyes rounded as she watched Dorothy's widen with insult at the challenge.

"So what do you say about demon-possession?" she continued.

"I'd say the accounts of demon possession in the ancient and medieval worlds are what we recognize today as the various mental illnesses," Dorothy explained.

"But the Bible says Jesus cast out devils," Lorene said emphatically.

"I think it would be foolish to take that literally," Dorothy smiled.

"We're *supposed* to take it literally," Frances began.

"The Bible is inerrant," Lorene reminded her.

"Well, if you think so, Lorene, you'd better be willing to concede the Catholics' interpretation of Lord's Supper," Dorothy said. Grace caught her teasing tone.

"What?"

"The sixth chapter of John does not equivocate. It says the bread and the wine literally are the body and the blood. Do you believe you partake of flesh and blood at the Lord's Supper?"

"Of course not!" Lorene cried.

"Well, don't swear you believe in inerrant scripture," Dorothy concluded, the fire in her eyes softening as she realized she'd won.

"What's equivocate?" Frances whispered loudly to Lorene.

Grace sighed, closed her eyes and leaned her head on the back of the chair. She could imagine the word games that went on between Dorothy and Rosemary every Sunday morning.

Later that day, she couldn't resist grilling Rosemary. "Have you sneaked behind my back to see *The Exorcist?*"

Rosemary grinned. "It's a stupid movie, Mom. You wouldn't like it. There aren't any Sonny and Lucy scenes."

"Very funny. So you saw it? When I told you not to go to R movies?"

"I'm almost eighteen. I don't need your permission."

"I hope it scared the pants off you."

"It didn't, although the hospital scene was pretty bad. Do you know how doctors check to see if you have lesions on the brain, Mom?"

"Did any of your friends ask you anything about it afterward?"

"Yeah. It's all everyone's talking about at school."

"And?"

"And what?"

"Didn't it give you a chance to say anything positive about your Christianity?"

Rosemary paused and sighed.

Grace saw she'd hit a nerve. "Or don't you think it's important?"

"Remember what you told me when I was in the tenth grade and that nut played the rapture tape? That it's wrong to terrify people? When a bunch of us talked about it, I said I thought demon possession of the old days was probably schizophrenia or something. Something people didn't know about."

"Even though Jesus cast out demons?"

"I can believe Jesus healed the guy, Mom, but I can't swallow the rest of the story."

"I know someone else who doesn't, either," Grace sighed.

"Miss Dorothy? Oh yeah, she went to see it about a month ago. Said she hadn't seen so many teenagers pass out at a movie since Lon Chaney was the Wolf Man. How many years ago was that?"

Grace gasped with surprise. Dorothy at an R movie? She smiled. The blackmailing was over! *The Godfather* incident was truly finished now.

*   *   *

The church's immediate need for a minister was filled in the interim by a retired professor of theology from the seminary. From the moment Grace saw him she was certain Rosemary would be impressed. Even at the age of seventy he was ramrod straight and dignified. When it was time for his first sermon he walked slowly to the pulpit, lit a single candle and said, "Christ said, 'I am the Light of the World.'"

For the next thirty minutes the congregation was treated to a sermon of intense research and eloquence. There were no terror tactics, no histrionics for the sins of the world, simply a brilliant essay on Christ's compassion.

Rosemary sang his praises all the way home. "Oh Mom, he was great, wasn't he? Why doesn't the pulpit committee insist he stay?"

"He's retired, Rosie. He doesn't want the responsibility of a church."

Rosemary was silent only for a brief moment. "I wonder if he's sure about that. Think what it would mean to have someone like him, Mom! Maybe the congregation would actually *learn* something for a change."

"Church isn't supposed to be a classroom, Rosie."

"I don't understand that, either. If we aren't there to learn, what are we there for?"

Grace glared at her. "The whole idea of Christian fellowship is completely beyond you, isn't it?"

"It has to be more than that for me. It's supposed to open our minds and stimulate the intellect. That's what Miss Dorothy says, you know."

Yet however impressed she, Rosemary and Dorothy were, the congregation, on the whole, was not. At the monthly Circle Meeting the complaints went around.

"He just doesn't preach soul-winning sermons."

"He thinks he's still at the seminary."

"Talking above our heads! What a snob!"

"All that talk about compassion! Sounded a lot like a social gospel to me."

Grace was stunned. She ventured to glance at Dorothy, wondering if the older woman was as surprised. Dorothy, however, shook her head and looked away.

        *   *   *

By late spring the pulpit committee's choice fell on a middle-aged Southerner. He was a soft-spoken man who, in the first weeks of his ministry, gave ample evidence the pulpit would not be what it had been in the interim.

"When he sees how the wind blows he'll fall into line, you can bet on it," Dorothy prophesied.

It didn't take long for him to find a subject, either. One of their sister churches had recently ordained a woman deacon. Grace suspected there would be opposition. Women's places were in their homes with children. That was the way things were but even so nothing prepared her for the fire and brimstone from the pulpit.

It undid every positive emotion Rosemary had regained since January. There wasn't a word spoken all the way home.

Dorothy was right. Rosemary's troubles were far from over.

*   *   *

Grace set down her pen and smiled at the neat stack of addressed envelopes on the dining room table. Done at last!

She reached for a left over card. Miss Rosemary S. Lee. How grown-up it sounded! How sophisticated!

The graduation invitations were lovely, too. Of course, it would have been much more satisfying if Rosemary herself had taken an interest but she only offered to lick stamps.

"Why aren't you excited?" Grace demanded, trying to understand her daughter's disinterest.

"It's just high school," Rosemary said off-handedly. "Everybody graduates from high school. Now in four years when I graduate from college I'll really have something to celebrate."

She was so restless, like a thoroughbred at the starting gate, bucking and jumping to dash away. "Don't you feel at all sad? You may never see some of your classmates again."

"I'm only sad Gretchen and Laura won't be starting to college with me and that I have to wait until August for classes to begin. I wish school would start Monday after we graduate on Saturday!"

It was nothing more than the conclusion to the confusion Grace had felt the entire school year. She'd argued a senior year was something to cherish forever but Rosemary was unimpressed. She tried to emphasize the social privilege of senior status, hinting she could go with Kevin to the prom but Rosemary ignored her.

Why doesn't she want to go to the prom, Grace wondered. She herself had been unable to attend her own prom and the wound went deep. She promised herself her daughter could attend the prom if she wanted to but as the spring slipped by and Rosemary said nothing, Grace took matters into her own hands.

She spent hours talking with Kevin's mother, planning a lovely evening around the two teenagers. She managed to have everything ready before Rosemary had time to think about balking. Grace congratulated herself the two of them were dressed and photographed without reality having dawned on Rosemary.

She went to a neighbor's baby shower. When she returned three hours later there was Rosemary, out of the beautiful gown and the flowers, in her jeans and tee shirt watching television with Harry.

Kevin felt ill after dinner so they canceled their plans, she explained. Rosemary didn't seem at all disturbed.

Grace was furious. All that time and money! When she hinted at her displeasure, Rosemary turned a level glare on her and said simply, "I didn't want to go in the first place."

She wasn't eager to participate in commencement exercises, either, but somehow knew better than to rock that boat. With the sourest of faces but uttering no complaints she brought home the invitations and the cap and gown.

"It's the beginning of the rest of your life," Grace reminded her.

"It's boring," was the only reply she received.

"You'll get some nice gifts."

"I feel bribed. Remember when you and Daddy gave me quarters and toys for bringing home good grades in elementary school? That's how I feel now, only the loot is worth more."

Grace glared at her. "Maybe someone will give you something for your hope chest."

"Hope-less chest, you mean."

"Well, if you tried to cultivate a boyfriend, maybe you'll get married in a couple of years—"

"No way!" Rosemary cried. "I'm not giving up my life to wait on some man."

"Is that what Gretchen's doing?"

Rosemary blushed. "I have no idea what Gretchen's doing, Mom. I know I'm too young to get married. She is, too, but who can tell her anything? I can't imagine getting married now when everything is finally right."

Grace watched her for a few days. When Gretchen's engagement was announced at Christmas she was sure that Rosemary was jealous. Now she wasn't so sure. The friends came together happily as Gretchen included all of them in her wedding plans but Rosemary seemed to stand apart.

It must be very hectic for Gretchen's mother, Grace thought, having to address Gretchen's graduation and wedding invitations at the same time. How quickly the two girls grew up! Gretchen getting married soon, how soon, if ever, for Rosemary?

*   *   *

The five hundred and some-odd seniors made an impressive showing at their graduation and Grace was sad. Some of the children had started first grade with Rosemary. How strange some of them changed so little, only growing taller!

It was over now and when Rosemary started college in August she would chart new territory. Her parents hadn't gone to college. Her success or failure would ride on what she'd learned the last twelve years.

Rosemary was astonished at the graduation gifts she received and wrote thank you notes without any prompting from Grace. Her Sunday School class of older women gave her a luncheon plate from a popular china pattern. Dorothy gave her a place setting of sterling silver.

"I can't believe they gave me something for a hope chest," Rosemary muttered.

"Well, even single women entertain," Grace reminded her.

"That's true," Rosemary agreed and looked closer at the china pattern. "You know, this is very pretty. I might just add to this, after all. And did you see Miss Dorothy's silver, Mom? It's so beautiful!"

"You'll have to wrap up those pieces so they won't tarnish."

"Where can I store them?"

"Well, your father could make you a hope—"

"Don't say it," Rosemary warned.

"—*less* chest?" Grace grinned, remembering Rosemary's pun.

Rosemary smiled in spite of herself. "Yeah but only if everyone is told that's what it is. Hopeless."

∗   ∗   ∗

Gretchen's wedding day dawned sunny and warm, a perfect late spring day with the first hint of summer in the air. Rosemary awakened early and unzipped the bag to look again at her bridesmaid's dress.

Grace watched as her daughter started poking around her dresser drawer, searching for the makeup she seldom wore. "Why are you getting into that so early?"

"I want to be ready."

"If I didn't know better, Rosie, I'd say you're nervous."

"Well, if anyone trips over a hemline and rolls down the aisle, it'll be me."

"You'll be fine."

"Weddings sure are complicated, aren't they, Mom?"

"What do you mean?"

"I still can't believe we rehearsed only one time. Everyone seemed so anxious to go to dinner I didn't have the nerve to ask them to do it again."

Grace paused a moment and frowned at Rosemary's pallor. "What's the matter with you? You practically ran down the aisle to show off when you were in GAs."

"This is different. What if I start too soon? I just wish Angela were first! And I have a problem with these shoes, too, Mom. I couldn't tell Gretchen I'd never worn heels this high before. She'd think I was nuts."

Grace glanced at the dyed pink shoes on the floor. "High heels are lovely, Rosemary. They'll slim your ankles."

"What difference does a fat ankle make when the dress is long?"

"Rosemary—"

"I dreamed I was allergic to the flowers—"

"Rosemary," Grace said sternly, "the only person allowed to be nervous today is Gretchen."

"Gretchen won't be nervous."

"How do you know?"

"Gretchen's never nervous. She knows how to handle all the social occasions. She'll be just fine. *I'm* the one who'll probably faint before I get down the aisle. Last night it seemed longer than a football field."

Grace chuckled. "It's a good thing today isn't your wedding."

"Even if it were, I wouldn't get married in church."

Grace's smile vanished. "What do you mean?"

"That ugly place? Never. I'll get married in the living room—"

"Oh no, you will not," Grace cried, her voice rising angrily. "You'll not be married at home as though you had something to be ashamed of!"

Rosemary opened her mouth to argue then closed it suddenly.

Grace wondered if she'd won or if Rosemary simply chose not to press her point. How silly to fight over this, she thought, yet her heart raced. No matter how long it is before she marries I'll worry about this. I wonder if it's only the color scheme of the sanctuary that's poisoned her mind this way.

Enough of this, she thought, returning to the present. Gretchen was getting married today, little Gretchen, the first of their group.

The wedding was sweet and simple. Rosemary made it safely down the aisle, even though she was first and didn't sneeze once.

Gretchen was breathtaking. Overnight the tall gawky girl had changed into a slender beauty, her heart in her eyes, her smile not fading once.

The ceremony was a rapid eighteen minutes long and then it was suddenly over and Grace found herself whisked away to the Finny home for the reception, where she next saw Rosemary and Laura having their pictures made as they served fruit punch.

Grace smiled as she watched the bridesmaids. Gretchen was wise to put them in rainbow colors: Angela and Laura in peach and yellow, so suited to their brown eyes and chestnut hair; Jill in a cool mint green; Christine in blue; Rosemary in pink and the maid-of-honor, Gretchen's sister, in lilac.

Gretchen and her husband cut their cake and smiled for more photographs. Grace felt tears slip out of her eyes. How could any of Rosemary's friends be old enough to marry?

She looked back at the reception table and noticed something slightly amiss. Laura, who was a few inches shorter than Rosemary, seemed so tall and elegant in her yellow dress. Then it dawned on Grace with a chill. Rosemary had taken off her shoes.

Grace's heart sank and she went cold all over.

After eighteen years of seeing her mother endure a girdle and stockings and tight shoes in order to be properly dressed, Rosemary certainly knew better than to take off her shoes in a public place. Grace fixed her most terrible maternal glare on her daughter, willing her to look at her.

Rosemary did look up but instead of noticing the glare and responding to it, she only smiled and waved. Grace turned away from her. Impossible. Hopeless. How could Rosemary be so ready for college and so ill prepared for what society expected of her?

*   *   *

The summer dragged on and by July advising conference, Rosemary was definitely champing at the bit and fighting Grace on a point. "This brochure invites the parents of incoming freshmen to attend," Grace said firmly, "so I'm going."

"To hold my hand and register me?"

"What are you so worried about?"

Rosemary blushed. "I just don't see the point."

"Well, miss, the point is your father and I are paying for this adventure so we're going to see where every cent of it goes."

It wasn't a popular decision but on the morning she and Rosemary went to campus she didn't see a single teenager alone.

The parents looked determined and their children wore expressions similar to Rosemary's.

Most of what Grace learned was no surprise. A university setting would be traumatic for some students. Those who were shy or who hailed from smaller secondary schools were expected to find the changes difficult.

I don't have to worry about Rosemary on that score, Grace thought with relief but there were other things she wasn't prepared for.

If girls were eighteen they could request birth control pills from student health and parents were not consulted. There wasn't as much supervision of comings and goings from the dorms as there used to be.

She's living at home so I can enforce a curfew but what if she wants the pill, Grace wondered. My God, how would I know?

Rosemary, beside her, frowned deeply and shifted in her seat. "Why are they bothering us with all this? I want to get upstairs and fill out my schedule while classes are still open!" she whispered loudly.

Grace exhaled with relief. The old competitive Rosemary was, for once, something to be cherished. Birth control pills were obviously the last thing on her mind, at least for now.

*   *   *

"She has classes on Mondays, Wednesdays and Fridays," Grace explained to Dorothy, "so she's home all day on Tuesdays and Thursdays driving me nuts."

Dorothy laughed. "College is a different ball game than high school, you know. Have you encouraged her to go to the library and study?"

"She does that the three days she's in school."

"The feeling of freedom will rub off, Grace. Give it time. In a few weeks she'll probably be spending more time on campus with new friends."

That happened, too, before long, and what Grace dreaded.

"Mom, I want a part time job."

"Why?"

"I don't like coming to you and Daddy for spending money. If I make a nice amount I want to pay for my books and supplies."

"Where do you plan to work?"

"The art library."

Grace held the silence, surprised.

"By the time I really need to get in and dig up material for term papers, I'll know the place inside out, and if I don't know where the right thing is I'll know someone who does."

"It sounds so methodical," Grace explained to Dorothy. "She's making her contacts early."

"That means she's serious," Dorothy said. "It would be terrible for all of us if she were doing nothing about her career."

After Rosemary started working at the library she wasn't home as much. She loved her job and the people she worked with. She was as smug about her meager sixty-four dollar biweekly check as though she were a bank president.

"What are you going to do with your first check?" Grace asked, trying to keep the teasing sparkle out of her eyes.

"Save it."

"For what? New clothes?"

Rosemary frowned and shook her head. "Books."

Books and supplies, exactly what she'd promised before she got the job. It seemed Rosemary knew what she was doing.

*　　　　*　　　　*

"Laura and Rick are getting married at the end of December," Rosemary announced one day after school.

"Are you going to be in the wedding?"

Rosemary shook her head. "Her little sister's going to be the only bridesmaid. She asked Christine to serve at the reception. I guess she doesn't need a lot of us for a small wedding. Getting married at home shows how smart she is."

Grace decided to ignore the remark. "Do you want a new dress?"

"I don't know yet."

"You're behaving better with Laura's announcement than you did with Gretchen's," Grace observed.

Rosemary nodded. "I've always felt that Laura knows what she's doing. The rest of us don't have our feet on the ground yet."

"Even you?"

"Especially me. College is so strange! It's hard, Mom, seeing so many talented kids in my art classes, people who are better than I am. It's hard to smile at them much less be nice when they're so good. There's one guy, a senior. He's so gifted!"

Grace smiled, wondering if Rosemary knew her eyes shone. "What's his name?"

"Andrew." Rosemary blushed.

Grace laughed at her expression. "So, why don't you ask Andrew to take you to Laura's wedding?"

"He has a girlfriend. Besides, he's vain as a peacock and doesn't know I exist."

"Doesn't know you exist?"

"He looks right through me."

Grace could stifle her laughter no longer. "I can't imagine anyone looking through you, Rosemary. And not knowing you exist? Only if he's dead!"

Rosemary's blush deepened. "You've got the whole thing wrong. I admire his talent. That's all."

Grace forced herself to stop laughing. Teasing would only make things worse, she knew. "I only thought—"

"I know what you thought."

"Who are you going to take along to Laura's wedding?"

"If I don't get asked, I'll go alone. It doesn't bother me. Good Lord, I'm only eighteen, hardly ready to worry about not having a date!"

"Why, Miss Lee, I thought you were such a woman's libber! I didn't think it would bother you to ask a boy for a date."

Rosemary blushed again and folded her arms. "Men are so conceited. I have no intention of giving them a reason to think they're the cat's meow. And that's *Ms.* Lee, if you please."

She was blustering again sure as the world.

Later, Grace was still smiling about the so-called mere admiration for Andrew's talent. Possibly but whoever Andrew was, he'd made her daughter blush and her eyes shine. College was indeed more than academic experiences, exactly as Dorothy had predicted.

*   *   *

It was also unbelievably stressful. After finals Rosemary came down with a terrible twenty-four hour bug. Her transcript arrived. Not the straight As she hoped for, she was bitterly disappointed but too exhausted to be worried. "Next semester," she promised, "I'll get those A's."

She forced herself to dress up for Laura's wedding and because she hadn't pursued the mysterious, elusive Andrew, went alone. Grace waited up for her.

"Was it pretty?" she asked when Rosemary came home.

"Gorgeous," Rosemary smiled. "There was a fire in the fire-place and candles all around. The Christmas decorations made for a beautiful room and Laura was a beautiful bride. Ah me, if I thought I could be as happy as she is, I'd give marriage a whirl, too!"

Grace smiled but kept her mouth shut.

Was it Andrew's influence softening Rosemary or was she just growing up? Whatever the reason Grace decided she liked the change.

*   *   *

Rosemary started her spring semester in mid-January and the snow came. Grace couldn't resist teasing her that had she still been in high school she'd have missed a few days due to the bad weather. Rosemary shrugged. "I wouldn't trade places with any high school kid for a month of snow days!"

She settled into her classes a bit faster that time around and once sighed deeply. "I can't wait to get started on those education classes. Why do they make me wait until my sophomore year to begin, I wonder?"

"Well," Grace offered, "maybe because of all the freshman drop-out rate you mentioned."

"True. So many kids did poorly last semester, Mom, and for reasons that are completely beyond me. One of the kids in my Latin class got over here and simply couldn't handle it."

"The class work?"

"The different environment. Professors aren't going to call you down for chewing gum and aren't going to make a fuss if you skip a class."

"Skip a class?"

"Think about it. If you're grown-up enough to go to college you're grown-up enough to take the consequences of skipping."

"Have you skipped classes?"

Rosemary grinned. "Once or twice. You have to remember what a paragon-of-attendance-virtue I was in high school and take it into account for my present delinquency."

Grace pointed to the back door. "Go to school. I have work to do."

She considered what Rosemary said about her high school classmate being unable to handle the college environment. She remembered the story about a boy in a sister church who, almost failing high school, was admitted to the university only because of its open door policy for state residents. He was suddenly motivated, bloomed in the academic environment and graduated Phi Beta Kappa.

There was no understanding it.

＊   ＊   ＊

Grace was suddenly faced with the young adult who would make her own decisions when Rosemary came home one day with a handful of brochures from student health. She motioned for Grace to sit down at the kitchen table and Grace's heart raced.

She pushed the brochures closer to her mother and said matter-of-factly, "I'm going to have a Pap smear tomorrow."

"You don't need a Pap smear until you have your pre-marital check-up," Grace argued.

Rosemary shook her head. "Cervical cancer doesn't respect virgins, Mom. I need to do this and have the professional breast exam that goes along with it."

"You check your breasts every month."

"Yes, but a doctor checks, too, when I get the Pap smear."

Grace swallowed hard and felt tears rising. "What are you planning to do? Go on the pill?"

"I'm not interested in birth control," Rosemary snapped then softened her approach. "You always made sure I went to the dentist and the ophthalmologist every year, right?"

Grace forced herself to nod.

"This is the same thing, Mom. Preventive medicine."

It makes sense, Grace thought as she cleared her throat and forced herself to be calm. "Do you want me to go with you?"

Rosemary shook her head. "I don't think so. But I *am* scared to death."

"What's made you so worried, Rosemary? Are you discharging blood or anything?"

"No, but from what I've heard, by the time you have symptoms of cancer you're dead with it."

"Where did you get the brochures?"

"Lisa." Rosemary smiled. "She takes her nursing stuff very seriously and barrages us with paperwork all the time. It feels good to have someone looking out for us."

Grace sighed. "You know, the generation of girls a bit older than you went to their pediatricians until they were ready to get married. Then they went to an ob-gyn."

"That's kind of sickening. Makes me think they were children one day and married the next. Sort of passed from parents to husbands."

Grace frowned, seeing Rosemary's point for the first time.

"Women need to be on their own awhile before they marry," Rosemary said softly.

"You mean to do that, don't you?"

"I believe it will make me a better wife when I do get married, probably when I'm a hundred and fifty!"

Grace laughed. "Not that old, surely?"

Rosemary shrugged. "Don't hold your breath."

*   *   *

As Rosemary tackled her world, Gretchen and Laura got on with married life. They generously invited Rosemary and a date over for dinners, experimenting with the dozens of cookbooks they'd received as wedding presents.

"It's time I returned the favor, Mom, so I'm going to send you into a stroke because I plan to cook and mess up your kitchen. I want to give two dinner parties."

"I'll be happy to cook—"

"No. *I'll* do the cooking."

"How will you have time?"

"I'll entertain over spring break. That should give me plenty of time to do everything just the way I want it."

"You could have one big party—"

"No. Since I hardly know how to boil water to make a cup of tea, I don't think I should take on a lot at one time."

She gave herself plenty of time to learn. Besides, Rosemary noted one day, glad to have a scoop on some gossip, Gretchen was pregnant. "So we have something to celebrate and look forward to," Rosemary said cryptically.

"You don't sound very enthusiastic."

"I'm trying to take this better than when she announced her engagement."

"You aren't doing so well."

"Once again, Mom, I can't believe Gretchen took such a big step at her age."

"She's four months younger than you."

"I know. And I'm too young, too."

"Don't you want to have a family one day, Rosie?"

"I can concentrate on only one thing at a time. Education first. I want to teach a couple of years then get married. I'd like to have a few years before I have any kids, if I do it at all. I can't imagine myself with a baby."

Grace frowned. That certainly hadn't been her own case. She'd wanted children ever since she played with baby dolls. "Whatever you do," she said gently, "make sure you don't have a baby until you want one and are prepared to do everything necessary to provide for it. I want my grandchildren to be educated like you and have opportunities Harry and I didn't."

"That's what I mean, Mom," Rosemary said. She grinned suddenly. "I notice you said that without mentioning having a husband first."

Grace blushed deeply. "You know what I meant."

Rosemary laughed merrily.

11

Grace had nearly forgotten about Vietnam but it was suddenly in the headlines again as the United States pulled out. It wasn't the jubilation she expected. People around her accepted the news grimly. The emotions that divided the country diminished from rage to simmering hostility. People said the status of the United States was compromised and Americans were capable of being defeated for the first time.

Not a first defeat exactly, Grace thought. The Confederate army was made up of Americans and they were defeated. And this isn't defeat! We finally woke up and realized we shouldn't have been over there in the first place.

It wasn't what we were told, wasn't the defense of a country against communism. It was involvement in a civil war. What would we have done if Britain or France meddled in our war? We wouldn't have taken it very well, that's what!

The people in her church didn't understand and Grace wondered if their bitterness, silenced now, would find a new outlet later.

Did mankind never weary of war?

✶   ✶   ✶

Rosemary gritted her teeth and signed up for three courses during summer school. "I can get these horrible math and science requirements out of the way in a hurry," she explained, "and also take one fun course. It shouldn't be all drudgery with no reward."

So the reward class was English Romantic writers. Grace expected her to be quoting Keats, Byron and Shelley before the end of the summer.

The artwork continued and shortly before the summer term ended, Gretchen had her baby. "A darling baby boy," everyone said. Grace asked Rosemary about the baby since she'd been invited to visit mother and son at the hospital and at home.

"He's a baby," Rosemary said blandly.

"Don't you think he's cute?"

Rosemary paused, wondering where the conversation was leading. "Well, he's got ten toes and ten fingers and everything that's supposed to be there—"

"Rosemary!"

"He looks no worse than the other babies who were born around the same time. How's that?"

"Don't you think he's sweet?"

"At this age? All he does is eat, pee, poop and scream. There's nothing interesting or cute about that."

"You're hopelessly unmaternal."

Rosemary shrugged. "I can't imagine getting bent out of shape about newborn babies, Mom. Other women do, I know, but it just isn't me."

"It's different when the baby is your own."

Rosemary paused for a long moment. "Hormones are powerful things, obviously. I saw some mighty ugly babies in that nursery and if their mothers thought they were pretty, well, as I said, hormones must be very powerful."

"You'll be the most sickening type of mother, you know. You'll think any child you give birth to is the most beautiful baby ever born."

Rosemary blanched. "That's a truly terrifying thought."

*   *   *

"Now I feel like I'm *really* getting into the heart of things," Rosemary announced when fall semester began. "I can get this first education class out of the way this semester!"

The class wasn't what Rosemary expected. Frustrated, she took her material to Dorothy who later confided to Grace she didn't know what to make of it, either. "I'm trying to do the right thing, Grace, and encourage her to be patient."

"What's the problem?"

"Rosemary thinks the idea is absurd that an individual can be taught to teach."

Grace felt a knot grow in the pit of her stomach, the same knot she felt every time Rosemary shot off her mouth at church. She held the silence for a moment then asked quietly, "Is that what you think, too?"

Dorothy raised guilty eyes to her. "Let me say this is in my defense. I think the curriculum is good for elementary school teachers."

"But Rosemary doesn't want to teach small children."

"I know."

"What's she going to do, Dorothy? She's got her heart set on teaching."

"We have to hope this first class will be the only problem one," Dorothy paused. "I can't believe how things have changed since I retired!"

"Do you miss teaching?"

"I'm intellectually challenged every Sunday when Rosemary and Christine fire a barrage of questions in my direction."

Grace smiled. "Does anyone else in the class ever get to talk?"

"Of course! We're very vocal. Rosemary doesn't let anyone sit on the fence."

Why did Dorothy think that was a good thing? So many people liked sitting on the fence. It was comfortable and to be forced to decide on issues of faith, well, she wouldn't have liked it, not one bit! The knot in Grace's stomach tightened but she forced herself to smile.

"I wonder if she's as aggressive in school as she is in my class?" Dorothy wondered aloud.

Grace shrugged. "Probably but since the university has no such things as deportment grades I'll never have a way to know, will I?"

"You worry too much, Grace. It's good for Rosemary to take her education so seriously."

Grace tried to push the worry out of her mind. Rosemary may have run into a brick wall but if she wanted to teach badly enough she would either have to knock it down or find a way around it. Grace was certain Rosemary, being Rosemary, would much prefer to knock it down.

*   *   *

"Mom, the nut's back on campus."

"What nut?"

"The evangelist. He's regular as clockwork so you'll have to come have lunch with me on Wednesday so you can see him."

"Have you told me about him before?"

"No. I didn't think he'd have the nerve to show his face again."

Grace looked deeply into her daughter's sparkling eyes. "Is it anyone we know?"

"God, I hope not!" Rosemary cried before remembering herself. "I have no idea what he's supposed to be but it's so much fun to argue with him. I'd never been called a whore before, at least not to my face, until he got started."

"What do you—called you a—what—"

"Because I wear jeans. Don't worry, all the women on campus are whores." Rosemary laughed. "Guess you will be, too, if you get in his line of vision."

Grace sat down quickly and tried to control her racing heart. After a long moment she felt calm enough to speak. "What's a man like that doing on the campus, anyway?"

"He talks in the free speech area."

"He sounds dangerous."

"He's not dangerous. Nuts, yes. Rich, too. He wears this gorgeous London Fog coat and alligator shoes. Looks like he stepped right off the cover of *Gentleman's Quarterly*."

"Aren't you supposed to be in class after lunch?"

"Not until one o'clock. I rush through lunch just so I can get on the front row for his ranting and raving. Now promise me you'll come have lunch with me on Wednesday."

Grace couldn't believe she actually agreed to do it.

*　　　　*　　　　*

It was unusual for late September to be so cold and rainy. Grace thought Rosemary would let her off the hook because of the bad weather but the phone call in between classes was only to remind Grace to bring an umbrella.

She rode the bus to the campus and there was Rosemary, huddled under her own dilapidated umbrella, waiting for her. "Hope you're hungry," she smiled.

They rushed to the student center without a word to get out of the weather. Grace sniffed the air. Stuffed peppers! "That smells good," she said, following the aroma.

Rosemary caught her jacket. "Not that way, Mom. I can't afford the cafeteria. My budget only allows for a sandwich at the grill."

"Don't be ridiculous, Rosemary. I'll pay for lunch. I can't resist that stuffed pepper."

The food was mouth watering. She and Rosemary added green beans and a baked potato to their pepper entree and because they were wet and cold, some coffee. At the last minute, just before Grace paid, Rosemary helped herself to a generous slice of cherry cobbler and remembering her manners too late, grinned sheepishly. "Would you like some, too, Mom?"

"No, thank you," Grace said politely, paying.

"Do you want to eat by the window?" Rosemary asked.

"Where do you usually eat?"

"Anyplace I can find a seat."

"The window is fine."

As they sat down Grace looked around at the various students. It dawned on her the cafeteria line was indeed something of a luxury. Only the faculty members and a handful of students were served from there. All the others, like Rosemary on other days, ate sandwiches.

Almost missing the implication, Grace turned a second time to see what she thought she did not. The black students sat exclusively in one wing of the student center. "Rosemary."

"Umm?" came the almost inaudible sound as Rosemary ate her cobbler first.

"Is there an unwritten code of segregation in here?"

Rosemary's mirth vanished and she swallowed the cobbler. "So you noticed that?"

"It's hard not to."

"I don't know what to tell you, Mom. Occasionally I'll sit over there and try to make small talk. Sometimes it works, other times it doesn't. On bad days I think whatever went on seven or eight years ago came too late."

"Maybe so but I hope you're never too caught up in your schoolwork to be polite."

"I do what I can, Mom." Rosemary started digging into her meal. "Shake a leg there. We don't want to miss the show."

*   *   *

The weather was so bad Grace was certain the evangelist would cancel. As Rosemary guided her across the windy campus the gathering crowd told her not only was he there but they were too late to get the front row Rosemary so craved.

The evangelist pointed at a rather bedraggled young man. Grace noted there was none of the anticipation of a confrontation about the boy, unlike Rosemary who almost jumped up and down in her desire to fuel the growing fire. "Are you a Christian, son?"

"I'm a Catholic," the young man replied softly.

"But are you a Christian?"

Utter bewilderment passed over the young face and Grace, knowing exactly where the argument was going, felt nothing but a fierce maternal desire to protect him from the coming tirade. "I'm a Catholic," he said again.

"That doesn't save you, son."

"No, it doesn't," came another voice and Grace watched as a laughing young man with waist-long red hair elbowed his way into the free speech area along with the evangelist. "You see, son," he teased, "you have to believe just as the good brother here says you should. The Book of First Imaginations says so!"

"The Book of First Imaginations," Rosemary giggled to Grace, "I love it, don't you?"

"It's blasphemous," Grace replied.

Before the evangelist could retort the young man slipped an arm around his shoulders. "Christ said it was impossible for a rich man to get to heaven so doesn't that leave you out, *son?*" he grinned, referring rather obviously to the London Fog coat Rosemary had mentioned.

The evangelist, already red in the face from his warm-up tirade and terribly, terribly upset that such a heathen would interrupt him, was momentarily caught off-guard. "You're a fool as well as being hell-bound," he replied.

"That's the standard come-back," Rosemary whispered to Grace. "Everyone is ignorant and hell-bound."

"God rewards His faithful," the evangelist continued. "If you suffer and are poor it's because you are obstinate to the Will of God."

To Grace's horror Rosemary piped up, "The J.C. who said that was John Calvin, mister, not Jesus Christ."

The crowd roared with laughter at her remark.

Grace's knees went weak as she saw the evangelist turn furious eyes to Rosemary but before he could say another word the red-haired young man and several people on the front row surrounded him. Gently taking hold of him, they tossed him into the air as easily as though he were a rag-doll.

"Where are they taking him?" Grace cried as they broke rank and started away.

"I don't know but come on, it ought to be good," Rosemary laughed, raising her umbrella against a fresh sheet of rain.

Grace followed numbly. What did Rosemary find so funny about that horrible man? None of the other students seemed to be offended, either, just very, very amused.

There isn't anything funny about it, Grace thought frenziedly. He makes a mockery out of everything I believe, the damned fool. No telling how many young people will abandon Christianity altogether because he was their only reference point.

The crowd followed the evangelist-nappers to the quadrangle where the joyous young men merrily tossed their irate victim into the splashing fountain. Rosemary nearly collapsed with laughter. "That should cool him off," she laughed.

Grace reached for Rosemary's hand. "Get me out of here. I can't take any more of this."

Rosemary, for once, didn't argue and led her mother into an office building to sit down.

Grace waited awhile before saying anything. "Why did you want me to see that?"

"I think he's funny, don't you?"

"He *isn't* funny. Did you ever think he might be the only evangelist some of your classmates will see? Those boys who threw him in the fountain, can you imagine what they think of Christians now?"

Rosemary shook her head. "One of those guys who pitched him in the fountain, the one with the red hair down to his waist, goes to the seminary across the street. Another guy who usually makes it but couldn't today, plans to be a Catholic priest. Jewish students have joined us, too."

"A divinity student with waist-long red hair," Grace repeated, shocked.

"Mom, Mom—"

Grace forced herself to look at her.

"Mom, the guy is an idiot. No one takes him seriously. When kids show up who don't know what's going on it's pretty obvious the ones of us who argue make the case for tolerance and respect."

"But why argue with such a fool, Rosemary?"

"Because of what you just said. If I don't someone might think he's telling things the way they are." Rosemary grinned. "Besides, a little torture can be a lot of fun. Maybe that's why the Inquisition went on so long."

"Rosemary!"

"I didn't mean it seriously."

Unbidden came the memory of the evangelist's face as he sat up in the cold fountain water and unbidden, too, came Grace's sudden giggle. Thrown in the water by a divinity student and his friends.

Tears mixed with her laughter. I would never have made it through school in such a crazy environment, she realized. The lack of discipline and this free speech nonsense would have distracted me from my studies.

She glanced at Rosemary. Kids had to be tough as well as smart to survive a university atmosphere. Somewhere along the line, Rosemary learned to be tough. Or was she, Grace wondered as Rosemary took her back to the bus stop, just born that way?

＊   ＊   ＊

"I knew that bitch couldn't resist punishing me for my opinion," Rosemary said lethally, examining the C for the education course on her transcript. It was a terrific blow when she discovered it and the hours hadn't softened the shock at all.

"For heaven's sake, Rosemary, you make it sound like she had it in for you."

"She did. It was surely the most asinine class offered in the history of higher education."

Grace frowned as she wrestled Christmas paper around Harry's gift. "Hand me the tape," she said. "How can the class be asinine if so many kids take it and do well in it?"

"I've talked to a lot of them after class, Mom. In private they agree it's stupid but in class they pucker up and kiss—butt—when it comes to discussion and exam time. They make me almost as sick as she does."

"Was it necessary to disagree with the teacher?"

"If I didn't, who would? God, the crap they spew in that class! There were times I really thought she put forward the most idiotic stuff to see who would swallow it hook, line and sinker," Rosemary retorted, tearing off a long piece of tape in her fury. "The next class *has* to be better, that's for sure."

"What if it turns out to be asinine, too?" Grace asked sharply.

"I don't know."

"How many of them do you have to take?"

"Fourteen."

Grace finished the package and looked at her. "What's it going to take, Rosemary, for you to learn to keep your mouth shut?"

Rosemary flashed defiant blue eyes at her and smirked. "Death."

"Very funny. But you'd better start thinking about your future. If you want to teach you may have to put up with more classes you don't like."

"Guess I just have to hope the next one improves."

"What have you heard about it?"

"Nothing good. My supervisor at work suggested I ask to be transferred to the education library. She thinks I might do a little better with total immersion in the discipline."

"Are you going to?"

"Not yet. If this next class turns out bad I want something good to face when I go to work."

"Well, your other grades were As," Grace tried to soothe.

Rosemary forced a weak smile. "No wonder Miss Dorothy loved teaching literature," she said, remembering her electives. "It's neat."

"Would things be better for you if you decided to teach English?"

"Nope. I'd still have all this crap to do regardless of what I choose to teach."

"Would it be better at another university?" Grace asked, remembering another state university specialized in teacher education.

"You only go there," Rosemary said high-handedly, "if you can't cut it anyplace else."

Grace flinched at her superior tone. "Well, miss, if you get very many more of those Cs, chances are you won't be able to cut it, right?"

Rosemary blushed to the roots of her hair.

"May I have a proper response, please?"

"No ma'am, I don't care to go anyplace else. I don't want to stay in a dorm and have a roommate."

Grace almost laughed. "I thought surely you'd be begging us to stay in the dorm this year."

Rosemary snorted. "Give up my privacy? Not me."

"Have you forgotten everything from your days in the Beginner department? About sharing?"

"I'm happy to share my lunch money and my class notes with anyone who asks but that's as far as it goes. I'd have to kill anyone who laid a finger on my books and records."

Grace shook her head with a smile. That goes with the territory, she assumed, of being an only child.

*   *   *

During the holiday break Rosemary again touched base with her married friends. She ended a telephone call with Laura cheerily but her expression was far from happy. Grace followed her into the kitchen. "What's the matter?"

Rosemary leveled suspicious eyes on her. "Laura wants me to come over for dinner Friday night."

"What's the matter with that?"

"Rick has a single friend they're inviting, too."

"A blind date!" Grace laughed.

"It's not funny."

"It can be nice, Rosemary."

"Mom, this is the *one* thing we promised each other we'd never do!"

"Did you remind Laura of that?"

"She said she couldn't remember back that far."

"Then go to please her and be nice. People like foursomes for dinner."

"So I gather," Rosemary said tiredly. "There are never any tables for one in fine restaurants, no cars made for one person. No, this world is made for couples, all right. Single people ought to stand up and raise hell."

"The world goes on because of couples, Rosemary," Grace reminded her.

She made some sort of unintelligible sound between a grunt and a growl and dropped the subject.

On Friday afternoon Grace was utterly flabbergasted when a florist's van stopped in front of the house and a freezing young man hurried a box of flowers inside. Rosemary appeared from her room wondering what all the fuss was about. Grace closed the door and handed her the box. "Look! For you!"

Rosemary sat down on the stairs and opened the box. Grace gasped as she beheld a dozen long-stemmed red roses. Rosemary opened the note and read aloud, "'Hoping to meet you tonight. Jack.'" For a brief moment her face was as blank as the card's envelope then she blushed; from embarrassment or shock, Grace couldn't tell.

"How sweet," Grace responded properly.

Rosemary looked up at her. "*Sweet?*"

"He's only being thoughtful."

"Or manipulative. If I feel guilty enough he might get another date, mightn't he?"

"That was a mean thing to say."

"I didn't mean to be mean. But gee whiz, this is just a bit much, don't you think? I haven't even met the guy. He may be horrible. He probably is, if he's twenty-six and still in the market."

"Rosemary!"

Rosemary set the flowers aside and rubbed her head. "I think I'm going to be sick."

"No, you're not. You're going to be the perfect guest even if he's the most horrible man you've ever met. You wouldn't dream of disappointing Laura or hurting her feelings, would you?"

"No," came the weak reply.

"Then go upstairs and finish getting ready. Your father or I will drive you—"

"No way. I'm driving myself."

"Rosemary, I don't want you out in this snow and ice after dark."

"I don't want this guy to feel obligated to take me home. If I have the car I can take off if things get crazy."

Grace shook her head. "Now how crazy would things get in Laura's home?"

"I don't want to look like I need him to take me home. Like I'm fishing for time alone with him. On my own I call the shots. Can't you understand that, Mom?" she asked tiredly, leaving the roses on the stairs and going back to her room.

Unfortunately, Grace did.

What sort of man was Rosemary interested in? What sort of man wouldn't be offended if she drove to functions in order to call the shots? What sort of man would know sending flowers too early in the relationship pressured her then made her furious for feeling pressured?

Ah, it was a new world and traditional roles were changing fast. Grace decided sadly there'd be very few men who would understand and appreciate Rosemary because men, like boys, matured ever so much slower than their female counterparts.

*   *   *

Grace couldn't sleep. It had started to snow again and at eleven o'clock she seriously considered calling Laura and telling Rosemary to come home. For fifteen minutes she wavered between calling and taking the risk of embarrassing her daughter.

As though I don't trust her driving skills. I do, it's the other nuts out there on the road, too!

She was looking up Laura's phone number when the car softly crunched into the driveway. She peeked out the heavy old Venetian blinds, amazed it was so light outside in all the fury of the blowing snow.

Rosemary trudged carefully into the house. She gasped when she saw Grace waiting for her. "Why are you still up?"

"I was just about to call Laura and ask you to come home."

Rosemary gave a short snort of laughter as she took off her boots. "You'd better not ever do that to me, Mom," she warned. "I have sense enough to know when to come in out of the snowstorm."

"I thought you might be having such a good time—"

"Yeah, it was nice. Laura and I had a good chance to catch up on a lot of stuff. Mom, that dinner was something else. Laura could cook professionally, I haven't a doubt. She put all her sculpturing skill to work and did this dessert. I have no idea what it was. Anyway, I spent the rest of the night hounding her about checking into chef's credentials."

Grace shook her head sadly. "What about Jack?"

"Oh yeah, him. He's very nice," Rosemary said softly, as though being nice was a damning thing.

"And?"

"And what?"

"Tell me about him."

"He's nice. I thanked him for the flowers, he turned red as a beet and didn't look me in the eye the rest of the night. I never knew anyone could get through twenty-six years and be so shy."

Grace helped her out of her heavy coat. "I guess you overwhelmed the poor little thing?"

"I guess I did. He and Rick are typical engineers so they sat around and talked electronics and stuff while Laura and I took a nice little stroll down memory lane."

"What's a typical engineer, Rosemary?"

"Oh, the guys who wear calculators on their belts, don't know how to color-coordinate, that sort of thing."

"That's a condescending attitude, don't you think?"

Rosemary nodded. "Rick's attitude toward creative people isn't so hot, either. So I just talked to Laura. I think she's had enough practical level-headed-thinking crap to do her for awhile, too."

"Anything new?"

"Yeah, she's going to have a baby in August."

"Does her news upset you like Gretchen's?"

"I'm not upset but I hope this baby turns out to be wildly impractical and the furthest thing from an engineer old Rick could ever imagine. It would do him a world of good to father a concert pianist or a ballerina, don't you think?"

Grace shook her head. "Well, you know the old saying: 'opposites attract.'"

Rosemary started up the stairs. "Another truly terrifying thought."

12

Early one weekend of the new semester Rosemary pushed aside her homework without finishing it. Grace, reading about the first batch of presidential primaries, caught her expression from the corner of her eye. "What's going on in there, miss?" she asked, trying to sound light-hearted.

"A losing battle, that's what," Rosemary replied dismally.

"With what course?"

"Fundamentals of Education. That's a pretty name for a big waste of time," Rosemary answered bitterly.

"Why don't you come in here and look at these articles? You'll want to be well informed for your first presidential election."

"I already know who I'm going to vote for."

"Who is that?"

"Morris Udall. He appeals to me on a gut-level."

"What have you heard about Jimmy Carter?" Grace asked, surprised her daughter wasn't supporting the Southerner.

"Jimmy who?" Rosemary teased.

"I'm leaning very strongly towards him," Grace continued, ignoring the catch phrase all over the media.

"You'd better check him out good, Mom. What if he's one of the stupids we see so often at church?"

"Rosemary!" Grace cried. "He can't be stupid and you know it. He was governor of Georgia."

"George Wallace was governor of Alabama, too. I'd see if Carter is a Dixiecrat if I were you, Mom. You're getting so you're as radical as a northeasterner, you know. A Dixiecrat won't be to your liking at all."

"I am *not* a radical."

"You're kidding, aren't you?"

Grace bit down on her lip. "Now look here," she said sternly, "radicals are the ones who destroyed the Convention back in '68 with all that nonsense."

"What nonsense?"

"Well..." and Grace caught her breath, realizing suddenly that the Vietnam conflict she'd so hated was the defining element. "There were other ways to get points across."

"Right," Rosemary snorted. "If the college kids hadn't taken to the streets we'd have been in Vietnam forever and you know it."

Yes, I know it but does that make me a radical, Grace wondered.

"I can't see a Southerner winning this election," Rosemary went on. "You know how the rest of the nation perceives us: only one jump above *The Beverly Hillbillies.*"

"I think people want a change," Grace said. "Jimmy Carter is a Christian man, not just spouting religion to win an election but involved, Rosemary. That's bound to be a comforting thought after this Watergate nightmare."

"I'm really raining on your parade, huh, Mom? I don't think the American people want a Christian for a President. That's too pacifist."

"You make it sound despicable."

"Blood and thunder, that's what we prefer."

"It's not what *I* prefer."

"Well, we'll see come the primaries. I'll hold out for the rene-gade with the environmental programs and you put your money on Carter."

Grace felt herself rising to the challenge. "Carter will win the nomination. You mark my words."

"Betcha he doesn't," Rosemary grinned.

"What do you want to bet?"

"If he wins the nomination, Mom, I'll take you out to lunch and I'll wear pantyhose. How's that?"

Grace nodded. "Would you like to do it after the May primar-ies or after the convention?"

"Whichever you like," Rosemary laughed.

Grace nodded toward the kitchen. "Don't you have homework to finish?"

Rosemary made a face. "It can wait."

"It only gets worse with waiting."

"That's impossible," Rosemary sighed, heading back toward the kitchen table, "it can't get any worse."

*   *   *

Rosemary compromised her principles and wrote her mid-term paper exactly as she thought her education professor would want to see it. To the benefit of her transcript but to her personal cha-grin, she received an A with a plus beside it. Grace smiled at the blue book full of footnotes and the painstakingly gathered bibli-ography. "Did anyone else do as well?"

"No," Rosemary replied shortly.

Grace set the book aside and looked at her long and hard. "This is the first time I've ever known you to be disappointed with a top grade."

"This isn't about a top grade," Rosemary said softly. "I sold myself for this grade as surely as though I'd gone to bed with that professor. I wrote the biggest pile of bullshit ever put on a page." She thrust her hands in her pockets and sighed again. "I'll never get over this. Never."

"How many more of these kinds of classes do you have to take?"

"In the fall I have pre-student teaching that bounces me to one of the local high schools a couple of days a week, as well as a practical course about media and materials. I can stand both of them."

"Well, maybe they'll continue to get better."

"It doesn't end after graduation, Mom. Teachers are expected to get masters' degrees and a few hours beyond that. I've seen the curriculum. I don't think I have the stomach for it."

"What's giving you so much trouble?"

"The faculty isn't interested in seeing to it I'm a qualified artist going to work in the public schools. They're all bent out of shape about the theory of education, how students learn and treating the little darlings like porcelain. 'Reward the good behavior and ignore the bad.'"

"Don't you agree?"

"I don't care how the human mind learns or what's a bad or good theory. If a student is in my class there's work to be done. I have no intention of making myself a glorified baby-sitter and putting up with discipline problems. There are too many motivated students whose time is wasted with teachers arguing with bad kids."

"Are there really bad kids, Rosemary, or bad circumstances?"

Rosemary shrugged. "I don't care. Yes, I know it sounds harsh. By the time a problem kid gets to high school it's too late."

"You sound so cruel."

"That's what I was told in this last class. The taxpayers will pay me as a teacher, not as a child psychologist or a nurse. If I'm paid to teach the public will get my best effort. I deserve the proper atmosphere to do my work."

"So in this paper, you wrote the opposite of what you believe?"

"Yes."

"Sold yourself?"

"Hypocrite, Mom, that's the word you're looking for."

"I don't want to call you that. You did what was necessary to become the teacher you want to be."

"Ends justify the means? Didn't Watergate teach you any better?"

"I hardly think it's the same thing."

Rosemary nodded. "Sure it is. But you can be sure of one thing. I'll never, *never* do it again."

"We won't speak of it again," Grace said gently, handing the blue book back to her. "I'm glad you have the summer free. It'll give you time to get your feet back on the ground."

*   *   *

Time to recuperate from the stressful semester and spend with her friends was just the prescription Rosemary needed to restore her spirits. True to Grace's predictions and prayers, Jimmy Carter continued to sweep Democratic caucuses and primaries. To her delirious joy he won the convention's nomination. Pretending to be utterly miserable Rosemary took her mother to lunch wearing a dress and the much-loathed pantyhose.

As Grace continued to read and listen to media coverage of the campaigns, however, two things happened to shake her smug confidence. Gay rights were mentioned in the Democratic platform. "What are gay rights?" she asked Dorothy.

"Rights of homosexuals."

Grace cringed, her lip curling in distaste. "I don't like that."

"So I see. But they're American citizens and they deserve the same rights and protection as anyone else under the law."

"As Americans they have it," Grace retorted coolly.

"Did black Americans have rights just because they were citizens?" Dorothy challenged.

Grace blushed and looked away. "How can Jimmy Carter, being a Christian, support such a plank in the platform?"

"Never underestimate that fine man," Dorothy said glowingly. "I think I'm going to have more peace of mind and joy in voting for him in November than anyone before. Even Roosevelt." She grinned mischievously.

Her point was lost on Grace. "He can't support these gay rights and be a Christian."

"Why not?"

"It's immoral."

"Hmm." Dorothy frowned. "These people have a right to work and live in this society free of fear, Grace."

"Yes," Grace agreed, "I can see that."

"All right," Dorothy nodded. "In saying so you support gay rights, too."

"If it stops there."

"What do you mean?"

"Just what I said."

Dorothy laughed. "I see. You won't support them if they demand a little boy in every bedroom?"

"That isn't funny."

"Yes, it is. Have some sense, Grace, and don't panic. Homosexual members of our society want the same things you do: safe neighborhoods, workable government, a sound economy and good schools."

"You make them sound...normal."

Dorothy laughed again. "Forty years ago I said black families wanted the same things white families wanted and almost lost my job. It's hard to believe we were so backward, isn't it? When we speak of gay rights I hope forty years' time will make as happy a difference."

Grace could only stare at her. How in the world had Dorothy come to such conclusions? She wanted to press but the mischievous twinkle in the older woman's eyes stilled her tongue.

Did Rosemary share her views? Grace was afraid to ask.

*   *   *

Out of the blue Jimmy Carter almost tumbled off Grace's pedestal. He gave an interview with *Playboy*.

Grace went to bed and hid her head under the pillows. God, God, how could he? No one would ever support him again and everyone, yes, all those non-Christians would think it was fine to read *Playboy*.

She had to get up and face the world. Yes, and face Rosemary's certain teasing. If she did normal things maybe she'd forget.

Rosemary, who was planning Laura's baby shower with Christine, returned home with a paper bag with Grace's name written on it in red marker. "I stopped by the book store just for you!" she said with a smile, handing her the bag.

Grace opened it and her heart nearly stopped as she found the *Playboy* issue inside. She swallowed hard and handed the bag back to Rosemary.

Rosemary's smile vanished and she frowned deeply. "For God's sake, Mom, grow up," she said sternly. "This article is excellent and will reach thousands of people."

Grace fought back her tears. "I don't know how he could have done it."

"I hate to admit it but when men say the articles in *Playboy* are great, they're telling the truth. You probably won't get a better interview anywhere. A lot of people are going to buy this thing just because of the controversy, you know."

Grace moistened her lips and took a second look at the bag. "Do me a favor."

"What's that?"

"Keep it in your room. I don't want your father to know I'm reading such a thing," Grace whispered.

Rosemary exploded in laughter. "Great excuse, Mom! Don't you think Daddy might want to read the article, too?"

Grace turned scarlet. "Will you just do as I ask, please?"

Rosemary grinned. "It'll be on my desk in the brown paper wrapper. How's that?"

Grace swatted her with a dishtowel. "Put it up and tell me about this shower you and Christine are concocting."

Rosemary went to her room and Grace heard her laughter all over the house.

*   *   *

The article did exactly what Rosemary said, reaching and informing many, many people. "There's been more achieved with this article than you can ever imagine, Mom. People will learn he's no foaming-at-the-mouth ideologue. He's kind and compassionate and sincere, exactly the image Southern Baptists paint when they mention a Christian man," Rosemary said triumphantly.

"November next, please God," Grace prayed.

"Gerald Ford seems mighty snug," Rosemary reminded her.

But Gerald Ford hadn't won very many hearts pardoning Nixon and extending amnesty to young men who went to Canada for the duration of the Vietnam conflict. He chose Robert Dole of

Kansas as a running mate and for the first time Grace heard the rumblings of forces she knew nothing about. There were those who called for a repeal of the law that made abortions safe and legal and returning prayer in public schools.

The president of the Southern Baptist Convention refused to politicize the organization and made a statement that both Ford and Carter were fine men. In spite of the fact Jimmy Carter was himself a Southern Baptist, the president of the Convention maintained the neutrality of his position.

Grace didn't know if such neutrality was good or bad. Some people, the people she didn't like anyway, thought the refusal to endorse Carter was as good as a vote for Ford. Other people praised the decision and said a wise man never used religion to interfere with other people's voting preferences.

Perhaps it didn't make any difference in the long run. When she and Dorothy praised Carter every chance they had, few people dared utter a challenge. The two of them were, Grace felt guiltily, perhaps too strident.

She once opened her mouth to discuss the abortion issue with Rosemary, scolded herself for thinking of bringing up so unsuitable a subject, and then had second thoughts. Why on earth shouldn't she talk about it? One of Rosemary's friends had a baby and another was going to. "Do any of your friends talk about the abortion debate?"

Rosemary raised surprised eyes to her mother. "Yeah, sure. Why?"

"How many of them plan to stand behind these people in the Republican Party?"

"I have a few Catholic friends at school. I imagine they'll consider the issue very seriously."

"What do you think?"

"About abortion?"

Grace nodded shortly.

"Well, I guess I take the coward's way out and hope I never have to face the problem."

"That might not be an option."

"True. I don't know, Mom, I haven't really thought about it."

"Why not?"

"Because I'm not in a position to get pregnant."

Grace swallowed hard and looked her daughter in the eye. "You could be raped."

Rosemary almost stopped breathing. "I try to be very careful. You know I don't like taking dangerous chances. If I got pregnant as a result of rape, yes, I'd have an abortion."

"I wish I didn't have to talk to you about such things."

Rosemary's mouth twitched. "What do you mean, Mom? Do you think because Gretchen's got a baby and Laura's pregnant, I'm going to start wondering where babies come from?"

Grace blushed again. "I don't mean that! Talking about rape is...well, distasteful—"

"Indelicate," Rosemary interrupted and added with a grin, "unladylike."

"Yes."

"No." Rosemary shook her head. "Anything that provides information is not unladylike, Mom. Women simply can't be as green as you and your generation were. Ignorance isn't a virtue."

"Your Catholic friends, what do they think?"

"Well, they think even artificial contraception is a sin, much less abortion. If a woman's life is in danger then an abortion is sanctioned."

"I can almost agree with that...about the abortion, I mean."

"The issue is choice. You wouldn't want anyone interfering with your decision if you had to make it. Protect that right for other women."

"Even if they use abortion as birth control?"

Rosemary paused. "I don't like that but if we start chipping away, which reason will fall next?"

Grace swallowed again and frowned. Why couldn't people leave such emotional issues alone?

       *   *   *

Shortly after school started again, Laura had her baby. A girl, Rosemary announced, who looked exactly like Rick. She wanted to spend time with her friend but schoolwork began at once and Rosemary, for the first time in her life, seemed to have difficulty organizing her time.

She was excited about the pre-student teaching course, almost unable to contain herself until late September when she received her posting. The other education course was, as she hoped, practical and unstressful.

Her art courses were demanding and she found she didn't have time for the literature course she wanted if she insisted on Italian. Italian won the day.

Grace realized the pre-student teaching course was doomed to fail within the first week. Sent back to her old high school, Rosemary met the new art teacher who was also the girls' tennis coach.

"All she wants to do is coach tennis. She gives talented kids busy work to do…oh, if that job were mine, how I'd motivate those kids! I'd offer an art history course, and for those talented kids, keep raising the bar higher and higher to help them see what they're capable of!"

In October she asked her professor to be transferred to another school where she wouldn't be so frustrated.

"All I got for my pain was this horrified expression and a lecture that we could never do such a thing and offend teachers. Well, why not? If they're bad teachers, offend them and get them out so good teachers like me can get in!"

Grace fully expected her to stamp her feet in rage. Wasn't college supposed to be a positive experience?

*   *   *

On Election Day Grace and Rosemary went to the polls with Harry who voted early in order to be to work on time. Rosemary emerged from the voting booth with a Cheshire cat grin and left for her pre-student teaching assignment, leaving Grace to vote alone and go home to prepare for Circle Meeting.

She and Dorothy could hardly contain themselves until the meeting was over and they could go to lunch. "It will be a fine thing for Rosemary's first presidential vote to be a winning one," Dorothy smiled. "I lost my first two. They were quite devastating experiences."

"I won my first one," Grace smiled back. "Voting for Truman in '48 made me feel wonderful."

Dorothy laughed. "Me, too. Although I must confess I knew very little about him when Roosevelt died."

Grace's smile vanished and she nodded soberly. "He came into office at a bad time."

"And a critical time," Dorothy agreed. "I often wondered why God let Roosevelt die just a few short weeks before Germany surrendered. It seemed so unfair. But when Truman ordered the atomic bombs to be dropped, I think I knew why. Truman said he made the decision and never looked back. I think Roosevelt may have looked back or not dropped them at all."

"Did you think it was the right thing to do?"

"There were estimates we would lose one million boys if we invaded Japan, Grace, and no telling how many more Japanese would have died. Perhaps I'm defending my own point of view but I think if the Allies had invaded there wouldn't have been a Japanese left alive. We were so much more furious with them than we were with the Nazis."

Grace shook her head. "I've never understood that. Japan was such a different country then, the emperor treated as a god! The Japanese people didn't know any better. The Germans did."

Dorothy frowned for a moment. "Have you ever stopped to think why the Germans allowed Hitler in, Grace?"

"Rosemary said Hitler made it very clear, even in the early '20s, that if he gained any power, he planned to kill Jews."

"That's true," Dorothy said. "You remember the Depression. Imagine it ten times worse and you and Harry were a young German couple. There was no work, inflation destroyed the economy and you had a baby daughter to feed. Wouldn't you, Grace, and answer me truthfully, have supported *anyone* who promised to end such a nightmare?"

Grace twisted in her chair. "I hope not."

"If I had a hungry child I probably would have done anything. The hell of the German situation is by the time the people realized what kind of corner they'd painted themselves into it was too late."

"You almost sound sympathetic to the Nazis, Dorothy."

"Make no mistake, Grace, about my fear and loathing of Nazis, in any shape or form."

"What's there to be afraid of now?"

"Oh, my friend, how young you can be at times! What the Nazis were has been with us all through time and will be with us until the end of the world. It simply wears a different label and targets a different group in the different places it emerges. I fear people who hate others so thoroughly, not because of what they do but because of who they are."

"That can't happen here."

"Really?"

Grace's heart went cold. She forced herself to smile and tried to shake off the feeling. Dorothy was, after all, old and probably given to fears.

Who could fear anything on such a victorious day? She'd won! She couldn't wait until the inauguration.

13

Grace watched Rosemary carefully over the semester break. As usual, she was exhausted at the end of finals and perked up a little for Christmas but as soon as the holiday decorations were down she was again quiet and preoccupied.

When school started in mid-January in the coldest weather they'd suffered in years, Rosemary didn't seem interested in a single class, not even the art. Even when Grace reminded her that next year she'd be doing her student teaching, it seemed to fall on deaf ears.

Dorothy was worried, too. "This is a vulnerable time, Grace. So many women drop out of school when they're twenty."

"Has she told you what's the matter?"

"No."

"Is she getting to a point where the classes are harder?"

"She isn't above her head yet."

"I can't put my finger on the problem. She isn't dating seriously. That usually accounts for moods like this."

"Well, my dear," Dorothy said gently, "she'll tell us in her own good time."

*   *   *

At the end of January, Rosemary finally came to her. "Mom, I have to drop out of school this semester, just this semester. I'm so tired and confused I don't know what I'm doing."

"Drop out? Why?"

"I want to go on a museum tour for four weeks in Europe. It'll help clear my mind and I'll get myself pulled together. When I get home I'll know what I have to do."

"About what, Rosemary?"

"Please don't ask me any questions about this just now. I know this is a wasted semester. I'll pay you and Daddy back for it, I promise, but let me go on this museum tour."

There was something in her tone that stilled Grace's torrent of questions, something that made her realize it wasn't a childish whim but something very serious, indeed. "When is this tour?"

"The beginning of March. I have to get a passport and don't know if I can get the thing processed in time."

Grace found herself nodding. "We'll have time." She suddenly noticed the dark circles under Rosemary's eyes. "It'll be cold in Europe, you know. Are you sure you wouldn't rather go to a beach somewhere and get some sun?"

Rosemary laughed, the first real mirth Grace had heard in weeks. "I'm no sun worshipper, Mom. I'd die of boredom. No, I want to see the museums and churches in Italy and France. They ought to help me more than anything."

Grace nodded again. As Dorothy said, Rosemary would tell her all about it in her own good time.

*   *   *

Racing for the passport and scraping the money together for the magic four weeks was almost fun itself but nothing seemed to ease the strain and discontent that emanated from Rosemary. "Won't this trip make you happy, Rosie?"

"Yes, of course it will! It's a turning point of sorts, Mom, so I'm...anxious...I guess that's the best word."

"What sort of a turning point?"

"About the art."

"Rosemary," Grace cried, fearful suddenly, "promise me you won't quit school!"

Rosemary laughed. "I'll never quit. Not on your life!"

That was faintly soothing, at any rate, but what was *really* behind the crisis? Boy trouble, maybe? Was Rosemary trying to heal a broken heart by running off to Europe?

Grace was shocked at how suddenly quiet her life was without her. When the first postcards arrived Grace sighed with relief then blushed deeply as she looked at the pictures.

"Dear Mom and Dad: I'll send the lewdest ones on the rack so you'll be too embarrassed to take them to church. Ha-ha. Rosemary."

Later messages were informative and seemed to reflect a restoration of Rosemary's sense of humor. Once in awhile she sent cards that were not too embarrassing to share.

From Italy and France they came, then Germany.

"The locals can't understand a word of my horrible German with this blasted Southern accent, so we struggle in my much worse French and their perfect English. It's too beautiful here for words. I'm starved for junk food. England to go then *home*!"

Dorothy laughed long and hard over the vulgar postcards and handed the collection back to Grace. "She seems in much better spirits."

"Only five days to go until she gets home! Then maybe I'll learn what this is all about," Grace said, slipping the cards into her purse.

"You brought her up with a fine sense of self-esteem and responsibility. You should trust your work."

"She's only twenty-one, you know."

"She's an adult, Grace. When she gets back it will be a good time to move your relationship in a different direction."

"What do you mean?"

"You've been too involved with her decisions. If you continue, you'll paint yourself into a corner and make a lot of grief for yourself in the process."

"Why?"

"It's time for Rosemary to make her own decisions. She may make some you won't like."

Grace frowned and felt a deep stab of apprehension. "What do you know that I don't?"

Dorothy shook her head. "Nothing."

"I don't believe it. I've always thought Rosemary left because of something bad—"

"That is *not* true, I promise you."

"Something more than a career crisis," Grace shot, hoping to hit pay dirt and wring a confession.

"Well...it isn't bad."

"Why did she tell you and not me?"

Dorothy gasped at the pain on Grace's face then smiled. "Did you tell your mother everything when you were twenty-one?"

Grace glared at her. "Of course not. But you're old enough to be her grandmother—"

"My students always said I was easy to talk to," Dorothy interrupted.

Grace read the message loud and clear. Rosemary had sworn the old battle-ax to silence and there she was nothing she could do to get her to share the secret.

Before Grace could pout, however, Dorothy sighed. "It will be so good to have her home."

✳   ✳   ✳

Grace realized Rosemary's absence consumed her every waking moment when, at Circle Meeting, the conversation around her took her by surprise. She shook her head to clear her thoughts.

"We're not supposed to watch it," Frances Taylor said haughtily.

"Imagine a communist making a movie about Jesus!" Lorene Wright exclaimed.

"Franco Zeffirelli is not the sort of communist you're imagining, Lorene. Not every communist is an atheist and some of them actually have worthwhile things to say," Dorothy teased. "I've heard his *Jesus of Nazareth* is exquisite."

Grace glanced quickly at Dorothy and her heart calmed a bit. Nothing seemed to erase the old schoolteacher's permanent mocking smile.

"You don't plan to watch it, do you, Miss Dorothy?"

"Yes, of course. I can't see how any religious epic can be any worse than that travesty with Max von Sydow."

"Who?" someone close to Grace whispered.

Dorothy's hearing was too sharp to miss the question. She smiled. "The blue-eyed blond Swede who played the part of Jesus in *The Greatest Story Ever Told*."

Lorene Wright glared at the older woman. "I cannot believe my ears when I hear you actually plan to watch something we've been asked to boycott."

Dorothy's smile faded somewhat. "My dear, I'm *well* over twenty-one. I make my own decisions about my leisure activities."

"It's a sin," Lorene warned her.

"Because our minister says so?"

"Yes—"

"It amazes me how often Baptists are turning to their ministers as spiritual authority figures these days," Dorothy noted.

"That's what a minister is for—"

"No, my dear," Dorothy said levelly, "it is *not*. Our minister is supposed to be our pastor, a shepherd to offer help and guidance. That's all. If you want to be told every little thing to say and do, you really aren't a Baptist, are you?"

Lorene's face went scarlet but she was unmoved. "If everyone goes around making their own decisions why have a church at all?"

"What is your definition of a church, Lorene? When I was a girl, we defined it as a group of people who held in common only a few specific beliefs. I'm beginning to think Southern Baptists crave a creed."

"What's that?" Lorene asked suspiciously.

"A list of things to believe in order to belong," Dorothy explained.

Lorene and several others nodded.

Grace's mouth fell open. "How can any of you believe that? Don't you realize what it means to us, historically, *not* to have a creed?"

Lorene shrugged. "I'd just like to know who is a real Christian and who isn't."

Dorothy's mirth vanished instantly. "You must read from a different Bible than mine, too, Lorene. I was under the impression God is the only judge."

Frances Taylor interrupted. "Let's have refreshments, ladies, and tell us, Grace, when is Rosie coming home?"

Grace smiled, knowing Frances must have been desperate for a distraction to ask about Rosemary. "We pick her up at the airport tomorrow."

"Has she had a good time?"

"I think so."

"Will she be at church on Easter?"

"Yes, of course."

"It's always good to have the children home for the holidays."

Children! Grace repressed a sigh. Rosemary was a child no longer. If Dorothy had succeeded with no other point, she had at least brought Grace to that sad conclusion.

Yet it wasn't sad, too. She and Rosemary had clashed so violently the last few years. Surely, as adults, their relationship would improve.

I already have the jump on most of these women, she thought omugly. I at least realize my child isn't a little girl anymore.

*   *   *

She expected a ragged scarecrow to deplane in the early spring afternoon and was quite surprised when a neat and clean Rosemary, straining under the weight of her carry-on baggage, struggled down the corridor.

Harry laughed for what Grace supposed was the first time in four weeks. He rushed to help her with the awkward cases.

She consented to only the briefest of hugs, too wound up, Grace realized, to be tearful.

"Will we need a fork-lift to take home the big suitcase?" Harry teased.

"No, that one's pretty light. This stuff is full of film that I didn't want going through x-ray machines."

Grace laughed. "How about junk food?"

"I'm ready to eat McDonald's down to the foundations," Rosemary confessed.

"Don't they have them in Europe?"

"They're not the same, Mom, just not the same."

"What did you bring us?" Harry asked, excited as a child for gifts.

"For you, a ton of chocolate from every city," Rosemary grinned, "and an authentic designer scarf for Mom. It'll look great with your red suit," she said to Grace and began talking for what seemed to her mother two solid hours without breathing once.

*　　　　　*　　　　　*

Early the next morning after Harry went to work, Rosemary got up. She motioned for Grace to sit down at the breakfast table. "I have to tell you about my decision, Mom."

For a brief moment Grace's heart constricted. Here it was at last, the end of the mystery. "Before you left you said something about a turning point with the art," she said gently, wanting Rosemary to understand how important the crisis was to her, too.

Rosemary grinned and reached for a mug. "Is there any more coffee?"

"Yes."

"I'll get it." As she made her way around the kitchen Grace noted how very changed she actually was.

"You promised me you weren't going to quit school."

Rosemary laughed as she set the steaming mug on the table and curled up in a chair opposite her mother. "How does another three years on top of a bachelor's degree sound to you?"

"Graduate school?"

Rosemary met her eyes calmly. "Law school."

"Law—" Grace almost strangled on the word. "What on earth made you think about that?"

"I have to back up to give you the whole story. You know I've always loved English and history. No one could be friends with Miss Dorothy without knowing politics."

"Politics…you want to go into politics?"

"I don't think that's in the cards for me," Rosemary admitted. "The art hasn't been working for a long time, Mom. I've been beating my head against a brick wall in the college of education. I argue with the professors all the time. It's senseless. Whatever I am, it isn't teaching material."

"Dorothy always said you'd be a wonderful teacher."

"Well, the teaching profession has changed a lot since she retired. Even since I got out of high school. I don't like what I see there and in order for me to graduate with a teaching certificate, I'd have to conform." She grinned again. "You're well aware of my problems with conformity, Mom, so I'm sure you understand why I'm at the end of the road with art."

Grace sighed. "I have the feeling that isn't the only thing, though."

"No. What I'm going to tell you now, Mom, goes no further than us. You can tell Miss Dorothy but I lay you odds ten to one she probably knows it already."

Grace gritted her teeth.

"Just before finals last year Lisa invited me to have lunch with her and she offered to show me the hospital," Rosemary began.

"As we walked past the emergency room cubicles guess who was inside one of them?"

Grace shook her head and her heart began to pound.

"Gretchen."

Grace's eyes widened. "What was the matter?"

"Her sweetheart of a husband opened a gash in her scalp that required stitches."

"Oh God, Rosemary, do her parents know?"

"I don't know how they could miss that wound. Anyway, the doctor forgot to close the curtain and that's why we saw her. Lisa and I stayed with her. You know, Mom, all of a sudden I was ashamed of being an art major."

"Why?"

Rosemary paused a long moment. "Because I was so damned useless in the crisis, I think. Even though Lisa's only a third year student she was really a help to Gretchen. She's already making a difference in the world with her nursing.

"As for me," she continued, "I'm not good enough to bring the world to its knees with something beautiful and earthshaking. My art will never make a difference. What was I good for that day? Just to sit there and hold Gretchen's hand, wishing I could kill that husband of hers!"

Grace looked long and hard at her daughter's flashing blue eyes.

"I realized I have to do something important with my life, too, Mom. Law school will do that for me. I can help women like Gretchen, I know I can."

Grace sighed again then smiled a little. "It seems like you had your mind made up last year, Rosemary."

"For the most part. But there's something really scary about switching horses mid-stream. All the pre-law majors are so far ahead of me. They've been reading history and political science as long as I've been scribbling on a drawing pad."

"I never saw you back down from a challenge before," Grace teased.

"You're not likely to see it anytime soon, either," Rosemary promised.

"Why did you go off to Europe?"

"It was a sort of farewell."

"You don't have to completely give up your drawing, Rosemary," Grace said after a long silence. "I think it would be a perfect hobby for you. A good way to relax when the pressures of law school nearly get you down."

Rosemary nodded. "I think so, too, but the only thing that worries me, Mom, is the expense—"

"Expense?"

"I'm going to have to get a full-time job—"

"Not so fast, miss," Grace interrupted. "Remember, your father and I saved for your education thinking we were going to send you to the Baptist college. You cut the expenses more than half by going to the university and living at home. There's still a lot left in the account. It will pay for your law school."

Rosemary smiled. "Unless I get accepted to Yale."

Grace's smile froze. "You want to go to Yale?"

"I'm just teasing, Mom. My life is here. This is where I'm going to school."

Grace smiled. "Dorothy knows this?"

"She knows I was at the end of my rope with the college of education. I never told her about Gretchen, though, but as I said before, I think she probably knows. Nothing gets by her."

"True," Grace said softly.

"And Mom?"

"Mmm?"

"This coffee's awful. No wonder you're hyperactive."

"You're quite welcome to start making your own."

Rosemary smiled. "I'll get a jar of instant."

Grace sighed and relaxed. The mystery was solved and her relief was overwhelming. Not something tragic, after all! In fact, good...*very* good!

*   *   *

As Rosemary predicted, the designer scarf was perfect with Grace's red suit. Grace fluffed it higher around her neck, wondering why a neck showed a woman's age so much worse than anyplace else.

"Mom, do you have any hair spray?" Rosemary called from her bedroom.

"No. Sorry."

"That's what I get for trying to be stylish."

Grace slipped into her daughter's room and almost laughed. Rosemary's impossibly straight hair refused to feather around her face, although one stubborn lock held a slight curl, making it ridiculously out of place.

"I'm a fashion nightmare," she complained. "My hair never cooperates and this stupid makeup is so dark that I look like a streetwalker."

"Rosie!" Grace rebuked, reaching for her daughter's lipstick. "This is a beautiful shade."

"In the tube," Rosemary sniffed angrily. She took it from Grace and applied it to her lips. "When the style goes back to pale shades I'll buy this stuff by the case." She wiped the lipstick on a tissue and handed Grace the tube. "It's yours if you want it."

Harry called to them from downstairs. "Okay you two, the old Easter Bunny's been here!"

Rosemary grinned, shaking her head. "Some things never change."

Grace hurriedly set the lipstick on her dresser and followed Rosemary down the stairs. "Especially when it comes to you and your father." It was somewhat reassuring in a world that wasn't quite so steady these days.

*   *   *

Grace's festive spirit was shaken between Sunday School and church when she noticed Rosemary deluged by the crowd of kids she'd had little to do with the last three years. She tried not to overhear but couldn't help herself.

"So you went to Europe?"

"Yep, a four week museum tour," Rosemary replied.

"We're having a retreat in July—"

"I'm sorry. I have this semester to make up so I have to go to summer school."

"Oh, writing papers on all those nice museums?"

"I'm changing majors so I have a lot of catching up to do."

Grace bit her lip and ducked into an empty classroom. How would her peers accept her news, especially those who never knew Rosemary to do anything but draw?

"What to?"

"History or political science. They're the best pre-law majors I can think of."

"Law? You, a lawyer?"

"I can see it now, old Rosie the hangin' judge!"

"I'm glad you think it's a natural calling," Rosemary said lightly but Grace caught her sarcasm.

"Oh, Rosemary, how exciting! What sort of law are you going to practice?"

"I want to be a woman's advocate."

"A what?"

"I want to go after men who don't pay their child support, men who use women as punching bags, that sort of thing."

"Feminist stuff?"

"Rosie, don't you think it's...well, just a bit sordid?"

"Absolutely. I can't think of a more sordid thing than domestic violence."

"No, I mean getting involved with people like that."

Grace crept deeper into the shadows and wiped the sudden dew of perspiration off her brow.

Rosemary laughed. "You kid yourselves if you think it only happens to 'people like that!'"

Grace heard her walk away but the conversation continued in her absence. "I know she was baptized and everything but there's part of me that's convinced Rosemary Lee isn't a *real* Christian."

"She's been stirring up trouble since she was sixteen."

"No one can ever win an argument with her."

"Well, you know what they say. The atheists and the communists know the Bible better than anyone so they can destroy it."

Grace gasped, feeling nauseated. What in the world do atheists and communists have to do with Rosemary, she wondered, and why are these kids, the very kids Rosemary grew up with, so violently opposed to her plans?

She knew Gretchen's situation was partly responsible for Rosemary's career crisis. Suddenly, she was strangely relieved. She peeked out the doorway to make sure they were gone and started walking slowly to the sanctuary.

All Grace's old dreams about a missionary daughter had faded long ago as Rosemary slipped further away from the church. Yet wasn't Rosemary's determination to be a good lawyer, a deeply committed lawyer, missionary zeal of another sort?

A woman's advocate, she thought with pride, that has a nice ring to it, doesn't it? What a fine difference she will make to so many women! She'll help them stand alone and unafraid as she stands herself!

My daughter, the lawyer. Yes, it *was* a good decision.

           *   *   *

She smiled as she saw Rosemary and Gretchen sitting together. Did those two ever suspect sitting near the front gave their mothers perfect supervision? It wasn't so hard to imagine them as children again…it really hadn't been so long ago, had it? Yet Gretchen was divorcing her husband and had a baby son beyond in the church nursery!

The congregation stood to sing *He Arose*. Grace couldn't help but smile again at the two of them.

However, once the sermon began the old apprehension returned. Before it progressed five minutes, Grace felt her jaw tightening. Any euphoria she'd enjoyed was gone.

"Our country is under siege…our fundamental Christian values…politicians who cater to left-wing rabble and the homosexuals who seek to destroy the American family with their 'alternative lifestyles!'"

What is he trying to do, start a war, Grace thought miserably, her head spinning. God, God, how inappropriate for an Easter service! The hostility of it all!

Her heart beat rapidly and she wished fervently that she'd left her long-line bra in the bottom drawer of her dresser.

Suddenly, before her eyes she saw Rosemary slowly stand. The action was slow and deliberate. All eyes turned on her and the preacher, distracted, fell momentarily silent.

Rosemary stepped across Gretchen into the aisle. Grace forced herself to look at her daughter's face. She was absolutely furious and deathly pale. She paused to adjust her shoulder bag and walked up the aisle and out the door.

Grace felt all eyes in the congregation turn toward her. For a fleeting moment she wanted to get up and leave, too, leave that pompous jackass in the pulpit with something to *really* preach about!

But she couldn't move. Whether or not the same blood-and-thunder pattern continued, she never knew. She was too grieved, realizing Rosemary had walked out not only on an inappropriate sermon but the church, as well.

Grace knew she'd never return.

14

Rosemary refused to go back to church under any circumstances. Her leaving provided Christine the opportunity to find a church closer to home. "Since the two of them left it's like the life has gone out of the class." Dorothy sighed deeply, mourning Rosemary and Christine's departures from her Sunday School class. "Where will she go, Grace? First or Central?"

Grace couldn't bring up her eyes to meet Dorothy's. "She's brought home a lot of books from the library."

"Why?"

"She told me she's not a Baptist anymore."

Dorothy grimaced. "I was afraid of that."

"She's leaning toward Disciples of Christ."

"At least they aren't Episcopalians," Dorothy teased gently.

"Still a bunch of radicals," Grace said tartly.

"Well," Dorothy retorted, "so is she."

"I don't know how or when she grew so far away from what I raised her with."

"You encouraged her to *think*, Grace."

Grace turned suddenly angry eyes on Dorothy. "You encouraged me to encourage her. This is all your fault."

"My fault?" Dorothy challenged, her hazel eyes sparkling. "What's that supposed to mean?"

"If I hadn't listened to you, maybe she'd be where she's supposed to be!"

"And maybe she wouldn't!" Dorothy snapped then suddenly softened. "Oh Grace, for heaven's sake, why try to second-guess it? A generation ago, Rosemary might have been happy. But things are different for her, not only in our church but in society, too."

Grace squirmed in her chair. "I don't like what's happening in our denomination, Dorothy," she confessed.

"What do you plan to do about it?"

"Do?"

"I've always believed in challenging what I dislike. It's about time you take a page out of my book and start doing it, too. I won't be around forever, you know. I need someone to follow in my footsteps who'll keep the silent majority nervous and upset."

Grace couldn't help but smile. "I always suspected that was your game."

"Now it seems Rosemary won't be around to follow me."

God, how depressed she sounds, Grace noted.

Dorothy sighed again. "Maybe she knows a fight is hopeless. I have to respect her for looking for a church more in tune with her personal beliefs but dear God, how I shall miss her!"

*   *   *

Dorothy seemed to be the only one. Rosemary, in spite of gathering up reading material, was in no hurry to plunge into a new church. Grace didn't like it when she slept late on Sunday mornings without betraying the slightest bit of guilt that she enjoyed herself.

She scheduled a full class load during summer session and spent two days with the necessary paperwork changing her college from education to arts and sciences. "I think the secretaries were ready to have a thanksgiving service when I filled out the last forms and bade them good-bye," she teased.

Grace felt a little weak in the knees, harboring her secret that most people in church felt the same way. "Maybe you'll have better luck in arts and sciences."

"It would have to be better than this last year," Rosemary chuckled. "By the way Mom, do you remember Melanie? I saw her father when I went to the history department for an advisor. He's still teaching reformation studies and I'm going to take one of his classes this fall."

Grace paused, feeling her heart constrict at the thought of an unwelcome religious influence at such a vulnerable time. She glanced quickly at Rosemary, wondering if she should voice her doubts. "And how is Melanie?" she asked instead.

"An engineering graduate!" Rosemary laughed. "Of course, I shouldn't be surprised. She was always a math whiz."

"Is her father your advisor?"

"Of course not, Mom. I have to have an advisor who teaches the history of American law."

I feel like a complete fool for that, Grace chided herself.

"I couldn't stand the thought of more theory and stuff in political science," Rosemary explained.

"Oh," Grace said, hoping her expression looked appropriately impressed. "So it's history then."

"It's where I should have been all along."

*   *   *

Immediately after Rosemary began class work in pre-law her attitude changed. Her predisposition to lively argument brought her to the attention of her professors and seemed to be exactly what was expected.

She began spending her free time with six or seven students in her classes, learning and questioning beyond the classroom. She was so content she fairly glowed.

In the meantime Grace and Dorothy, who hoped to share their political happiness with their peers at church, found themselves challenged for their support of Carter. Unbelievably, the very denomination Carter belonged to repudiated him.

It started in Florida. Whipped into a frenzy by a group led by Anita Bryant, demands were made in Dade County to eject homosexual teachers from the public school system. Moreover, the group demanded a return of Bible reading and prayer.

Now this is one time, on this homosexual issue, Dorothy and I are going to lock horns, Grace thought nervously. She probably sees nothing at all wrong in it.

The older woman was certainly in a mood to be reckoned with. "How dare Baptists take such a stand? Why isn't anyone standing up to them with privacy rights?" she demanded, shaking with fury.

"Maybe rights to privacy aren't the same for people who work with children," Grace countered.

"Aren't the same? Since when did we start having two sets of laws in this country, Grace?"

"We shouldn't talk about this, Dorothy. I agree with them."

"Agree—I don't believe it!"

"Believe it. I understand how these parents feel. The thought of a homosexual touching Rosemary...why I would have lost my mind!"

"A homosexual man would have no interest in Rosemary, my dear."

Grace's face went scarlet but she held her ground. "You *know* what I mean."

"No, not really, but let me try to guess. At what age would you put an unmarried teacher on notice that he or she is suspected of being homosexual?"

"What?"

"Thirty? I'll never forget how society gave up on me after I turned thirty."

"Society didn't give up on you."

"Of course it did! I doubt anyone suspected I might have been a lesbian but that horrible label 'old maid' was attached to me and changed my life in ways I didn't like at all!"

"It's different. You know it."

"Would you use the limp-wrist theory to sniff out your gay men, Grace?"

"What?"

"Men with feminine mannerisms. That's a dead giveaway, supposedly."

Grace tried to calm her splitting head.

Dorothy continued, "The Nazis had various and sundry ways of finding homosexuals. Of course they thought they could identify Jews by the way they walked, too."

Grace went rigid with fury. "How dare you compare this to something the Nazis did?"

"Why not? *Isn't* it something the Nazis did?"

"The Nazis killed them. I simply think they shouldn't be teaching school."

"Once you lock them out of the teaching profession, where else will you expect them to go away?"

"Well…"

"Do you feel like a fool yet?"

"No," Grace argued. "We've always had special rules for teachers. I don't see why homosexuality doesn't fall under moral turpitude and they aren't dismissed for it."

"I knew three men teachers during my career who molested little girls. They weren't homosexual."

"You *know* what I mean!"

Dorothy shut her mouth and forced herself to calm down. "This is nothing short of a witch-hunt, Grace. When a teacher crosses the line of professional behavior I say throw the book at him or her. But until there are specific charges aimed at a specific teacher, you simply can't act this way. Don't you see what this is? A war-cry!"

She *did* see it and felt her burning convictions crumble away. Before she could admit as much, however, Dorothy started pacing again.

"I thought we were finished with the school prayer issue, too, and here they are trying to revive it!"

"I agree with you on that one."

Dorothy paused and frowned. "I had a colleague, a horrible old woman, how I pitied the children in her class! Anyway, Grace, she took particular pleasure tormenting a Jewish child to pray in the name of Jesus."

Grace's blood went cold. "No!"

"Oh yes. I was so glad when the Supreme Court resolved the issue; glad it put the muzzle on people like her. It put prayer and religious education into the hands of the parents, where it should be."

"These people obviously don't appreciate the separation of church and state."

Dorothy forced a weak smile. "You expect a lot out of people, Grace. If you asked one hundred people on the street about the separation of church and state, I guarantee ninety of them would look at you as though you'd just breezed in from the moon."

Grace shook her head. "I don't think so but I'm beginning to think Baptists aren't as on the ball as we used to be!"

*   *   *

The semester break was different for Rosemary that year. Although she was tired she seemed blissfully content and when her transcript arrived full of As, she tossed the flimsy paper into the air with a squeal of delight. She was well on her way.

It was a wonderful Christmas with Rosemary so content.

Christine graduated in December with her music degree and right after the holidays, left for a five city audition tour. Rosemary went with her to the airport to see her off and returned home rather downcast.

"I hope you didn't let Christine see that long face," Grace said, pouring cinnamon tea for the two of them.

"I forced myself to smile." Rosemary sighed. "She'll get one of those jobs, you know, and Lord knows when I'll ever see her again."

"What kind of job, exactly?"

"Playing in an orchestra," Rosemary explained.

"The two of you will have letters and occasional phone calls. When you get out of law school, you'll have the money and the time to travel to see her. And she'll come home every now and then to see her parents."

"Yeah but things change once people start into their careers, Mom. Christine will be surrounded by all sorts of people as talented as she is. I'm happy she's pursued her career to these ends, I really am, but she's been around for seven years and this is going to be hard!"

"It's a pity there wasn't something here for her."

"She needs to be someplace where the fine arts are better rewarded."

"Would you have left home if you'd stayed in art?"

Rosemary laughed shortly. "Probably. Think what you've gained by me staying here and planning on law school!"

Grace smiled. "I'm glad it's worked out."

"Me, too," Rosemary said and smiled, too. "I think I'll be a real hot-shot lawyer."

*   *   *

"Last year we started back to school in the deep freeze and this year we have a snow that will never end," Rosemary complained, pulling on her man-size parka. "I notice everything in town has come to a dead halt except the university."

"Maybe it's because so many of the students live on campus," Grace reminded her.

"Yeah, but the professors don't. If I go to classes today and the professors don't show up, I'm seriously thinking of demanding the university reimburse me for my time."

She's already thinking like a lawyer, Grace noted. She frowned at the picture she made. "Does anyone else dress the way you do? You look like you're ready for duty in Antarctica."

Rosemary glared at her. "I don't care how it looks, as long as it works."

"Where's your bag?"

"On my shoulder inside the parka. If the professors don't show up, I'll come home."

"Be careful in the snow."

"When I'm elected mayor, I promise to get snow-removal equipment into the city," she said melodramatically as she closed the door behind her.

Grace watched as she swept the heavy snow off the car. She wished she'd insisted on taking her but Harry said she needed the experience of driving in the bad weather. How hard it was not to worry!

Bad weather in the figurative sense assaulted Southern Baptists the same month. Charges were made that the seminaries were full of liberal heretics. The statement was grasped, Grace noted, with the same sort of fervor that propelled along Anita Bryant and her friends.

Clarifying their stance, the accusers said the issue at hand was Biblical inerrancy and infallibility and professors in the seminaries were falling woefully short. Grace hoped to discuss the issue with Dorothy over lunch after Circle Meeting but for the first time in years Circle Meeting was canceled due to the bad weather.

She called her. "I've only heard the term infallible as it regarded the Pope," she tried to explain. "What about you?"

"Oh, I've heard the term before, Grace, but not among Southern Baptists. Other Baptists have believed this sort of thing since Heck was a pup."

"Inerrant means without error, right?"

"They mean scientifically and historically, too," Dorothy reminded her.

"Now I'm completely confused."

"It means the Bible speaks correctly about matters of science and history, too."

"Oh, for heaven's sake!" Grace cried. "That sounds like something from some backwater tent revival!"

Dorothy held the silence.

"What I mean—"

"I know what you mean, Grace, but maybe you and I should pipe down a little. We seem to be in for some rough times."

*　　　　*　　　　*

The controversy of infallibility and inerrancy was all the talk at church functions. Quite suddenly, people's opinions revealed their roots. Most of the church members who'd grown up with Grace and shared the same programs believed the way she did.

There were many others, though, people who joined their church in their adult years, who did not. It was especially telling among the new people who'd joined her church, en masse, since its relocation.

Grace could think of little else. Coming back to haunt us! No intensive study about what Southern Baptists believe! We let them walk down the aisle, fill out a card, gave them the obligatory dip in the baptistery and took them in as active members.

This is what we get, allowing these ignorant people positions of authority. God, dear God, Rosemary noted they weren't Southern Baptists when she was only thirteen!

*　　　　*　　　　*

The bad weather lasted until March with the most paralyzing snow the area had ever experienced. But when spring finally came, how glorious it was!

"I've never seen so much color!" Dorothy declared.

"I can't wait until May to see if the dogwoods will be as lovely. No place is as beautiful as Kentucky in late spring!" Grace added.

Rosemary was grateful for the beautiful spring, too, using her break to go outside to enjoy the fresh air and chilly sunshine. Unlike other years she didn't have the luxury of

completing midterms and so had two term papers to finish
before she went back.

"I've got a bad case of spring fever," she admitted.

"Get on with those papers. What are they about, anyway?"

"Roman law, which is excellent. I love ancient history! Those
old Romans really talk to me. Maybe I've been a pagan rather
than a Christian all these years and am just now finding it out."

"Rosemary!"

"I'm writing a paper about women's rights under Roman law. It
makes me sick that women never saw such freedom again until the
late nineteenth century. Kind of makes you wonder about
Christianity and what it's done for women."

"It doesn't make *me* wonder," Grace huffed.

Rosemary shrugged.

Grace decided to change the subject. "What's the other one?"

"Oh, it's for the radical teaching the history of American law. I
think I understand his game now. He's a rabble-rouser and says
the most horrible things just to get people started."

"Like what?"

"Well, before the break, he brought out the fact that compassion isn't written into the constitution. Did that open up a can of
worms!"

Grace's eyes widened. "What sort of person is he?"

"He's not really bad, Mom, he just loves to get something
started. He won't stand for it if you emote. He'll only listen if you
have the facts to back yourself up." She smiled again. "I didn't
think I'd ever meet anyone who loves stirring up a hornet's nest
like I do. He's a scream!"

"Do you do well in this class?"

"He's a tyrant," Rosemary said simply. "On one exam I got a B
and the only thing he wrote across it was 'not at all bad.' Now if
that was supposed to mean good, why didn't he give me an A?"

"Why not, indeed?"

"Because I didn't plug up the last hole in my summary," Rosemary sighed. "I told him he could have written it on the page but the smug twerp told me I'd spent so much time making the essay legible he didn't want to deface it."

Grace laughed. Could this smiling, successful student be the same Rosemary who, last year, was so miserable? The change was unbelievable.

*　　　　*　　　　*

During summer session Rosemary joined forces with other students preparing to enter law school. They exchanged notes and met for discussions, hoping to bolster each other's confidence and make themselves invincible for the dreaded law school admissions test.

She came home one afternoon with the *LSAT Study Guide*. "It gives tips on studying and has four or five sample exams from the previous years," she explained to her mother.

"When do you have to take it?"

"It runs on the same schedule as the college admissions tests. So I'll take it in December and again in March if I don't like the score," Rosemary explained.

"You'll have finals to be studying for in December and the March one probably coincides with mid-terms."

"Don't worry, Mom. I've planned six months to study for this thing. I'll be okay, really I will."

Grace kept an eye on her to make sure she wasn't taking on too much. Perhaps this is the type of pressure Rosemary actually enjoys, she decided, like competing with the other girls in GAs to be a queen-in-service, learning all the Bible verses and things. Yes, this was the child in her still striving to be first.

She was just a little more subtle at twenty-two than she'd been at twelve.

*   *   *

Then the unbelievable happened. Jimmy Carter brought Menachim Begin and Anwar Sadat to Camp David and there would be peace between Israel and Egypt. Who would have thought it?

Rosemary watched the news and nearly danced with joy. "What a triumph, Mom! This is even better than getting a Supreme Court justice nomination. This act will live forever."

Grace was pleased, too. The more she read, the more she liked Anwar Sadat. The things he said about how he knew he would have to change to move his country forward showed her he was a man to admire.

Unlike her daughter, however, Grace's peers at church didn't take the news so well. A solitary Israel, persecuted from all sides, seemed to them the more appropriate example of God's will.

"They can't be at peace with Egypt," some people said. "Egypt cannot be trusted."

"They shouldn't make peace at all. All that land is supposed to be Israel's anyway, from the Euphrates to the Nile."

"Did you hear what else is in the agreement? Israel will have to give up some of its land for those Palestinians!"

"How can Carter claim to be a good Christian and ask the Jews to give up the claims on land that's theirs?"

Grace felt her head spin with the frenzy and fury motivating the women. Why couldn't they see what she saw?

Rosemary sarcastically evaluated the situation. "Well, if the Middle East becomes peaceful where in the world will we sell our arsenal?"

Grace glared at her. "You make it sound like a game of war is behind everything!"

"Remember what the kids in the '60s called it, Mom? The military-industrial complex? Think about it. If we couldn't export arms, what would happen to our economy?"

Grace remembered the pride she felt in being part of Roosevelt's arsenal of democracy but also the sting of shame and disapproval that her country was now the arsenal of the world. "Well," she said defensively, "*I* approve of what Carter's doing and I don't really care what anyone says!"

15

"Boy, do I have a lot to do this month!" Rosemary exclaimed, poring over the kitchen calendar. "My first stab at the LSAT and hooking up with Christine so I can meet this Prince Charming of hers."

"Christine's coming home for the holidays?" Grace asked with a smile.

"Yes and no," Rosemary hedged. "She has some time before Christmas but her orchestra actually plays on Christmas Day and through the holidays."

"Tell me about her Prince Charming."

"She's been pretty secretive about the whole thing," Rosemary said. "All I know is his name is David and he's a percussionist in the same orchestra she's in. That's a drummer."

"I had a rough idea." Grace glared at her.

Rosemary laughed shortly. "I wonder what he's going to think of Christine's hopelessly unmusical friend?"

"Is it serious?"

"I think so." Rosemary grinned. "Ah me, there they are in New England making music together. Doesn't that sound sickeningly, deliciously romantic?"

Grace paused. Was that a little envy in Rosemary's voice? Not of Christine's boyfriend, necessarily, but of her happiness?

"Anyway, they want me to go to an opera with them," Rosemary continued. "After the show's over we're going to dinner—excuse me, *supper*. Boy oh boy, will this ever be a pantyhose occasion! If I didn't count Christine as one of my dearest friends, I'd head for the hills right now."

"Will you need a dress?"

Rosemary gasped. "I don't have anything for something like an opera, do I?" She paused. "I want to think about this. If I'm going to invest in something sort of formal, I may as well get something classy so I can wear it for years. Maybe on the long side so I can cheat and wear knee high hose—"

"You're not going out of this house with a good dress and knee high stockings."

"Sure I will. But only if I find the right dress."

*   *   *

"I think I did well," Rosemary declared after the Law School Admissions Test. "In fact, I seemed to know what I was doing on those awful math problems."

"When will you know?"

"End of the month. Nice little Christmas present."

"How can a law school accept you if you haven't graduated?"

"I use my grade point average and the test score to see if the combination is acceptable for admission," Rosemary explained. "Then I have to harangue three people into giving me academic references, apply and hope for the best."

She doesn't seem nervous at all, Grace noted. It was just as well. She herself was nervous enough for both of them.

*   *   *

Opera night arrived and Grace was downstairs when Rosemary groped her way down the steps, trying to look dignified. If Grace hadn't been aware of the fact that Rosemary wore knee-highs, she might have considered the effect very stunning.

Rosemary had chosen a silk dress that was, as she hoped, very classy. Extravagantly, she bought and dyed a pair of shoes to match. Spike heels were back in style again and she practiced for hours with her new shoes, howling and complaining with every strained step she took.

She wore Grace's sparkly clip earrings, a little lipstick and peered at herself in the hall mirror. "Well, I hope they don't mind what they see, because this is as good as it gets."

The doorbell rang promptly at six and Rosemary answered it, waving in Christine and David from the sudden rainstorm. Grace said a quick hello and disappeared into the kitchen. She heard a bit of garbled small talk then Rosemary's sudden, "Oh Christine, it's gorgeous!"

That has to be an engagement ring, Grace decided, straining to overhear.

"Mom, come here and look at this rock!"

So Grace emerged from the kitchen again and almost plunged headlong into David. She smiled but the smile froze on her face. Jewish, she thought. He has to be Jewish, he looks exactly like Motl the Tailor. She forced herself to turn to Christine and the beautiful outstretched hand. "Good Lord," she gasped, "that's the most exquisite diamond I've ever seen! It's beautiful, dear, just beautiful. Have the two of you set a date?"

"Next December." Christine fairly glowed with happiness.

Rosemary shook her head with a smile. "I guess I'm definitely going to be the cow's tail to the altar."

"Well, we'd better be going. We have a long drive," David said. "Good night, Mrs. Lee."

"Good night, David…oh, I didn't catch your last name—"

"Levy," he grinned as Rosemary and Christine started out the door under Rosemary's huge umbrella. He closed the door after them and Grace stared at it.

Do Christine's parents know she's planning to marry a Jew, Grace wondered frantically. Has Christine converted him? Christine was always so much more devout than Rosemary.

Could David have converted Christine? God, what a sobering thought! Of course, up there in New England, away from everything she was raised with, it was possible for her to get mixed up with people who would confuse her.

Grace looked at the clock. Rosemary said not to expect her before three or four in the morning. It was a terribly long time to wait!

*   *   *

"What a night!" Rosemary sighed languidly the next day, making an appearance after noon. "I cried through the whole thing, it was so romantic! Oh Lord, only once to be able to sing like that girl did!"

"Which girl?" Grace asked.

"'Musetta.' What a role! If I could sing opera, that's the role I'd want to sing!"

Grace paused and put the teakettle on. "Is David Jewish?"

"Yep. Mom, if this opera ever comes here, you've got to see it. I think I'm hooked."

"Tell me more about David."

"He's very nice. Christine couldn't have done any better, I'm convinced. Where did I put my program, Mom? I got a couple of autographs and I want to show—"

"Has he converted?"

Rosemary paused a long moment, realizing where Grace's line of questioning was going. "No," she answered firmly.

"Doesn't it bother Christine?"

"Conversion isn't an issue between them."

"Where will they get married?"

"I didn't ask. They plan to have a minister and a rabbi officiate at the wedding. I think it sounds terrific."

"How will they raise their children?"

"Good God, Mom, that's hardly any of my business. Or yours either, for that matter."

"You didn't say anything to her about it? About raising her children without confusion?"

"Christine's a grown woman and knows what she's doing. She and David have a year to work out any problems."

"I don't understand you and Christine at all. Doesn't it matter to you this boy isn't a Christian?"

"Truthfully?" Rosemary asked sternly. "No, it doesn't."

"You and Christine know this isn't the way you were brought up to think."

"Perhaps Christine and I decided, somewhere along the way, we didn't like that aspect of the way we were brought up."

Grace shook with rage and pain. "You'll come to regret that one of these days."

Rosemary only shrugged. "Maybe. I can imagine the gossip that's going to start making the rounds at church when people find out about David. Let me warn you, Mom, I'd better not track any of it back to you, do you understand?"

"I have the right to talk—"

"You heard what I said. If Christine is hurt by anything that comes from that adder-tongued gang of yours, someone's going to be mighty sorry. So dwell on it a few minutes before you burn up the phone line." She turned on her heel and left the room.

Grace sat down and frowned. She surely wouldn't mind me talking to Dorothy, she decided. And what will Dorothy think of the situation? She called immediately and was comforted by the pleasant sound of Dorothy's voice. "It's Grace," she said quickly, "do you have a minute?"

"No, not really, dear. Christine has brought her fiancé over and we're having some tea and scones."

"Oh."

"I'll call you when they leave," Dorothy promised and hung up.

Not a trace of disappointment or shock in her voice, Grace noted. She was the same old cheerfully pleasant Dorothy who always had time for Christine and Rosemary and their problems.

If anyone else brought up the subject of Christine's fiancé, she would have to smile and not say anything. It was a sad state of affairs when a daughter's threats could so unnerve a mother!

*　　　　*　　　　*

Rosemary's LSAT score pleased her very much and she noted she was already within admissions standards with her current grade point average. "Of course, getting this last semester full of As will only make it look better," she explained and plunged into her final semester with gusto.

Christine and David left for New England again but not before Christine told Rosemary she wanted her to be her maid of honor. Rosemary was euphoric. "Eleven months to wait, I don't think I can stand it!"

To Grace's chagrin, Dorothy reacted to David just as Rosemary had. "He's a fine young man and has plans where he wants to be next year and five years after that," Dorothy explained. "The two of them seem to have everything arranged."

"Rosemary told me she didn't care whether he converted or not," Grace said.

Dorothy laughed. "Grace, you'd be just as upset if Christine were marrying a Methodist or a Presbyterian."

"You know I'm not like that!"

"Why are you taking on so about this? Christine isn't your daughter."

"I've always wanted Rosemary to be like Christine."

"Why?"

"Christine is sweet and gentle. She never stirs up trouble or enjoys an argument. She's feminine and what I wanted Rosemary to be."

"Rosemary is feminine, too, Grace, in her own way."

"She is not. She's like a steam roller and has no sense of decorum or subtlety at all."

"The world needs all kinds of people."

"If Christine could make such a radical decision, can you imagine what sort of man Rosemary might choose?"

Dorothy paused a long moment then frowned. "What would you do, Grace, if Rosemary decided to marry a Jew? Or maybe even a Catholic?"

"I don't think I could stand it."

Dorothy nodded curtly. "Although Rosemary isn't serious about any man right now, there'll come a day when she is and I can promise you one thing: she'll never marry a boy from our church!"

Grace's blood went cold. It's true, she realized. And if Rosemary doesn't choose a Southern Baptist, what will I do?

*   *   *

Graduation. Grace looked at the extra invitation she'd set aside for her scrapbook and smiled with delight. Five years ago Rosemary hadn't been excited about her high school graduation ceremony. Oddly, she didn't seem all too eager about today's grand event, either.

"Mom, there'll be billions of us. You'll never see me."

"Tell me which side of the auditorium you'll be on and we'll go early so we can see you."

"I don't know that, either."

It seemed incomprehensible to Grace. How could so many graduates be organized at the very last minute?

She agreed with Rosemary that the university's caps and gowns could have used a bit of pizzazz. Rosemary shook out the heavy black gown and looked at it soberly. "It's supposed to be hot with a chance of rain Saturday," she said softly. "I'll die in this thing."

"White tassels?" Grace sighed, picking up the mortarboard.

"For arts and sciences," Rosemary explained. "Boring, isn't it?"

"Well, boring or not, you've earned the right to wear it."

So on the big day Rosemary pinned the mortarboard onto her short hair and carried the gown over her arm, claiming she couldn't bear to put it on until the last minute because it turned so hot and steamy.

Harry and Grace arrived early to find seats close to the front. Grace gasped as she noticed all the hundreds of chairs for the graduates.

In they marched, a little late. Grace's heart sank as she noted the group who came to sit on her side of the auditorium wore orange tassels on their mortarboards. Where were the white ones?

Harry discreetly pointed to the other side and Grace squinted over the top of her bifocals to catch sight of her daughter. No luck. They all looked alike.

They were graduated by college and stood while the university president addressed them. There were so many of them...so many...how could all of them ever find jobs?

It was finally over and Rosemary found her parents at the appointed meeting place, again carrying her gown over her arm. She'd taken the mortarboard off and swung it gently.

"Where's your diploma?" Grace asked.

"In the mail."

You would have thought, Grace thought with a frown, there could be a little pomp and circumstance to the occasion even if there were so many of them.

*   *   *

In Houston, Southern Baptists met for their annual convention. There, reacting to two years of problems, voting members chose one of the conservatives who called for the purge of seminaries and a commitment to an inerrant, infallible Bible.

What will the ramifications of such actions be, Grace wondered. Before, Baptists hadn't meddled in the specifics of people's beliefs; a relic, no doubt, of the times when they themselves were persecuted over the particulars.

Now, God in heaven, what would happen to the seminaries and to missionaries on foreign fields? In some countries, where their presence was only barely tolerated, having to preach a particular party line would guarantee them a one-way ticket out.

Everything, yes everything could come apart.

It was called the most blatant display of power politics in the history of the convention. Grace, shocked and furious, wept in her kitchen. Rosemary bounced in at that very inopportune moment and Grace hastily dried her tears.

"What's wrong?" she demanded.

"Haven't you been reading what's happened at the convention?"

"The—oh, that." Rosemary shrugged. "It doesn't concern me anymore."

"Well, it concerns me and Dorothy. I thought you would be at least a little sympathetic."

Rosemary opened the refrigerator and pulled out a pitcher of iced tea. "I'm not surprised."

"Well, I am. I don't see how these people have made such inroads in the last two years. Pour me a glass too, please."

"You and your friends have been asleep at the wheel, Mom. Face it, this stuff was hanging over the horizon as far back as 1971," Rosemary said, handing her a glass of tea.

"No, it wasn't."

"Sure it was. Remember when that gang of girls started to the Baptist college in the fall of '71? They came home spouting some of this same foolishness that year." She paused. "Seems to me Southern Baptists are looking for their heretics on the wrong end of the spectrum."

"Are you happy in the church you're going to, Rosie?"

"Yeah, I guess so. The things that bother me have nothing to do with theology…Lord, but they're a disorganized bunch! I guess it goes hand in hand with being a liberal."

"How liberal?" Grace dared ask.

Rosemary grinned. "Well, Mom, our associate minister is a woman. Doesn't that shock you?"

Little hussy, Grace thought. "No, it doesn't," she said clearly. "I'm beginning to think we missed the boat on that issue, too, you know. If we'd been more progressive and ready to embrace new things, you might have been going to seminary to be a minister instead of going to law school."

"Me, in seminary? I don't think so!"

"I meant if things had happened differently."

"Everything seemed to lead up to me making the decision to leave and considering the way the Southern Baptist Convention is headed, I think it was all for the best."

"Christine didn't find it necessary to leave."

"Christine's questions were never basic to Baptist doctrine like mine, Mom. Like you and Miss Dorothy she has no time for this ultra-conservative movement."

"Do you tease her the way you go on at me?"

Rosemary laughed and stood, taking her glass to the sink. "Sure I do. What are friends for?"

*   *   *

"Mom, I've applied to live in graduate student housing this fall," Rosemary announced early in July over lunch.

Grace stared at her, not really comprehending what she'd said.

"I ought to receive confirmation in the mail pretty soon and I wanted you to know what it was when you open the mailbox."

"You're not living over there," Grace cried without thinking.

Rosemary paused and set her sandwich down. "I don't think you understand. I wasn't asking for permission."

Grace's stomach tightened. "Why do you want to leave home?"

"I'm twenty-three. It's time for me to be out of here."

"You still haven't told me why."

"Because it's time for me to go."

"Why now instead of last year or last semester?"

"I'm in professional school now. It doesn't look good to still be living with Mom and Dad."

"Since when did you care what other people think?"

"It's not what other people think. It's what I think."

"Will you have a roommate?"

"Yes, probably a foreign student."

"You once said you would hate living in a dorm."

"Well, I hope to God I've grown up a little since then. You ought to be glad, Mom. On campus I won't need a car so you'll be able to come and go as you please without me asking for the wheels. This is different than dorm life, too. I'll have to be responsible for my own cooking and cleaning and washing and ironing. Aren't you glad your maid service days are coming to an end?"

Grace tried to imagine it but couldn't. "I didn't think you'd leave home until you got married, Rosemary."

"I need to live on my own. You and Daddy have done everything you needed to do, now it's up to me."

*   *   *

Rosemary's roommate was an engineering graduate student from India. Grace imagined a lovely dark beauty, ethereal and exotic in a sari.

Rosemary called Grace. "Mom, I want you to come over for lunch tomorrow. Sarala thought you might want to sample some Indian food. Come at noon."

"Shall I bring anything?"

"Just your appetite and I mean it, too. She's a sensational cook and you're going to love this stuff."

She agreed and worried the rest of the day about what to wear. First impressions were so important and the girl *must* think well of her.

Since Rosemary's departure from church, Grace assumed she wouldn't have discussed religion with her new roommate. The thought depressed her. Didn't Rosemary care the girl was a Hindu? Well, I care and I may be the only Baptist this girl has ever seen so I have to be on my very best behavior, Grace told herself.

She only knocked twice on the door before Rosemary opened it. Grace gritted her teeth then gasped with surprise as she saw how beautifully the two of them had decorated their apartment.

Framed alongside Rosemary's impressionist rip-offs were Indian batiks. Grace wondered if the pictures were classical or folk-art. There wasn't a speck of dust on the pictures or the lamps or the rest of the furniture.

From the kitchen a petite young woman entered the room. She was in jeans and a tee shirt! Barefoot, too. Grace shuddered, noticing Rosemary's shoes were gone as well.

Sarala stepped forward and extended her hand. "Hello, Mrs. Lee," she said softly, the slightest trace of an accent in her voice.

Grace smiled back and shook her hand. "Hello, Sarala. Something smells good."

Sarala's smile grew wider. She pointed to the sofa. "Please sit down. Would you like some tea before lunch?"

"No, thank you," Grace smiled.

"Lunch won't be ready for awhile."

Rosemary pointed to the clock. "You see, I told you she'd be early."

Grace surreptitiously glanced at the clock. Twenty minutes early...was that bad?

Sarala smiled down at Grace. "She told me you run on Baptist standard time."

Grace felt a lump rise in her throat. She glared at Rosemary. "What's Baptist standard time?"

Rosemary grinned. "Being at least twenty minutes early so you can unnerve your hostess."

"It's rude to be late," Grace scolded, embarrassed.

Rosemary grinned, ignored the remark and looked at Sarala. "Everything smells done," she said.

"What are we having?" Grace asked, her curiosity about the unusual fragrances getting the better of her manners.

Rosemary put on her most serious face. "Thought we'd start with a little crocodile canapé followed by roasted elephant and tiger claws—"

Grace glared at her. "That isn't funny. I know most Indians are vegetarians, so there."

Sarala nodded. "Yes, everything today is vegetarian."

"Were you raised vegetarian?" Grace asked.

Sarala smiled and nodded. "Yes."

And the lunch was excellent. Rosemary, finicky Rosemary, spooned generous helpings of all dishes onto her plate and inhaled deeply. "Food of the gods," she said quietly.

"Since when did you start eating vegetables?" Grace cried, unable to believe her eyes.

Her daughter turned mischievous eyes on her. "Since they started tasting so good, that's when."

"I could never get her to touch vegetables," Grace confessed.

Rosemary glanced again at Grace and wore an I-am-lying-through-my-teeth look on her face. "Sarala and I decided there's definitely a maternal conspiracy afoot to force kids to eat what they hate. Once in awhile her mother used to curry some pumpkin and when this little brat turned her nose up at it, she was told to think of all the starving children in Appalachia."

Sarala laughed but stopped at sight of Grace's stern face. Hoping to get her point across that she didn't find their scathing humor amusing, Grace turned away from Rosemary and started eating the meal.

At the end, Sarala offered Grace some homemade yogurt. She declined but noticed Rosemary did not. Sarala mixed hers with a heaping tablespoonful of leftover rice then opened a jar on the table.

"What's that?" Grace asked.

"Mango pickle," Sarala explained, spooning out a small amount. "It's traditional to have a little of this condiment with rice and yogurt at the end of a meal."

"Are you having that, Rosemary?" Grace asked.

Rosemary added three generous teaspoonsful of sugar to her yogurt. "I prefer it sweet but you may like it, Mom. It's a salt-and-sour combination."

Grace agreed to try a little but the overpowering strength of the hot oils, garlic pieces and the fruit set her throat on fire.

Sarala smiled apologetically. "It's an acquired taste."

"I can't believe you're eating yogurt," Grace said to Rosemary.

"With a lot of sugar it's right tolerable."

"'Right tolerable,'" Sarala teased. "I love the way she speaks!"

*   *   *

As Rosemary and Sarala cleared the lunch dishes, Grace realized the afternoon wasn't going as smoothly as she'd hoped. Her nervousness had made lunch conversation a disaster but maybe she could redeem herself during dessert.

She wandered across the small living room, recognizing some brass figurines as Hindu idols. A chill crept up her spine and she wondered how Rosemary, brought up the way she was, endured the sight of them.

"Beautiful, aren't they?" Rosemary asked.

Grace turned with a start to find Rosemary and Sarala smiling at her.

Sarala joined Grace at the coffee table. "I simply had to bring a little of home with me. These belonged to my grandmother."

"They are...beautiful," Grace conceded. Her curiosity got the better of her. "Do—do all Hindus leave them setting around like this?"

"At home they're usually in a small room or a niche," Sarala answered.

Grace looked at Rosemary. "She displays the essentials of her religion. I don't suppose you'd considered leaving your Bible out, too?"

Rosemary folded her arms across her chest and frowned. "Well, since we never did anything so ostentatious at home I didn't think it would be expected of me now."

That shot home with a sting, Grace noted.

"Please don't misunderstand, Mrs. Lee," Sarala said. "These figures are only sentimental heirlooms as far as I'm concerned."

Grace frowned.

Rosemary started for the kitchen, calling over her shoulder, "Listen to what Sarala says, Mom. You never heard this in WMU."

I'm afraid to find out, Grace thought with fear, following Sarala to the sofa and sitting down beside her.

"No two Hindus practice their religion the same way," Sarala explained, "because we lack a codified text."

"But you have books?"

"Epic poetry and commentaries," Sarala replied. "You see, Hindus have no dispute with Christians. When Christians first entered India and said Jesus is God, Hindus were willing to accept the fact. One more doesn't make any difference to us."

Grace's eyes widened. "But it does make a difference! Rosemary, where are you?"

"Starting some water for tea."

"I didn't mean that as snobby as it sounded," Grace tried to apologize, almost breathless as another fit of nerves claimed her.

Rosemary appeared from the kitchen and dropped into a chair next to her. "But it *is* snobby," she emphasized. "Christians have a terrible time grasping the idea that other people just might have a claim on truth, too."

"That isn't what I mean—" Grace started to argue.

"I know it isn't what you *think* you mean, Mom. Look at it like this: in the mid-'60s you decided racism wasn't for you and took steps to try to eliminate it from your life. Right?"

"Right," Grace acceded, hoping she wasn't falling into a trap.

"You did it socially and politically...now, try it spiritually."

"Spiritual...racist? How can anyone be a spiritual racist?"

Rosemary shrugged. "White man's religion. Is it *really* superior to everyone else's?"

Everything in Grace shaped by the Baptist church screamed to shout 'yes!' but the word stuck in her throat.

Sarala leaned forward, smiled and patted Grace's hand. "You're being harsh and demanding again, Rosemary."

Grace turned to stare at Sarala. Am I a religious bigot, she wondered numbly. I don't want to be. I can't imagine anything more disgusting but how can I tell this girl that I think her religion is wrong in every way?

"Well, Mom, looks like you're going to have to take some of your own medicine now," Rosemary teased. "You always told me that I couldn't judge people by lumping them into groups; I could only make up my mind one person at a time. I'm going to turn it around on you and tell you to do the same with religions. You might find a Hindu or a Jew closer to the truth than a few Baptists. What do you think of that?"

"It makes sense," Grace said gently. "I only have to look at some of the women in my Circle and know their Christianity is lip-deep."

Rosemary grinned. "Now look what's staring you in the face. There might be other religions as valid as yours."

Grace glared at her.

"She's crumbling," Rosemary whispered. "The liberal domain of main-line Protestantism yawns before her like the Great Abyss."

"Stop teasing your mother," Sarala rebuked.

The teakettle started to whistle and Rosemary got up. "But it's so much fun when she's having a crisis!"

16

Grace couldn't tear herself away from the radio. The embassy in Iran had been seized and fifty-two of its members were taken hostage. She was unable to reach Rosemary and Dorothy and sat huddled in her quilt, rocking by the radio. Does it mean war, she wondered. This is awful, simply awful. What will happen?

Will people in the country pull together in the crisis and do what's right as well as what's necessary? What will Jimmy Carter do? Even in her fear, Grace trusted Carter and knew he wouldn't make a rash decision.

When the phone rang it nearly scared her to death. "Mom, do you have your radio on?" Rosemary cried.

"Yes!"

"God, it's awful over here! Some rednecks have stormed the housing complex and are fighting with any foreign student they think may be Iranian."

"My God!"

"Have you heard anything official? Are we going to war?"

"Not yet."

"What *is* Carter waiting for? Give those jerks forty-eight hours to release our people to a neutral country or suffer the consequences, that's what I say!"

"And plunge us into a third world war?" Grace argued. "Do you seriously think the Soviet Union will stand by if we massed across their border?"

Her words seemed to still the furious Rosemary's tongue only temporarily. "Maybe Jimmy ought to cut a deal with the Russians. They've always wanted a warm water port. Maybe we could go in together and clean house. Oil for us, a warm water port for them."

"I can't believe you're so blood-thirsty."

"I've always liked Teddy Roosevelt's big stick and think now is the time to dust it off and clobber a few people."

Grace changed the subject. "Have you heard from Dorothy?"

"No, why?"

"Well, I guess she must be out. I wonder what she's going to think of this."

"I'm sure she'll agree with you this time around, Mom." Rosemary laughed. "Of everybody I've talked to today, I'm the only one squalling like a scalded cat. Everyone else is for negotiation."

"That ought to take the sauce out of you a little."

"I'll call later, okay? I think I might meander on over to the engineering building and walk back here with Sarala. I don't want her coming across the campus alone with nuts all over it."

"Don't do anything provocative, Rosemary," Grace warned. "People are very upset now."

"I'll behave, I promise. But I'll be a lot better when we get a resolution to this mess."

*   *   *

The hostage crisis didn't resolve itself in the few hours Grace hoped. Or days. Or weeks.

In the meantime, Christine and David came home to get married and all the fuzzy, abstract wedding plans were suddenly brought into the sharp focus. The powers-that-be in Christine's home church hadn't been keen on her plans for a minister and a rabbi and a mixed religious ceremony. She settled instead on a restored Victorian home that belonged to the city and was becoming popular for weddings and parties.

"If David lived here they could probably have been married in the temple," Grace said to Rosemary, embarrassed that Christine had been discouraged from having her wedding at Grace's church, too.

"Well, now that they've had a little time I think they prefer the idea of neutral territory," Rosemary said.

At the Tuesday Circle Meeting after Christine's invitation appeared in the church newsletter, her wedding was all the talk. Grace consciously clamped her teeth over her tongue, remembering Rosemary's threat.

"Can you believe it? Marrying a Jew without converting him first!"

"What did you expect when she ran off to New England for a music career?"

"I wonder what her parents think?"

"I don't know why all of you are so shocked. She's one of Rosemary Lee's friends and you know what *that* means—"

The room fell so suddenly quiet that Grace could have heard a pin drop. Her heart thudded loudly in her ears as she searched the blushing faces for the woman who had been too hasty.

Dorothy's hazel eyes snapped with fire, her small body quivering with insult. "Just what's that supposed to mean, you gossiping hag?" she demanded furiously.

"Miss Dorothy—"

"Don't you 'Miss Dorothy' me! I'll have you know Rosemary and Christine are as dear to me as any grandchildren could ever be." She paused and fought to collect herself. "This boy Christine's marrying is a very fine young man. His faith is as important to him as Christine's is to her. It's a mark of their mutual respect for each other they're doing this wedding in such a way."

Grace breathed deeply. Mutual respect...was that what Rosemary had tried so unsuccessfully to get across to her?

"You may think it's mutual respect, Miss Dorothy, but *we* think Christine's faith isn't important enough to her to try to win him to Christ," Lorene Wright put in.

"Do you now?"

"Yes, I do. I'd never have married outside the faith or permit my children to do so."

"It's always so inspiring to see such examples of right thinking in my church as you and your family," Dorothy said acidly. "You wouldn't know a person of spiritual worth if he stared you right in the face."

"Dorothy!" Grace cried.

Dorothy ignored her and shook a long, bony finger at Lorene. "I mean for this gossip to stop here and now or I'll take you in front of the church and expose you for the gossiping back-biter you are. Do you understand?"

Grace wondered how many of them actually shook in fear. She was shaking enough for everyone in the room.

*   *   *

She thought it was necessary to tell Rosemary what happened at the Circle Meeting and made sure she added she hadn't taken part in the horrible scene. "Besides," she confessed, "the more time I've had to think about it the more I realize you and Dorothy are right."

Rosemary smiled. "I'm glad you came around."

"Tell me, though, did I act as bad as Lorene?"

"Not quite but almost," Rosemary answered honestly.

"Has Christine been affected by any of this?"

"She told me a few of David's relatives were upset, too, so your gang doesn't have the monopoly on bad behavior this time."

"Would you marry a Jew, Rosemary?"

"I'd marry any man who's open-minded, Mom, and doesn't try to make me share his views."

"What about him sharing yours?"

"Faith isn't a black-and-white issue. Now on the subject of politics I'm afraid I'll have to draw the line," Rosemary teased. "I can't see myself hooking up with a Republican."

"Have you met anyone lately you like...a lot?"

Rosemary smiled. "Mm-hmm."

"When are you going to bring him home?"

"I'm not ready for that yet."

"I'd like to get to know him—"

"I'm sure you would but as I said, I'm not ready yet." She smiled a this-conversation-is-finished smile.

*   *   *

Arguing with Rosemary to spend a few days at home over the Christmas holidays proved fruitless. She assumed Rosemary would miss Sarala who went to New York for the holidays but Rosemary claimed she had things to do and they'd never get done if she put them off any longer.

She'd seemed so tired Christmas, looking almost as exhausted as she did after the first semester of her freshman year in college. But it had been a successful, productive term in spite of her tiredness.

Grace wanted to ask Rosemary more about a gift she'd received. It was an old book about English Common Law and Grace wondered if it was from the young man that she'd mentioned earlier. Rosemary never reacted about a boy in such a way before, had never been secretive.

Grace's curiosity knew no bounds. Who was he? Where was he from? What did he do? Was she serious about him? Was he a Christian?

He obviously thinks a lot of her to give her such an unusual gift, Grace decided. Most men buy the first bottle of perfume or the first box of candy they see in a store. This gift involved time as well as money guaranteeing its appeal.

So why hasn't she told me about him, Grace thought, trying not to be hurt. Why didn't she ask him to Christine's wedding, she wondered. That would have been a perfect venue to introduce him to her closest friends and her parents. And to give her such a Christmas present, they'd known each other for awhile...how long, exactly?

I'll call her and find out if she wants to go out for lunch, she decided. Chinese food would be so good on this bitterly cold day.

The phone was busy when she first tried calling in the middle of the morning and still busy an hour later.

Impulsively, Grace decided to drop in on her.

The streets were slippery and the parking lot at graduate student housing was an icy mess. Grace finally found a place and gingerly picked her away over the ice patches and into the building.

She took off her gloves and knocked at the door. She heard voices laughing inside. Then a young man in a bathrobe answered the door. His merry laughter stopped abruptly. Over his shoulder Rosemary called, "Do you have enough money for the tip?"

"Who are you?" Grace breathed, unable to believe what her eyes told her.

"Oh my God," came Rosemary's voice. She stepped into the doorway, her hair mussed, her face flushed...like the boy's.

The young man closed his eyes and moaned softly.

If the two of them said anything, Grace never knew it. She had a faint image of Rosemary motioning for her to come inside but she turned and fled out of the stale hallway, out of the complex and into her car.

*   *   *

"They'd been in bed!" Grace sobbed, pouring out her heart to Dorothy.

Dorothy closed her eyes for a moment then sighed deeply.

"I wonder how long this has been going on," Grace went on. "That's why she wanted to get away from home, so she could shack up—"

"That's not true, Grace, and you know it," Dorothy said sternly. "Get a glass of water and sit down. You've had quite a shock. We need to calm down, both of us."

Grace obeyed. With trembling hands she filled a glass from the tap and went into Dorothy's sunny parlor and sat down across from her. "I shouldn't have burdened you with this—"

"Of course you should. That's what friends are for." Dorothy forced a weak smile.

"You know what's worse?" Grace said after a pause. "I don't think guilt entered the picture at all. I think she's upset I caught her but nothing more." She felt tears start anew and didn't bother to stop them. "I can't figure out how she can justify sleeping with that boy."

"Times have changed, Grace."

"I don't believe it. Trash is trash and Rosemary's in the gutter."

"No, Grace. Think about when you grew up. There was a very good reason you didn't indulge in casual sex. There was no birth control for unmarried women. When I was young there was no birth control at all."

"You can't believe it's all right!"

Dorothy sighed. "When I was teaching a few girls came to me and told me their boyfriends were pressuring them to have sex. I told them a boy could have sex, go home, take a bath and nothing would change. But for them there could be consequences unimaginable to any boy. I also told them teenage boys would screw a knot hole in a two-by-four if it had a little hair...well, not exactly in those words." Dorothy blushed as Grace winced at her language.

"My mother used to tell me the same thing...pretty much," Grace went on. "I told Rosemary that, too. I told her there was nothing good about being used merchandise. I told her virginity was a special gift for her husband on her wedding night. This damnable sex revolution, Dorothy! It'll be the downfall of our country!"

Dorothy snorted. "Don't be silly and don't fall for that nonsense about the strength of a nation riding on the virtue of its women. That's a lot of baloney designed to keep women barefoot, pregnant and naive."

Grace paused, stung at the rebuke. "You don't approve, you can't!"

"I'm old enough to be Rosemary's grandmother. I can't possibly imagine what's going through her mind."

"I guess she's decided to live like a tramp."

"Stop using words like that! We're so ready to brand women: whores, sluts, tramps and the like. Have you noticed we don't have such words for men? If she were a man, we'd probably say she's sowing her wild oats."

"No! If she were my son, I still wouldn't approve—"

Dorothy leaned forward and reached for Grace's hands. "I'm sorry. I should have known you'd never have employed a double standard for a son." She sighed and leaned back again.

Grace drank a little more of her water. "What am I going to do, Dorothy?"

"Do?"

"I'll have to tell Harry—"

Dorothy's eyes widened. "No, Grace. This conversation goes no further than us."

"He has the right—"

"He does not," Dorothy said sternly. "Remember, you intruded on a private moment between consenting adults."

Grace frowned. "I've heard too much of that term lately. A lot of foolishness, that's what it is!"

"It isn't foolishness. Rosemary is almost twenty-four. When we really get down to the basics, this episode is none of our business."

"I'm her mother—"

"She's a grown woman now and her life is entirely in her hands. Besides, she isn't stupid. She knows you disapprove of such a lifestyle. Remember the old adage about stirring in the muck?"

"Only makes it stink worse."

"Yes." Dorothy nodded. "Bear that in mind."

Grace sighed deeply, still heartsick.

"And, Grace," Dorothy continued. "Never drop in on her again. At least until she invites you to do so."

*   *   *

Grace took no interest in the first primaries and caucuses that year. Dorothy asked her to keep an eye on George Bush but Grace ignored her. If she waited long enough without calling Rosemary, maybe her prodigal daughter would make the first move.

It obviously wasn't going to happen. Dorothy finally made the move and invited both Rosemary and Grace for tea. It was strained but broke the ice and Dorothy pulled them both into political conversation that distracted them.

"The Republicans are gearing up for a war," Dorothy said lightly. "It's going to be a lively year."

"Sarala seems to have second sight for this stuff," Rosemary said. "She thinks Ronald Reagan will win the nomination."

"That's likely," Dorothy agreed. "He's certainly massing the right-wingers behind him. I haven't heard so much blood and thunder since Barry Goldwater ran against Johnson."

Grace shrugged. "Let them rant and rave all they want. Carter will win a second term."

"There are rumors," Dorothy said softly, "Ted Kennedy will challenge him."

Both Rosemary and Grace paused. Grace tossed her head. "Ted Kennedy doesn't have a chance."

"It will divide our party," Rosemary sighed. "If there's one thing I have to admire about Republicans, loyalty is it. No other Republican would dare challenge a sitting president."

On and on they talked and for a few minutes Grace temporarily forgot her injury. It was Dorothy's aim, obviously, and she realized Dorothy had no intention of letting her have it out with Rosemary in the form of an argument.

As her temper cooled, she realized Dorothy was right. Whatever choices Rosemary made, she was no longer in a position to influence her.

*　　　　　*　　　　　*

To further drive Grace to distraction, the leadership in the Southern Baptist Convention took a very definite stand that year. Not even in 1960, when rumors of John Kennedy's Catholic agenda swept the nation had the fear mongering been so intense.

For a brief moment Grace nurtured hope that George Bush, the moderate Republican, would win his party's nomination. He blasted Reagan in the first primaries by calling the much-touted Reaganomics voodoo economics and reminded Republican women of his record of pro-choice voting.

Then the change. Bush backtracked during the late spring and early summer. Somewhere in the Republican smoke-filled rooms, Grace suspected, a deal was cut. Bush's conscience for the promise he would be Reagan's running mate.

Grace could almost feel the tidal wave of fury and disgust against Jimmy Carter due to the stalemate in negotiations to bring home the fifty-two hostages. Ted Kennedy's bid to unseat him at the Democratic Convention was nearly successful. Skyrocketing inflation because of a united OPEC strategy to drove up oil prices.

There were complaints the President was too involved in problems to campaign. If he campaigned, accusations flew that he didn't take seriously the plight of the hostages... it was enough to drive anyone crazy.

This time the conservatives not only abandoned Jimmy Carter but devised a list, something akin to the Moral Majority rating, that would enable right thinking Baptists to vote for Christian candidates.

The agenda of the Christian candidate had to include his voting a specific way on certain issues. That meant being against SALT II and, by default, approve a massive increase in military spending; stand unequivocally against abortion; against busing to achieve racial equality in public schools; against the Panama Canal treaty; and promise to return prayer to public schools.

"And Jimmy Carter falls short of this agenda," Rosemary noted, "by a whopping one hundred per cent. Gee Mom, do you ever feel like you've been locked in a room with a bunch of horses' asses?"

Dorothy turned furious eyes upon her. "How dare you, Rosemary! Simply because these people are in control doesn't mean they're in the majority!"

"Doesn't it?" Rosemary needled. "One of those guys said people like you and Mom only represented half a million out of a total of thirteen million."

Dorothy turned her head away and sniffed her antipathy. "You must remember what Mark Twain said, my dear, about lies, damned lies and statistics."

"It's bad of you to tease Dorothy," Grace scolded her. "And all of this started with this inerrancy flap!"

Rosemary shook her head, chuckling. "Oh come on, Mom, inerrancy is just a smoke-screen."

Dorothy turned back to her. "What do you mean, Rosemary?"

"Push the rhetoric aside, Miss Dorothy. Look at the other thing these people stand for...or don't stand for, rather: their lack of commitment to missions. That was the one thing that drew all Southern Baptists together. The Cooperative Program is a cash cow, too. Think what would happen if right-wing preachers in churches got it slashed or done away with. Do you have any idea what twenty per cent of a big church's budget is? If it stays in the church, think how those preachers' salaries are going to explode."

"The issue is *not* money, Rosemary," Dorothy said haughtily.

Rosemary leaned forward in her chair. "Don't tell me this Christian agenda isn't about money and power. No wonder the Soviets are scared shitless. I would be, too, if I thought we were getting ready to usher in a Christian theocracy armed to the teeth with godless communism as a war cry."

"Your tone is as inflammatory as theirs," Dorothy pointed out.

Rosemary shrugged. "*Someone* has to be inflammatory, Miss Dorothy. Good God, what are you and Mom waiting for? A divine revelation?"

Dorothy shook her finger at her. "You go too far, Rosemary, insulting your mother and me."

Grace watched them nervously. "Exactly what do you expect us to do, Rosemary?"

"I know the two of you will never leave the church. But there's one thing I hope you do every chance you get. Raise hell."

Dorothy smiled and settled back into her chair. "That, my dear, you may certainly rely upon us to do…most cheerfully!"

* | *   *

Rosemary's Election Day party was scheduled to begin at five o'clock. "Don't cook, Mom. We'll kill ourselves on vegetables, potato chips, dip and pizza."

"You think Dorothy will eat pizza?"

"She seemed willing enough last night when I asked her."

Grace was late for the party. Rosemary opened her apartment door and laughed at her. "Well, Mom, you're ten minutes 'rude.'"

"The traffic was awful—" Grace began but couldn't finish. The look on Rosemary's face was much too comical.

Inside Sarala and Dorothy sat on the sofa engrossed in conversation and pizza. Grace followed Rosemary to the kitchen.

"What time did you vote this morning?" Rosemary asked, pouring iced tea.

"As soon as your father left for work. Why?"

"I didn't go until three. You know what? You and Daddy were the only two people on the page who voted in all that time. Can you believe that?" She handed her mother the glass of tea and Grace went to the living room.

Dorothy turned to her. "Grace, this young lady has been telling me how high the voter turnout is in India."

"Voting takes place over two or three days," Sarala explained, "so it doesn't work a hardship."

Grace sat in the chair across from the two of them. "One day or one week," she said soberly, "I don't think it makes a difference here. Americans are very lazy and irresponsible, Sarala, about their voting."

"So many people complain they don't really have a choice," Dorothy added.

"I'll always vote," Rosemary said, bringing in a tray of fresh vegetables and a bowl of dip. "Even if I lose, I figure I've renewed my bitching—" she blushed as she remembered Dorothy's presence, "—complaining license, that is."

"Well, let's get the television on so you can see how thoroughly you've been routed," Sarala smiled, standing to turn on the set.

"Quite an interesting observation, my dear," Dorothy said.

"Now, Dorothy—" Grace began.

"Don't make it sound like a *totally* lost cause, Miss Dorothy," Rosemary said gently. "After all, I have enough junk food to last until the wee hours of the morning. By the time we know we're beaten we probably won't care, we'll be so sick."

Sarala shook her head and sat down again beside Dorothy. "You're beaten already, my friend."

"How do you know?" Grace demanded.

"This hostage crisis, Mom," Rosemary sighed.

"I think most Americans wanted military action against Iran," Sarala observed.

"I did, too, at first," Rosemary confessed. "But if we really want those fifty-two people out of there alive, this is the only way to do it."

Sarala smiled at her. "I'm very glad Jimmy Carter is President, Rosemary. If it had been up to you there would have been a third world war within forty-eight hours of the siege."

Dorothy frowned and looked at Rosemary. "If you're considering a political career to follow your legal one, Rosemary, you simply must get your temper under control. This country doesn't need another saber rattler. Enough young men have been sacrificed to politicians' egos."

Rosemary blushed and shook her head. "Miss Dorothy, if there is anything I am *not*, political material is it. I'll be satisfied to be a judge. A good judge. A state supreme court justice." She grinned. "Chief Justice of the Supreme Court, maybe. Now I like the sound of that. The Lee Court!"

*   *   *

It was over by nine o'clock.

"He conceded," Rosemary said numbly. "He conceded before the West Coast polls even closed."

Dorothy sighed and shook her head. "We should have seen this coming, ladies."

"I did...but not at nine o'clock," Rosemary said. "It's those exit polls! How do they have the nerve to project winners based on one or two per cent of precincts counted?"

"If I lived on the West Coast, I'd be very upset," Sarala said.

The three of them looked at Grace who hadn't contributed to the conversation. They suddenly saw why. Tears streamed down her face. "I don't see how they could do it to him," she finally said, choking on a sob.

"I can," Rosemary said bitterly. "Appeal to the lowest common denominator and you have a successful platform for a winning ticket."

"Rosemary!" Dorothy scolded. "I daresay you wouldn't have said so if you'd won tonight."

Sarala was the voice of reason. "This issue about cutting taxes was very powerful, Rosemary. Margaret Thatcher rode to victory on it in Britain. Britain and the States are quite alike as far as voter temperament is concerned."

"Now that's one thing that was never explained in enough detail for me," Dorothy added. "If Reagan cuts federal taxes it seems to me that state taxes will only go up to take up the slack."

"I don't look for that to happen, Miss Blackwell," Sarala said. "Reagan is relying on the private sector to pick up the slack for federal programs he plans to abolish or reduce. That means," and she looked right at Grace, "American churches will have to get more involved with charity work."

Grace dried her tears. "Baptists have never preached a social gospel, Sarala."

"So Rosemary tells me. If you don't, however, I can promise you in a few years your city streets are going to look like Calcutta's with beggars and the homeless."

Grace caught her breath. Can it really happen here, she wondered.

Rosemary shrugged and helped herself to a piece of celery. "You're probably right, Sarala. We couldn't have some of these churches put their building plans on the back burner. Not have enough seating space for six billion at one church service? Not pay these preachers eighty million dollars a year? Not have a bus fleet to rival their sister churches? Why, my dear girl, that's blasphemy!"

Dorothy leaned over the sofa and sharply slapped Rosemary's thigh. "That's enough sarcasm from you, miss. If it turns out to be the case what do you plan to do about it besides…bitch?"

Rosemary's mouth fell open, from the shock of hearing Dorothy say bitch, or the blow and rebuke, Grace didn't know but Rosemary finally recovered herself and grinned sheepishly. "Well, Miss Dorothy, I promise to do what I can. When I can't think of anything else then I'll bitch. How's that?"

Grace expected Dorothy to lecture her but the older woman only laughed. As though, she thought dismally, there's anything to laugh about tonight!

*   *   *

She threatened not to watch the Inauguration. It was the first time she wanted to miss the event since she and Harry owned a television. Her curiosity got the better of her, however, and she watched. She saw very little through her tears.

As Reagan took the oath of office the Iranians released the hostages, the ultimate insult to Jimmy Carter. There was something strangely coincidental about the release and Grace was sure it wasn't because the Iranians were afraid of Ronald Reagan.

As the days passed and the new government came together, it was obvious Ronald Reagan was a different cat altogether than Gerald Ford and Richard Nixon. As much as Grace disapproved of the Republican old guard, one could at least respect its members.

What annoyed her so much was seeing the Moral Majority types in pictures with the Reagan people and reading their opinions in articles. It not only grated on her nerves, it frightened her.

In Kentucky, the school prayer faction moved almost immediately afterwards to post the Ten Commandments in public school classrooms. Grace cringed and would have given anything if she were thinner so she could hide under the bed until the nightmare went away.

"It's exactly what went wrong in our country," people at church said. "As soon as the atheists won that point over us, our children started having illegitimate babies and using drugs."

"Anybody who believes kids don't pray in school hasn't been around during mid-terms and finals," Rosemary laughed. "I've done some mighty powerful bargaining with the Almighty during exams on tax law."

Grace grinned in spite of herself but forced a stern look. The situation, after all, wasn't funny. "The kids will be praying before the end of the year."

"Yep, but whose prayer? I wonder what these good Christians would do if some sweet little Indian child got up in front of the class and led the daily prayer to the Hindu goddess Saraswati of education? That would be the end of school prayer in record time!"

Grace laughed too, knowing *other* prayer wasn't what the fundamentalists had in mind at all. But where would it end?

*   *   *

Then came the assassination attempt on Reagan shortly after he took office. Grace uttered her obligatory prayer of thanks he lived and watched as people around her momentarily forgot the divisiveness in the country and pulled together.

What was God up to? Could there really be a purpose in the destruction of everything she loved and held dear?

Reagan had the privilege of appointing a Supreme Court justice, the eternal legacy of a President, one Grace found herself fearing more than any other. His choice of Sandra Day O'Connor took everybody by surprise. Democrats, Grace was certain, were furious they hadn't had the privilege of nominating the first woman. Republicans, she decided, were divided too, because the right-wingers certainly didn't consider O'Connor orthodox enough.

She was a tough nut to crack; certainly wasn't the right-wing ideologue Democrats feared. As Grace listened to the hearings, she felt O'Connor would make up her own mind and Ronald Reagan probably wouldn't have a token rubber-stamp in her decisions.

But would the country be so lucky the next time?

*   *   *

Throughout 1981 Grace sensed a radical change in Americans. She always knew she was out of step but took comfort in the fact that between the extreme left and the extreme right, she was squarely in the middle. Or had been.

She didn't feel that way anymore. Had her political compass shifted dramatically to the left or had those erstwhile left-wingers gone into hiding? Dorothy and Rosemary were the only ones she knew who shared her convictions and she was frightened the numbers were so stacked against them.

In her calmer moments she realized most Americans had voted for Reagan for one reason only: tax relief. There were problems in the welfare system, she was sure, and blamed *both* parties for not addressing the problems before the issue threatened to polarize Americans on a racial basis.

I can't believe we're going to be singing that old sad song again, she thought. We made such progress in the '70s. We weren't in racial utopia by a long shot but we were getting there and I was so pleased!

As the year drew on, moderate Southern Baptists made a gallant though unsuccessful effort to take back the leadership of their convention. Grace read the accounts and was deeply troubled. How in the world had the conservatives become so firmly entrenched in only two years?

The moderates took no firm stand on the issue of women deacons and ministers and their fence sitting annoyed Grace. Didn't they realize it was better to make an unpopular stand than no stand at all?

How many young people would abandon Southern Baptists, like Rosemary, before the power struggle ended?

17

Rosemary finished law school and graduated with a respectable standing. Before she took the bar exam she moved back into her small bedroom at home. "After all I'm not a student anymore, thank God. I've had enough school to last a lifetime."

She studied intensively for the bar but didn't involve Grace. "You have enough to worry about without this," she explained.

"I don't like it," Grace said.

"Why not?"

"Pass or fail...whoever heard the like?"

Rosemary smiled. "At this point, Mom, pass or fail is fine with me. I want it over and done with so I can get a job and get on with my life."

"I thought you liked competition," Grace teased.

"I'll let my competitive edge take over when I pulverize my opponent on my first case. I wonder if there's anything like a B-1 Bomber of a legal brief?"

Grace shook her head. She wasn't even employed yet and talked about total destruction of her opponent. Some things never changed.

*   *   *

Rosemary passed the bar and immediately started looking for a job. She didn't want to deal with corporations or big money, she told her parents. She wanted to handle cases for legal aid.

"She'll never make a living doing this," Harry warned. "She can't really be serious about it!"

"She is," Grace said and smiled, remembering that if Rosemary had gone to a mission field she wouldn't have retired a millionaire, either.

In the fall, Rosemary finally began what Harry called her mission work for legal aid. She shrugged off the comment with a grin and found a cheap apartment and an ancient car well within her meager budget.

Grace helped her move in to the apartment and realized Rosemary couldn't have been happier if she'd just bought a penthouse suite and an expensive sports car. She wished the apartment was a bit nicer but it was a good start. For a young woman who teased about being Chief Justice of the Supreme Court, it was a modest beginning, a very modest beginning, indeed.

*　　　　　　*　　　　　　*

Grace had never known Rosemary to be nervous, not as a child and certainly not when she passed the bar. Of course, she always looked a little pale when something new took her by surprise. She confessed how shocked she was at the number of her colleagues' caseloads. Being the newest member of the team, all the unwelcome cases made it onto her desk and she attacked them energetically, if not too cheerfully. But it was a plunge into the great unknown and she was nervous.

Maybe it's because of her clothes, Grace thought. Coming out of the jeans and shirts of her student days wasn't easy. Rosemary valued her comfort above all else. For a young woman who numbered the pantyhose occasions of the last five years on one hand, it was shock therapy.

Her new wardrobe, so lovely in the department store, made her appear dreadfully uncomfortable. Grace pored over catalogues and fashion magazines, hoping to find something that would ease the distraction of dressing for success.

Her work, however, was very rewarding and she confessed she could almost forget the creeping crotch of her pantyhose in the excitement of bringing order to the snarled cases that she inherited. She wanted her first day in court to go well and didn't want a bulldog of a judge catching errors in her work.

Grace could almost see Dorothy smile on the other end of the phone. "She's been memorizing details since she was nine. I daresay something like the law won't intimidate her." The older woman laughed.

"Today's her first day in court and she's rehearsed herself into a case of laryngitis," Grace said.

"What's the case about?"

"A woman whose ex-husband is about three thousand dollars behind in his child support. She says she's worked up an airtight case. Tell me, Dorothy, why does this woman need Rosemary at all? If the ex-husband hasn't paid his support why doesn't the court do something about it?"

"I don't know the fine points of the law, Grace, but I've heard a lot of men withhold support because they claim their visitation rights aren't respected."

"I don't like this client confidentiality at all, either. She can't tell me anything!"

Dorothy laughed again. "When the case is over, Grace, maybe she'll tell you."

"I hope so. Well, I'd better get off the phone. She's probably out of court and should be home soon. She promised to call me."

Dorothy said her good-byes and Grace sighed as she hung up.

Rosemary won. Almost soundless with laryngitis, she gave her mother the news over the phone and Grace offered to take her out to dinner. It was a heady triumph.

*   *   *

For her own peace of mind, Grace tried to stop being so involved in politics, both of the country and in her denomination. In spite of hers and Dorothy's dread of what was happening in the Southern Baptist Convention, the congregation at the church continued to grow. It's unbelievable, Grace thought, we're in the middle of this crisis and no one seems to really know what's going on.

WMU felt the brunt of it. Although young families joined the church in record numbers, very few of the young women joined WMU. The Evening Circle had been reserved years and years ago for working women but its numbers had fallen off lately.

At an organizational meeting one Saturday, Grace noted there were nothing but old gray heads present. The image stayed with her for days.

"I thought all these young women went to Evening Circle," she said to Dorothy. "I went when Rosemary was little. She and Harry had a great time while I was gone."

Dorothy shrugged. "These women don't have time for WMU but I've seen at least fifty of them in the church gym for morning aerobics," she said tartly. "Our church is becoming a country club, I fear."

"Oh Dorothy, really!"

"Really. Organized sports for children, arts and crafts and aerobics for women. Dear God, that I'm part of such a farce makes me sick to my stomach! Why can't I wash my hands of this mess and go someplace else?"

"We have to hold on, Dorothy. Things will turn around."

"Will they? And when they do, how much damage will have been done? I don't know, Grace, it gets harder all the time—"

"I know. But you don't want to leave WMU."

"No, I have my life invested in WMU."

"You have to stay. I can't make it without you."

"Well, dear, I'm going to be gone one of these days. You must learn to stand alone."

"Things will turn around. They have to."

"Not necessarily," Dorothy said darkly and Grace was depressed the rest of the day.

Living up to Dorothy's initial suspicion of following prevailing attitudes, the preacher seemed squarely in the camp of Moral Majority. His sermons fed what his congregation wanted to hear, not what Grace and Dorothy *thought* they should have heard.

In the meantime Rosemary harangued Dorothy until she agreed to tutor children in a homeless shelter. She began her attack by mentioning the appalling fact that children without a permanent address couldn't go to public schools. It caught Dorothy's attention at once and Rosemary was ready to pounce. Initially, Dorothy resisted fiercely, swearing she was too old and unable to handle children. Rosemary, however, kept up the pressure and Dorothy consented, Grace supposed, simply for peace and quiet.

She was converted the first day. "I think a non-traditional setting helps," she explained. "We're set up in one corner of the room. With parents close by the children know they can't misbehave."

"What are you teaching?"

"The parts of speech. After they've mastered the basics, they're going to diagram sentences. By the time *my* boys and girls are back inside regular classrooms, they'll know more than their teachers!"

"So much for the kids being too out of hand and you being too old," Grace chuckled.

"Did I say that?"

Grace nodded.

"Oh," Dorothy said quietly. "Rosemary was right. Once a teacher, always a teacher. I was amazed how I'd missed the discipline." She paused. "You know, there are still quite a few of my old friends living. I wonder...with all of us tutoring we could almost provide an entire curriculum for those children."

Grace smiled. "Why don't you mention it to Rosemary?"

"Rosemary doesn't need to do things for me," Dorothy said haughtily. "The director of the shelter is a former student of mine. I'm sure he would be happy to implement the idea."

Well, Grace thought, with that sort of connection the deed's as good as done. We used to think such things were a social gospel and bad. How ridiculous! Getting people back on their feet and keeping their children educated in the meantime is extremely valuable and rewarding work, she decided. And Dorothy, nearly eighty, showed every sign of leading the charge.

         *   *   *

The older woman threw herself into her project with all the zeal of a teenager. Grace watched the years fall off and saw her soften a bit as she was exposed to the children.

Grace noted it took Dorothy's mind off the problems at church. Perhaps she should do something, too, but what? She wasn't a college graduate and had so little to offer.

Looking over the membership roster for WMU, she noticed how few girls were involved in Acteens. Every year the girls had a new leader. It seemed that Acteens in her church simply wasn't working.

WMU members had plenty to say about them, too. No attention spans. Only interested in boys and in youth choir. So ignorant!

Grace felt a twinge. If they're ignorant, she thought guiltily, whose fault is it? Maybe I should volunteer…no, no, no! Me in a room with teenage girls! That's a fate worse than death! But the idea continued to nag at her although she fought it valiantly every time it threatened.

Shortly after the new church year began, Grace was shocked when a new topic displaced the usual political rhetoric. The preacher praised their growing membership and started dropping broad hints about building a new church or at least enlarging the one they had.

Grace couldn't believe it. We're certainly bursting at the seams, she admitted to herself, but why take on a new building project now? Things are awfully uncertain economically, interest rates are so high…surely he can't be serious!

Their sister church had recently enlarged and boasted its capacity to double its current membership. Was that the reason her preacher suddenly decided they needed to expand?

"We've been in competition with them since at least 1960," Dorothy reminded her. "They got an associate minister so we had to have one, too. They got a new organ. So did we. You'd think after twenty years such petty goings-on would have ended."

Grace cringed, fearing she was right.

But the financial status of the membership convinced the preacher it was impossible for the time being. He finally settled, although not happily, on having two Sunday School services and two worship services. Grace liked the early one but wasn't ready for Rosemary's teasing.

"Do you remember what you used to say about Catholics who went to early Mass, Mom? Going to church at dawn so they could get to the lake," she reminded her, laughing. "Or do you like early service because the old wind bag has to shut up in thirty minutes?"

"I never said that about Catholics."

"Yes, you did."

"What would it matter to me what time they went to church?"

"I decided your point was if church didn't mess up your whole day it wasn't valid. If it didn't take up at least eight hours you'd somehow given the Lord short shrift."

"That isn't funny."

"Yes, it is."

Rosemary was right about one thing although she'd never tell her so. When she and Harry went to early services it *did* force the preacher to wrap up his sermon quickly.

*   *   *

Grace tried ignoring the political and religious upheavals around her. She and Dorothy decided to talk about their problems only one or two days a week. Dorothy suggested Grace find an outside interest to distract herself from the deterioration of the denomination she loved, unaware of Grace's torment over Acteens.

She suspected religious right-wingers would be very active in the election year. Shortly before the old year ended the President of the Southern Baptist Convention nearly sent the moderates into strokes when he announced the denomination would have a creed.

While trying to control her spinning head, Grace said a short prayer of thanksgiving all the old war horses of the Baptist faith were dead and gone. We're not Baptists anymore, she thought.

The real Baptists were sleeping on the job and this is the price we pay! Can we ever recover?

Ronald Reagan marched to certain victory for a second term but Grace pinned all her hopes on Walter Mondale. What she wasn't prepared for in the Democratic primaries was the venom directed against Jesse Jackson's candidacy.

"I like him," Rosemary confessed. "He's a dreamer but I don't care. When I listen to him, I feel there's hope."

"That's because he's a minister," Grace put in.

"It isn't only because he's a minister. He's sincere. I'm voting for him."

"Will he win the nomination, Rosemary?"

"I doubt it. Mondale seems to be the man but for an experienced politico he doesn't seem to be playing the game, does he?"

"What do you mean?"

"Well, when the subject of the deficit comes up he admits taxation is an answer. It won't fly."

Walter Mondale won the nomination and chose Geraldine Ferraro as his running mate. Grace nearly burst with glee. A woman vice president, maybe! It would send a message that women were finally receiving their due.

As if in retaliation the Southern Baptist Convention passed a resolution against the ordination of women. The backlash was swift but accomplished nothing. Grace believed she saw a darker message in the resolution: like it or get out.

The rest of the political campaign was an unfolding nightmare. There was only one issue on voters' minds and that was tax relief. There was only one issue for the fundamentalists and that was abortion. No matter how astute a candidate's ideas were, the religious right declared war if the candidate didn't fall into line about abortion.

"I've never seen this happen before," Dorothy said one day.

"What?"

"The issues of the day reduced to one or two topics. I find it insulting; I can't believe Americans are either so ignorant or so greedy they have allowed themselves to be painted into such a corner."

"You have to be a smart person to figure out the issues these days, Dorothy."

"You don't have to be *that* smart. But a person must be objective and look at these issues calmly. This abortion issue surprises me so. I can't help but believe it's a smoke screen."

"I've heard the first objective is abortion and the second is birth control."

Dorothy paused a moment then shook her head. "You know what I think, Grace?"

"What?"

"If women are stupid enough to sit by and allow it to happen they deserve the consequences. I remember when birth control became legal for married women. What a fight we had for that! If this young generation allows themselves to be taken back into such a time, I can't feel anything but contempt."

Grace frowned. Dorothy and Rosemary were the ones who usually preached understanding and compassion. How strange Dorothy would be on her high horse over this!

She looked at the spirited old woman and suddenly laughed. "You old feminist, you!" she cried and hugged her impulsively.

*   *   *

It was a lovely day, crisp and cool, as clear as October and almost as colorful. What was left of the leaves would disappear in the next storm and the chill in the breeze indicated winter was right around the corner.

Grace hoped Rosemary would schedule her lunch so she could vote with Dorothy and herself but things were so hectic at the office she'd voted when the polls opened. "You will come over tonight, won't you, and watch the returns?" Grace asked.

"I'm up to my ears in work, Mom," Rosemary replied, "but you and Dorothy have a ball, okay?"

"Think we'll have anything to celebrate?"

"I doubt it. I wouldn't want anything to upset this losing streak of mine," Rosemary said sourly.

Grace offered to drive Dorothy to her precinct. "Then we can have lunch," she said over the phone.

Dorothy agreed and was ready when Grace pulled into the driveway. Grace frowned as she watched the older woman hesitate on the porch stairs. She rolled down the car window. "Are you all right?"

"Just slow today," Dorothy said off-handedly. "I forgot to set my alarm last night and slept too long. I'm so lightheaded when I do that!"

"You tutor in the afternoons, why on earth should you set an alarm?" Grace asked as Dorothy got into the car.

"Now what's that supposed to mean?"

"Well—"

"My day is just as productive as yours even if I am retired," Dorothy said defensively. She softened and smiled a little. "I like your Mondale and Ferraro bumper sticker."

Grace couldn't help but smile, too. "I'm hoping for great things tonight."

"You're the only person in the country who thinks the Democrats will win."

"Why are you so convinced we won't?"

"I just am. I'm taking a book to bed tonight and leaving the television and radio off."

"You know the old saying, Dorothy," Grace reminded her, trying to be optimistic, "it ain't over until the fat lady sings."

*   *   *

The fat lady sang and the tune was dismal. Worse than dismal, Grace decided. It was disastrous. The networks at least had the decency not to announce winners before nine o'clock but Grace was too heartsick to care.

She reminded herself the process was fair and democratic and people had a right to vote as they pleased. But not fair, either. How could it possibly be fair when it didn't turn out the way she wanted?

Rosemary said people voted their pocketbooks. She'd heard that before and it seemed to be true. She expected the wealthy to again vote for Ronald Reagan.

But others also did and Grace was bewildered. The ones the media called "Reagan Democrats," didn't they see what Grace saw? Blue-collar workers backed Reagan almost to a man. Didn't they realize that with the successfully broken strike of air traffic controllers, the Republicans would willingly break their respective unions, too?

"Mom, it's the same story as four years ago," Rosemary said. "The Republicans boiled it down to two war cries: abortion and taxes. As long as they keep everybody whipped up on those two subjects they'll never have to face the music."

Dorothy told her, "Grace, everything moves in cycles. This too will come to an end, no telling how great the price will be but it *will* end. In the meantime there's no sense trying to second guess decisions or break your heart for something out of your control."

As more and more numbers came in verifying Reagan's second victory, Grace rocked more furiously in her chair.

Another four years, she thought angrily. Once again we have to sit on pins and needles every time a Supreme Court justice has a wheezing fit, trembling for fear of what fool will be nominated to the court. Will they really undo the abortion right? How much further will this school prayer mess get in another four years? Why, oh why didn't Dorothy watch these returns with me tonight? I'm so upset I'll never get to sleep!

         *   *   *

There was a different sound to a telephone when it rang with bad news. A ring was definitely not a ring.

"Mrs. Lee, I'm calling from Central Hospital. Miss Dorothy Blackwell was admitted this morning. She had a minor stroke last night."

"Last night and she was admitted just this morning?"

"Yes."

"I'm on my way!" Grace flew out of the house, almost forgetting how to drive in her distress. Why was it in times of emergency every traffic light was red and every railroad track had a slow-moving train passing by?

She learned that Dorothy had been moved to a private room. Grace gasped when she entered, in surprise as well as relief.

The older woman was sitting up, watching a young doctor's penlight. She raised a hand and waved shortly to Grace. "Come in, dear. This young man will be only a few more minutes."

As Grace came closer to the bed she realized she'd pulled on her raincoat over her bathrobe. Oh God, she prayed, please, please don't let anyone notice!

The doctor smiled at Dorothy. "I can't believe how little damage you sustained, Ms. Blackwell."

"That's 'Miss,' young man. This *Ms.* business sounds like a swarm of bumblebees."

"Yes ma'am," he said and laughed. "But you have to stay so we can begin physical therapy for your hip—"

"'We?'" Dorothy pinned him with a withering glare.

"Dorothy!" Grace scolded, stepping closer.

The doctor shrugged. "It's all part of the new bedside manner. I'm supposed to make you feel less alone and that your treatment is a group thing."

"A group thing?" Dorothy repeated.

"Stop being so rude to this doctor," Grace demanded.

The doctor put away his penlight and turned to Grace. "It's her revenge, I think."

Grace frowned.

"He saw my campaign button on my shawl," Dorothy explained, "and had the audacity to ask me if I was competent since I supported Mondale and Ferraro."

"I wasn't *that* rude," the young doctor teased.

"Well, you implied it," Dorothy sniffed.

His sense of humor appeared intact as he faced Grace. "I got a lecture I won't soon forget, either. Let's see, what was it? She's been voting since 1924 and hasn't voted for a Republican yet and however long the good Lord lets her live, that's how much longer she'll vote Democratic."

Grace cleared her throat. "What's this about your hip?" she asked, changing the subject.

The doctor nodded in Dorothy's direction. "It isn't broken but it's very badly bruised from the fall. A few weeks of therapy, Miss Blackwell, and you'll be back in the thick of things. But tell me, do you have a lot—I mean, many—stairs to manage in your house?"

Dorothy's eyes glinted with the minor victory of grammatical intimidation. "Yes, I do."

"You may want to think about building a ramp or two. Is your bedroom on the main floor?"

"No."

"Then you'll need to move downstairs. Everything should be on one floor. You may even want to consider moving to a seniors' facility."

That took the smug little smile off her face, Grace noticed.

The doctor sighed again. "It's a tough decision, I know, but your condition is weaker now and it may be better for you to be someplace where help is more available. You'll think about it?" he asked.

Dorothy nodded once and watched as he left the room.

Grace reached for her hand.

"A seniors' facility, that's what he said, can you believe your ears, Grace? *Me*, in an old folks' home!" Dorothy cried furiously.

"Well, you *are* eighty-one," Grace reminded her.

Dorothy turned surprised eyes upon her. "You say it as though it were old!"

"It is," Grace muttered weakly.

"It can't be," Dorothy argued. "I don't feel old...well, today, maybe...but until last night I always did exactly what I wanted to do."

"You're not an average eighty-one-year-old, Dorothy."

Dorothy smiled. "I know. I love shocking them, you see. Especially these young pups. The looks on their faces are won-drous to behold."

Grace smiled, too. "If not a seniors' facility, why not an apartment?"

"I think not," Dorothy said tartly. "Harry's still the best car-penter in town, isn't he? Well, I have some work for him. I'll build a ramp to my front door and open the first floor bedroom."

"But, Dorothy—"

"I won't hear anymore, Grace. Believe me, my dear, I'm far better off at home than condemned to an old folks' home. People begin to die when they go to places like that. I had enough communal living in the college dormitory."

Well, Grace thought, that obviously settles that. Dorothy always had her way.

Dorothy smiled again. "Grace dear?"

"Yes?"

"Why don't you go home and dress? Then come back and we'll have a nice chat before they take me away for more of those dreadful tests."

Grace blushed and pulled her raincoat closer but Dorothy laughed merrily.

*   *   *

Harry and a work crew completed the changes to Dorothy's house and the frail old woman went home to begin a new phase of her life. She exercised regularly, determined to recover her strength and mobility and return to her tutoring as soon as possible.

Rosemary continued her work with legal aid, learning and growing professionally, although not making the salary Harry expected of a lawyer daughter. She shrugged off his not-so-subtle suggestions she join a real law firm, telling him bluntly there was no place she'd rather be.

Grace suffered what Rosemary called a temporary fit of insanity and finally gave in to her screaming conscience, volunteering to be the church's Acteens leader. What kind of an influence would an old Southern Baptist like herself be on young minds, she wondered.

It was such a different program than Rosemary's GAs. There were only five or six girls involved. In a church as large as hers there should have been at least fifty of them, she calculated.

Missions were de-emphasized and anyplace where women were in positions of leadership changed or ignored. It was shameful.

At a Wednesday Night Business Meeting the president of WMU was told she could no longer address the congregation to give her report. She was instructed to hand her notebook to a deacon for reading.

Grace preached a sermon over the phone to Rosemary. "Just because she's a woman! Never in my whole life have I seen this! Even when I was little, when our preachers were so uneducated—"

"Mom, if this isn't your green light to go, I don't know what is," Rosemary said.

"It can't go on like this."

"Sure it can and it can get worse, too. Look, it's not like every church in the association is that way. Go someplace else."

"I can't."

"Sometimes your martyr complex is really hard to bear."

"I don't have a martyr complex."

"Of course you do. You'd much rather sit around and be miserable and hope you're gaining brownie points with God for staying on a sinking ship."

"It isn't a sinking ship."

"It's all over but the shouting. Don't you see?"

Things continued to deteriorate. At the end of the year one Florida minister told his congregation if they didn't vote his way they weren't voting for God.

In the spring of the New Year Southern Baptist moderates finally raised their voices to protest a statement that pastors were rulers of the churches. For all their fine writings, their detailed interviews, Grace knew it was too late.

The more she thought about it, the angrier she became. Rulers of the churches! Well, they're certainly beginning to live like royalty, why not say as much, she fumed to herself. Salaries nearly doubling in ten years. That's where all the Cooperative Program money went, yes indeed! Churches built to look like theaters...stadiums...monuments to vanity, that's what they were, providing everything from day-care to exercise classes. I wonder when one of them will add a golf course to the grounds, she thought sarcastically. Yes, too many of these preachers are indeed rulers of the churches. The Catholics call their higher clergy princes of the church, she remembered. Baptists, so hand-in-glove with Catholics these days, obviously want their share of the power and the glory, too.

Like rulers, their dictates were not challenged. More and more old Southern Baptist programs weakened beneath depleted funds. At the end of 1986 money was withdrawn from home missionaries who employed women in ministerial positions.

It would spell the end of the Southern Baptist presence in the less exotic mission fields: inner cities, Native American reservations, with migrant workers. Was it, as Rosemary said, all over but the shouting?

*   *   *

Praying hard that Rosemary was wrong, Grace carefully cultivated her Acteens group. She felt a thrill of delight as she tossed away their manual and began instructing them from Rosemary's old GA material. With minds so open and faces so trusting, they would learn what Southern Baptists were *supposed* to be.

It wasn't the standard line, telling the girls the emphasis was supposed to be on missions. All people should be allowed to hear and decide. Baptist doctrine did not involve minutiae; Baptists should not be involved crossing the thin line between church and state. Their minister was no more than any other member of the congregation. She told them most of the things they heard in

Sunday School and from the pulpit were wrong; they, as women, were full partners and absolutely equal.

She taught what the Cooperative Program was supposed to be: the *only* centrally controlled office within the convention. She emphasized its history and when she thought the girls were ready, taught them about the conflict within the convention, explaining everything they were learning and loving was under siege.

Those five, who grew slowly to ten, then suddenly to seventeen, would be her legacy. When one of them said casually, "I want to be a minister," and all the other girls applauded, Grace knew her small battle was successful.

It was why she felt compelled to stay on the ship, even if it was sinking. *Perhaps this generation of girls will be the ones to successfully reclaim our heritage: women and missions, from the men who wrested it from them and tried to destroy it,* she thought. *As besieged as it was, it belonged to them.*

It was the first ray of hope Grace had seen in a long time.

*   *   *

Realizing the fight to regain control of the Southern Baptist Convention was useless, moderate and liberal Baptists planted the first seeds of the Baptist Alliance. Churches could declare for the Alliance, which was highly unlikely in Grace's association, or individuals could belong to the group.

In the spring, a chapter began in Kentucky and Grace and Dorothy joined. It was wonderful to be with a large group of people who believed the same way.

Dorothy regaled people with stories of Grace's Acteens and Grace saw people smile at her approvingly for her dedication to the old ways. Dorothy claimed it gave her a thrill training these girls as though they were a cell of some underground movement.

"They *are* a cell in an underground movement," someone else declared with a laugh. "Good work, Grace! We'll need to create places for young Alliance members."

It seemed to be a glimmer of light at the end of the tunnel. If only her own church was a Alliance church! Other Alliance churches were rapidly ordaining women as both deacons and ministers...how lovely it would be to belong to one of them!

But I can't go, my girls need me, Grace thought smugly. And I need them, too. Thank you, God, for giving me a purpose even if they compare me to a radical training a cell!

    *   *   *

In late summer, Rosemary announced she was leaving legal aid for a more conventional job in a law firm. Harry couldn't resist teasing her. "Those big bucks finally talking to you, kiddo?"

"I need a wider range of experience. If I'm going to make my name a household word so I can be appointed a judge one day, I have to make a change."

"Why don't you run for office, Rosie?" Grace suggested.

"That would be a serious mistake, Mom. I'm afraid that underneath this liberal facade, I'm a tyrant. It scares me," she teased and smiled at her mother. "Besides, I want a better place to live and a decent car. Guess I'm getting materialistic in my old age."

"Thirty-one," Harry remembered, "that's not too old."

Rosemary glared at him.

He opened his mouth, Grace was certain, to hammer home his concern she wasn't married but Grace said suddenly, "Don't! If you say something, she'll never get married."

Harry glared, too. "I wasn't going to say anything about her getting married."

Rosemary shook her head. "Why don't you two relax? One of these days, when I'm good and ready, I'll get married. Okay?"

Harry clenched his jaw...Rosemary's jaw..."I wasn't going to say that. I wondered if you'd be interested in building a house?"

"A custom job?"

"Yeah."

"No, Daddy, I was thinking more on the lines of a condo. There's one I like that'll be available in January."

"A condo is only an apartment with a mortgage," Harry argued.

Rosemary looked him right in the eye. "I'm thinking on the lines of a condo," she repeated.

Harry gave Grace a frustrated glance as though she knew how to handle her when she was in that mood. Suddenly, Grace laughed. It was good for Harry to be railroaded by Rosemary, if it was only once in his life.

                    *   *   *

The fall foliage was beautiful. October, the most beautiful time of year in Kentucky, blazed with color. Cool crisp days, nights chilly enough for a fire...a perfect autumn!

Outside enjoying the beautiful weather, Dorothy slipped on the fallen leaves she was trying to rake and broke her hip. When Grace finally saw her after her surgery, she didn't know what aggravated the older woman more: the embarrassment of falling or the brutal fact her body was beginning to fail.

Delicate to begin with, Dorothy developed pneumonia and lost an alarming amount of weight. Her mind, however, was still as sharp as ever.

"She mustn't go home, Mrs. Lee. She needs full time nursing care now. Who is her next of kin?"

Grace had the presence of mind to tell them to take up the matter with Dorothy herself. She could imagine the explosion of temper if anyone tried to arrange the older woman's future without consulting her about it.

She noticed the staff seemed to walk on eggshells around Dorothy and couldn't help but chuckle. She still had the power to intimidate anyone she chose. Eventually, however, they wore her down with the logic of what they said and she tearfully agreed to sell her home, give away or sell most of her belongings and take up residence in a nursing home.

She would never take another step without the support of a walker, never again bounce up a flight of stairs with the agility of a twenty-year-old. The mobility she treasured and the smug independence were gone forever.

"All because I had to go outside and rake those leaves! Damn October!" she swore, furious her life had taken such a change.

Rosemary, who handled her legal affairs, found her the best nursing home in the area. Even so, Grace decided, it left a lot to be desired. She was appalled at the expense.

"Don't worry, Mom," Rosemary soothed. "Her pension is good and she made some smart investments over the years. She can live there a good ten years before money becomes a problem."

"When she had the stroke she swore she'd never live in a nursing home," Grace reminded her.

"She doesn't have a choice now." Rosemary said softly.

"If we didn't have stairs to manage I'd take her home to live with us."

"Well, you *do* have stairs and Dorothy needs professional nursing care. No matter how good your intentions are, Mom, you don't have that sort of background."

"I feel guilty."

"There's nothing to feel guilty about. When she gains a little more strength, you might want to take her home for a day now and then. But she has a long way to go before she's ready for that."

It was very difficult. Dorothy hated what she called "these old people who have given up," complained that patients who suffered from mental illness were allowed to wander the facility without supervision. She hated the food, most of the staff whom she swore stole her belongings, hated just about everything, Grace noted.

"About thirty years ago," Dorothy said one day, "I had an old tomcat named Byron. All of a sudden he developed arthritis and couldn't move the way he used to. Well, he thought he was still Don Juan with the pussycats and came home one day torn to pieces from a fight. I had him put to sleep that very day because he could no longer live the life he loved." She paused and looked at Grace. "Why is it illegal for me to be put to sleep? I can't live the way I used to. I hate this! It isn't living—"

"I can't believe you're saying this to me!" Grace cried. "You still have your mind, still know—"

"Knowing is the hell of it!" Dorothy looked away. "This is horrible, Grace. You can't imagine it. God, God, why didn't I die when I fell?"

Grace couldn't stop her tears. "What do you want me to do, Dorothy?"

"I want you to have Rosemary ask these doctors what I have to do to get out of here."

"But your home is sold."

"I don't care. I'll live in an efficiency apartment as long as I can live on my own."

The doctors were adamant. Dorothy was too frail to live on her own. Rosemary, usually so easily swayed by Dorothy, didn't budge, either.

"She hates it there," Grace tried to persuade her.

"It would be irresponsible to let her live alone, Mom. You've seen her. She's another accident waiting to happen."

It was the worst thing Grace had to do, telling Dorothy she was incapable of living alone. Dorothy swallowed the verdict in silence but before Grace left for the day, she turned fierce eyes up to hers and said quietly, "I suppose I have to get used to it. I've never flinched from doing hard things before...this is simply another one but...Grace?"

"Yes?"

"Will you bring me some of your corned beef and cabbage next time you visit? These fools around here can't cook and I've been dying for some corned beef and cabbage for days."

Grace smiled. It was her first admission of appetite and surely it was a good sign. Maybe, just maybe, Dorothy would settle into the nursing home.

But she thought about Byron the cat all the way home.

18

Grace couldn't wait for Rosemary to move into her condo. She had to admit that she herself would never have bought it but it was certainly going to be a beautiful place when Rosemary finished with it. She'd expected her daughter to furnish it with a flourish of blacks, whites and reds for accents, bold and daring like Rosemary herself. The sketches, however, took her by surprise.

Rosemary's new home would look more like something out of *Southern Living* than the stylish abode of an up and coming lawyer. With rich oak furniture and warm sunny colors, it made Grace cozy just thinking about it.

Inspiration for a Christmas gift struck early and she decided to spend some money and buy an antique roll top desk for Rosemary's study. She had a hard time staying quiet. The desk was an antique and all Rosemary's other oak pieces were new. Would the difference in the oak stains be acceptable?

And how were she and Harry going to present such an enormous gift on Christmas Day? Rosemary didn't take possession of her condo until the New Year. Where on earth would they store the desk in the meantime, however temporarily that would be?

This is what I get for being creative, Grace thought dismally. Instead of concentrating on Thanksgiving I'm all in a tizzy about that desk!

Thanksgiving is next week and I haven't even started to get ready, she remembered. Rosemary's begged me to go out and let a great restaurant do all the hard stuff but that just wouldn't be Thanksgiving.

She could almost hear Rosemary put in, "No, Mom, it wouldn't be Thanksgiving unless you've worn yourself out cooking all the junk no one eats."

The ringing telephone jolted her out of her reverie. "Grace!" the voice on the other end cried.

"Yes?" she asked suspiciously, not recognizing the caller.

"Have you got your television on?"

"No—"

"Well, turn it on! I can't believe *your* Rosemary would do such a thing!"

"Lorene." Grace finally placed the voice. "What's Rosemary doing on television?" she asked blankly.

"She's on the news. She's taking the case—that case everyone is talking about!"

"What case?"

"The queer who was fired by the school system. She's taking *his* case!"

Grace went cold. "I'll talk to you later," she said numbly and hung up the phone.

She cast her mind back to church conversations, trying to recall what Lorene was talking about. So often these days when the rhetoric started she tuned out but there was something familiar...

She remembered suddenly. A high school teacher with AIDs had been dismissed by the school board. A homosexual schoolteacher. That was it.

Grace went to her rocker and sat down heavily. She's taken that case, she thought. Why? She knows, she has to know how people will react, what they'll say!

She's new in the firm, maybe her bosses told her to take it, she decided. That has to be it. Rosemary has strayed far from what I raised her with but she wouldn't do this to Harry and me. It would be too much of a slap in the face.

Grace thought seriously about calling her but her fears got the better of her. If she'd been on television, she probably wasn't available to take any calls.

She glanced at the clock. Rosemary always got home around three o'clock on Fridays. Would she be on time today?

I'll go to her apartment and wait for her to get home, she decided.

*   *   *

The rest of the afternoon dragged by. The phone was mercifully silent but that in itself set Grace's heart racing. Would people in the church assume she and Harry agreed with Rosemary on this issue?

Finally, it was time to go. The day darkened suddenly and a cold rain started to pour. It matches my mood perfectly, Grace decided. How could she do this to me? After everything else she's put me through, now this!

What is she trying to tell me with this? Does she reject marriage and fidelity and sex differences, too? Is that her game? To rub my nose in everything?

The confusion of the early afternoon gave way to absolute rage. She will *not* take this case, Grace decided. I'll make it very clear to her. It's either the case or me. I've had enough in the last few years to kill me ten times over and I won't take this.

She pulled into the parking lot of Rosemary's apartment building and looked for a spot close to the entry. Nothing, of course. It was almost as though God was punishing her for something, making her fight the storm.

She ran out of her car to the building. The rain stung her face and the wind seemed to blow through to her bones. She tugged at the heavy entry door, fighting against the wind.

Once inside she shook her hair and paused to find a tissue in her purse to dry her glasses. She climbed the stairs to the third floor and walked to the end of the hallway to gaze out the long window to see if Rosemary's car was in the parking lot. Catching her breath, she noticed the rain had turned into a gully-washer.

As she watched, she saw Rosemary's car pull into the lot and the vigilant Rosemary find a spot she herself had missed, close to the building.

Lights and wipers off. Harry had taught her well. Then the car door opened and out she stepped without a raincoat or an umbrella in sight.

Trying to balance her briefcase and a bag of groceries, Grace watched with a small knot of malicious glee as Rosemary walked too fast, twisted her ankle on her precarious heels and dropped groceries and briefcase in her struggle to stay erect.

That's what she gets, Grace thought furiously.

There was no one in the lot to help and she could tell Rosemary was swearing as she gathered her soaked belongings. She disappeared inside the building and Grace sighed and walked back up the hallway to the apartment door, waiting.

Eventually, Rosemary appeared, soaked to the skin and still swearing softly. She noticed Grace and frowned. "Mom, what are you doing here?" she asked, setting down the torn bag of groceries, searching in her purse for her keys.

"I heard you were on television today," Grace said softly, hoping not to betray her feelings.

Rosemary nodded absently. "Yeah, you know the press."

"I heard you took that case."

"That's right," her daughter muttered, rifling the contents of the purse.

"Tell me you were assigned to the case, that your boss forced you to do it."

Rosemary met her eyes. "Forced me? What are you talking about?"

"Tell me you didn't want to take the case."

Rosemary paused and the light suddenly seemed to dawn on her. She set her purse down and drew herself up proudly. "Not only did I want the case, I asked for it."

Grace held the silence for a moment. "After everything else you've done in the last few years, how could you possibly put me through this?"

"Through what?" Rosemary demanded.

"You know what that man is. You know how I feel about it."

Rosemary frowned deeply. "Look, this isn't the time to be getting into this, Mom. Not here in the hall—"

"Yes, here in the hall. You're going to tell me what makes you want to humiliate me and your father—"

"*What*? The case I've taken involves a man's right to work, his dismissal without just cause leaving him facing a fatal disease without a dime's worth of health insurance. How do you have the gall to face me and suggest I'm doing something to embarrass *you*?"

"Because you are. Everything you've done in the last ten years has rubbed my face in everything I raised you to believe—"

Rosemary's face went deadly pale.

"You left the church, slept with that boy...God knows how many times or with how many others—"

"You've said enough."

"Oh, I'm not finished yet!"

"Yes, you are—" but Rosemary was cut off in mid-sentence as the creak of an opening apartment door startled her. The door only opened a crack; enough to warn the arguing women that every word they said was overheard.

"You take this case, Rosemary, and I'm finished with you. There are certain things I don't have to take and this is one of them. Now you think about it and call me later," Grace said, starting to walk away.

"I don't have to think about a thing," Rosemary called back.

Grace stopped but didn't turn around to face her.

"I'm going ahead with this case whether you like it or not. You've obviously done today what you have to do. Now I'll do what I have to do. I make no apologies, either. I like Ross Lawrence very much and I'm glad to represent him. You cut me off if you have to but understand you'll never hear me express any regret about this decision."

Grace started shaking. She forced herself to start walking to the stairs. She hadn't raised Rosemary, dedicated her to God, for this. Nothing had gone as she'd hoped and planned.

       *   *   *

All through the holidays the only thing Grace wanted to do was run to Dorothy for understanding. However, as her emotions calmed and she began to think more clearly it dawned on her that with every crisis she'd taken to the older woman, Dorothy consistently sided with Rosemary.

She couldn't bear the thought of Dorothy turning against her on this issue. So she was careful in her actions, visited Dorothy dutifully but never brought up the subject.

The holidays were miserable. Harry went out on Thanksgiving when he learned that Grace made no plans. She angrily wondered if he and Rosemary had lunch together but feared the answer. The silence between them grew long and anxious.

Dorothy seemed on edge, too, searching her face with demanding eyes and responding politely to Grace's suddenly casual conversations. She curiously held her tongue when Grace refused to talk about Rosemary.

When Grace thought she could stand the strain no longer, she and Harry were invited to a Sunday School Class Christmas party, the very one she'd sworn not to attend.

Harry sarcastically reminded her of it as he struggled with the necktie he so hated. "Didn't you tell me this gang is obnoxious and superficial?" he jeered.

Grace, squirming into her girdle, went scarlet with embarrassment and anger. "Well, maybe it's the way to get through life," she snapped bitterly. "If you never think about anything but what you're going to wear tomorrow or what you're going to eat tonight, you have a much less stressful life."

Harry adjusted the tie's knot and turned away from the mirror. "Is this the way you plan to live from now on?"

"Maybe it is. Being a thinking person has sure gotten me nothing but grief!"

"Mmm," Harry mumbled and closed the closet door. "I wish you'd make up your mind. For nearly twenty years you've been a bleeding heart liberal. All of a sudden you decide to cozy up to the very people you swore you couldn't stand. It must be the aftershock of menopause because there's no rhyme or reason to it."

Grace sat down on the bed and pulled her shoes closer with her toes. Tears stung her eyes. It's bad enough, she thought, to face people I've barely tolerated over the years. Tonight I want them to think well of me and realize I know where to draw the lines in my life.

Obviously, Harry didn't share her point of view but she didn't dare discuss it with him. Fathers like Harry would defend daughters like Rosemary on any issue.

He'd never been able to say no to her. Ever. That was why she'd grown into such a willful adult. No one had ever taken her in hand.

This was the price. When the battle lines were finally drawn there was no one on Grace's side because she herself abandoned those old friends years ago.

Tonight was the first step toward making up for those years. For nearly twenty years, she'd felt isolated from her church peers. Tonight, by God, it would change.

*   *   *

On the way home from the party Grace sat in embarrassed silence, so furious with Harry she could have clawed out his eyes. Driving home carefully, trying to whistle *Silent Night*, he obviously thought no more of his rudeness than Rosemary would.

The dinner was wonderful and Harry dug into his meal with gusto but Grace several times overheard him bragging about Rosemary: her salary, her professional reputation, her plans to buy the condo...it was enough to turn the strongest stomach. Then she heard Harry mention an expensive luxury car he was trying to talk her into buying.

So they *had* been in touch! Grace couldn't believe the intensity of the betrayal she felt.

The preacher had been invited to speak to the group after the dinner. Less than ten minutes into the speech Harry fell asleep, leaning back in his chair and snoring deeply.

The preacher wrapped up his topic quickly and amazingly Harry woke up. Grace seethed next to him, promising herself a fitting revenge.

The conversation moved onto the sensitive subject of politics and Harry said no more. The words Grace had learned to hate crept into the conversation, testing her, she realized, to see if she would react.

The pecan pie started churning in her stomach and she and Harry left shortly thereafter, with Grace claiming, "I just can't eat the good stuff the way I used to."

Now, going home, she realized Harry and the events of the night truly had conspired against her. She couldn't backtrack as easily as she'd thought but she'd have a few words with Harry if it was the last thing she ever did. He was exactly like Rosemary when she had a point to prove.

It was behavior she'd tolerated much too long. She was unable to control Rosemary at this stage of her life but Harry was a different story. In 1988 there would be different behavior in the Lee household.

*   *   *

Before Harry could stop her Grace called the furniture company to collect the antique desk. She received her refund without any trouble and planned to spend it redecorating her bedroom. To punish herself further, she resigned as Acteens leader. It was too much to ask, training other people's daughters when she was such a failure with her own.

Dorothy spent Christmas with her nephew and his family and seemed relieved to be back at the nursing home. "Am I getting old or are small children completely out of hand these days?" she complained to Grace, who visited her upon her return.

"I think it's the problem with working mothers. When kids are in day care all day they come home ready for bear and their mothers still have everything to do as well as cope with them. It's not a good life for the average working woman," Grace commented.

"Well, you certainly won't have to worry about *your* grandchildren. Rosemary—"

"Rosemary is much too self-centered to think about what it takes to be a good mother."

Dorothy frowned slightly and started to say something but Grace looked away, hoping her expression discouraged any probing of the topic.

She felt guilty for not sharing the problem with Dorothy but she couldn't bring herself to hear any defense of Rosemary. On any topic. *That* was asking too much.

                    *   *   *

Grace forced herself to be polite and mixed with church peers she hadn't seen socially for many years. Amazingly, they weren't the monsters she thought. They were so kind to her about Rosemary. They prayed with her and would have included Harry, too, if he hadn't left the house abruptly without so much as a hello or inviting them to have some coffee.

They kept abreast of Rosemary's case, sympathizing with her when Rosemary won points with the journalists at a press conference. They nodded with her in agreement that God sometimes gives a very hard knock to prove His point. More than once Rosemary's temper got the better of her and the judge cited her with contempt of court. Maybe God and the judge were on the same wavelength, Grace hoped.

Grace reminded the women how Rosemary seemed to have had so much promise as a church leader when she was a child. The newer members didn't know that. All they knew was an adult child of a church member was sorely distressing her parents.

"I wanted her to go to the mission field," she found herself saying. "She would have, too, if we hadn't let her have her away about the art."

While the women surrounding her sympathized and patted her hand, she wondered about the truth of her own words. Would Rosemary ever have ended up on a mission field? No, Dorothy said Rosemary would have mentioned a calling by the time she was twelve had it really been her goal in life.

"I remember little Rosie doing so well in GAs," one of the older women smiled. "She was the smartest one, oh yes, indeed."

"Then what happened?" a younger woman asked. "The church wasn't at fault."

Grace's face went scarlet and her heart beat erratically. It was exactly what everyone was saying, she was sure. If the church wasn't at fault, she and Harry were. It was so plain.

Bad parenting. Indulgence. It seemed so obvious now. Yet if I had it all to do over again, I don't know what I'd do differently. I would end up here again, so what was the right thing to have done?

Dorothy would know but Grace pushed the idea from her head. She'd come too far in the last few months to give up now. If she went to Dorothy it would mean the end of this rapprochement with these women, and it was so good to feel understood!

*   *   *

The dark winter days slowly lengthened and Grace found herself looking forward to spring with more than the usual excitement of wanting the flowers to bloom. It had been nearly four months since she'd seen Rosemary. Every single day was a torment, in spite of renewing old friendships.

Dorothy looked forward to spring, too, feeling the confinement of the nursing home more severely in the winter months. She and Grace were reduced to talking pleasantly about the weather and Dorothy's health.

It was hard to believe their lively conversations had been reduced to such a state. Grace refused to dig deeply into anything. The 1988 political primaries were running ahead with their usual mud slinging and rhetoric. This year she turned off the television and left her newspapers unread.

Dorothy only once ventured into the political arena when she mentioned her surprise that Robert Dole hadn't made a better showing. Grace shrugged and mumbled her disinterest and Dorothy let the subject rest.

Grace felt those alert hazel eyes digging deeply into her heart and sighed with guilty relief when she left the nursing home. Her visits were becoming more and more of a chore. How much longer before Dorothy's temper frayed and she would be subjected to one of her lectures?

So Grace shortened her visits a little at a time. She hoped that by summer she could manage to visit Dorothy only once a month without the old woman having noticed the change.

She drove cautiously through the slushy streets to the March Circle Meeting. A few other WMU members had already parked in front of Lorene Wright's house. Grace hoped she was early enough to get the spot right in front. It was threatening to pour again and with the thermometer hovering right around the freezing mark, it could as easily sleet as rain.

She slowed to see exactly where she could park. Everything that looked clear was too close to driveways and the one really open spot was in front of a fire hydrant.

Grace recognized the cars of her friends and preferred to park behind one of them but the only space available was behind an old rattletrap of a vehicle. Grace hesitated, wondering if the driver was as unsavory as the car itself.

Then something caught her eye: a 1984 bumper sticker with a Mondale and Ferraro slogan on it. She grinned broadly and her fears vanished. So there was at least one other person who'd backed that ticket besides herself and Dorothy!

Dorothy again! When will I ever stop thinking of her at every moment, she wondered.

Lorene met her at the front door with a smile. "We have a new member, Grace," she said pleasantly, taking Grace's coat. "The Tates moved their membership here from Providence, Rhode Island last Sunday. You do remember, don't you?"

Grace smiled, hoping her blushing face didn't confirm Lorene's fears that she'd indeed forgotten. She looked directly at the new member, a tall and somewhat gawky woman with snapping black eyes and steel gray hair. "Did you come from First Baptist?" Grace asked.

The woman returned her warm smile. "You know, Grace, you're the only one here who thought of that possibility," came the husky New England-accented voice.

"What possibility?" Frances Taylor whispered.

Grace shook her head. "You've been going to church more than fifty years, Frances, and still don't know Roger Williams founded First Baptist Church in Providence...the very first First," she punned mercilessly.

The new member stood and extended her hand to Grace. "I'm Sarah," she announced. "Come over here and sit by me and tell me when you were in Rhode Island."

The two women sat down in the middle of Lorene's sofa, effectively making it off limits to anyone else. Sarah leaned close and whispered into Grace's ear, "I feel as though I know you already. I've been getting quite an earful from your friends."

Grace's mirth dissolved and she went cold all over. "I see." She gathered the courage to look up into Sarah's eyes, finding no judgment but much warmth.

"We can't start until our president arrives," Lorene explained to Sarah.

"Of course," Sarah responded politely but Grace saw the corners of her mouth twitch with a slight hint of mischief.

"A bunch of them car-pool and when Nancy drives, they're always late," Lorene continued.

"Well, that lets me off the hook," Sarah said quietly to Grace, "because no one would dare get in my junk-heap!"

"You have the car with that old Mondale and Ferraro sticker on your bumper?" Grace whispered.

Sarah smiled. "Oh, you've seen it!"

Grace cleared her throat. "In this group it would be wiser for you not to mention that."

Sarah frowned. "Why not?"

"Because...well, it just wouldn't, that's all. Believe me, Sarah, you've got three strikes against you in the first place because you're from the northeast. Don't give them ammunition."

The new member frowned deeply. "I certainly wouldn't bring up politics, Grace, if that's what you think."

"I'm sure you wouldn't," Grace hastened to explain, "but *they* will. We never get through a function without something controversial coming up."

"Do all of them think alike?"

Them...me, too! Grace wanted to cry but the words wouldn't come out. "Yes—"

"The conservative party line?"

"Yes."

Sarah sighed. "You, too?"

"Well, I don't like what's happened to Southern Baptists in the last few years, no—"

"Are you, dare I ask," Sarah grinned, whispering, "a Democrat? A Jimmy Carter-type Baptist Democrat?"

Grace began to tremble. "I have no political convictions this year, Sarah."

"*This* year?"

"It's a long story—"

"Obviously!"

"And one I'd rather not discuss right now." She's a northeastern Democrat, Grace thought, knowledgeable and nice. They're going to hate her when they find out and here I am, sitting by her. They'll think I've back-slidden or worse.

She was hardly aware of the meeting when it started, only of the sickening lump building in her throat and the old tension in her stomach. Is God testing me or something, she wondered miserably. I'm trying so hard to get back to the way I used to be and bumping into one brick wall right after another.

Sarah contributed brilliantly to the class meeting and asked intelligent questions. They seemed to like her very much until the meeting was over and refreshments were served.

She praised the refreshments without a trace of flattery. "My husband swears he'll never live in the north again. I think the cooking down here has done more to convert him than anything else."

"You're going to like the milder winters and the longer gardening season, too," Lorene promised.

"And you're definitely going to prefer living in a more Christian community."

Grace couldn't bring herself to look at the woman who so brazenly assumed such a fact. Sarah, however, nearly dropped her luncheon plate in her surprise. "I beg your pardon?" she asked coolly.

Grace bent over her own plate, realizing she knew what was coming as surely as if she held a script in hand.

"Well, you're from the northeast. Real Christians are obviously few and far between up there from what we see."

"Exactly what do you see?" Sarah prodded.

"The Kennedys and those other liberals—"

"I don't understand your point," Sarah interrupted.

"Everyone knows our political system is managed by a godless northeastern liberal machine. Our church leaders call them secular humanists but they're actually a bunch of atheists out to destroy the moral fabric of our Christian society."

"And Jews, too, don't forget them," Sarah jeered.

"The Jews are only misled," Lorene said gently. "We are not anti-Semitic, Sarah, as you well know. All of us here support Israel without reservation."

Sarah stared at all of them for a long moment then forced herself to smile. "Well, I've certainly learned a lot today."

Grace sighed with relief and set her plate on the coffee table. As she straightened back in her seat, Sarah leaned toward her and softly whispered, "Coward."

It was the final straw.

She was suddenly aware her newly won status among her church peers was going to eventually cost more than she could give. Everything they demanded, she gave willingly, hoping each sacrifice would be the last.

The only way to truly belong was to turn over her mind as well. She couldn't do it, just couldn't do it. It's shaping up, she decided, to be a battle of my childhood faith versus my sanity. How in the Name of God can anyone win that one?

I can't think of this now, simply can't. It's too much to take. I agree with them about Rosemary and this case but nothing else. Nothing.

What were those stupid phrases we were taught as children? When God closes a door, He opens a window. God never gives you more than you can bear. What a lot of nonsense, Grace decided. No one ever prepared us for the fact that there are things that have no answers but like a great big fool, I keep looking for them! If God would open a window for me right now, I think I'd jump out of it!

Yet the thing that had startled her into such a reverie, she suddenly remembered, was the new member calling her a coward. Next to Rosemary's betrayal, nothing in the last four months hurt as much. Perhaps, just perhaps it was time to talk to Dorothy at last, even if she scolded and lectured for hours. Dorothy would know what to do.

How hard it will be, she realized, to breach this wall I've built! Even so, it's the only chance I have toward regaining my sanity and proving to this woman that I'm no coward!

$$* \qquad * \qquad *$$

Grace didn't have the nerve to visit Dorothy until the week before Easter. Even then, she shook in her shoes, trying to think of inconsequential things to relieve her distress.

She wondered what Dorothy would think of the preacher's plans to collect all the members from the nursing homes in order to attend Sunday service. It would give Dorothy a chance to see some of her old friends again, to be in church impeccably dressed and in her rightful place on the third pew from the front on the right.

As Grace walked down the sunlit corridor of the nursing home, she smiled as she thought of the plans. Dorothy would enjoy a break from the nursing home and its routines and rules.

She heard voices raised in Dorothy's room.

"Give it to me, you know where it is! Everyone around here is always stealing my things—"

"Now Miss Blackwell, if you don't calm down we'll have to give you a shot—"

"Look for my belongings and bring them to me at once!"

Grace entered the room, finding papers and clothes and underwear strewn everywhere and two strong nurses trying to hold the frail Dorothy in her bed.

"I don't think we have any choice but to order a sedative," one nurse said to the other.

"What's going on here?" Grace demanded, a lump rising in her throat.

Dorothy saw her and struggled against the hands holding her down. "Oh Grace, make them let go of me! I have to find it now and they've stolen it!"

Tears stung Grace's eyes as she realized Dorothy had probably suffered another minor stroke. She approached the bed and tried to be calm. "I don't think these women would have stolen anything—"

"Oh, not them!" Dorothy snapped and began to weep tiredly. "It's these damned old people around here! Nothing is sacred. They steal my underwear, my clothes—"

One nurse shook her head. "She's hysterical."

Grace reached for one of Dorothy's hands. "You must calm down, Dorothy, or they'll have to sedate you."

"Oh, damn them all!" Dorothy cried weakly, then turning furious eyes on Grace, "And damn you, too!" With that she turned away and sobbed bitterly.

One of the nurses left the room and the other glanced at Grace. "Will you be here awhile, Mrs. Lee? She'll probably fall asleep for an hour or so but it would be nice to have someone here she knows when she wakes up."

Grace nodded. "I'll stay."

The nurse returned with the sedative and Dorothy twisted in pain as the syringe's needle pierced her thin, delicate arm.

The drug acted quickly and Dorothy dropped off. Grace began collecting the papers and clothes. She sat down and watched Dorothy's shallow breathing. It was horrible what old age and sickness did to people. Especially to Dorothy.

Grace sighed, feeling drowsy herself. Sometimes it seemed there was no end to trouble.

19

"You mustn't let this argument come between you and Rosemary."

Grace jerked herself awake and squinted in the bright morning sunlight. She moved quickly to turn the blinds and looked at the frail figure in the bed, noting with relief the hysteria was gone. "Thank God you're better!" she cried, trying to hold back her tears.

"Panic seems to be at my shoulder these days," Dorothy said softly. "Passing the mid-eighty mark seems to have done me in." But her hazel eyes glinted with the old fire and she smiled.

"Well, I can't empathize with that," Grace teased.

"Impertinence, miss."

Grace dragged her chair closer to the bed and sat down beside Dorothy. "Exactly what were you looking for that caused all this trouble?"

"A beaded handbag."

"A handbag?"

Dorothy's eyes filled with tears and she looked away. "It isn't any ordinary handbag, Grace," she explained. "I bought it in Paris in the summer of 1939. I hoped to carry it later in the year when I married."

"I'll go through everything to find it for you."

"I want Rosemary to have it."

Grace shuddered but before she could say anything, Dorothy suddenly looked away, her cheeks flaming with embarrassment.

"I just remembered. I gave it to her last week. Oh God, how could I have forgotten?" She twisted the bed sheet angrily and looked back at Grace. "But enough about that. It's been four months, Grace, since the two of you have spoken. Are you *never* going to discuss this with me?"

"I—I planned to do it today, really—"

"How did things get so bad?"

God, it's like being called to the front of the class for bad behavior, Grace thought.

"Well?"

"How did you find out?" Grace demanded.

Dorothy folded her thin hands in her lap. "I watch television, you know, and our Visitation Committee keeps me quite up to date on your injured dignity. Their love for gossip is surpassed only by their desire for blood. I used to think you were too smart to fall into their trap. Now I'm not so sure."

"What do you mean?"

"I mean," Dorothy said sternly, "they're manipulating you. Whatever quarrels some of them had with Rosemary, they hadn't the courage to finish. Along comes this bitterly divisive issue, and—"

"I agree with them," Grace interrupted. "I don't see how you have the nerve to defend Rosemary's behavior in this. She knows what she's doing goes against every single thing she was raised with."

"This has nothing to do with Rosemary's morals."

"Of course it does."

"Must each of Rosemary's clients share her personal beliefs, Grace?"

"She's wrong to take this case. To defend that—that—"

"Queer? Faggot? Fairy, queen, pansy?" Dorothy paused only to catch her breath and lift her chin defiantly. "Cock-sucker?"

Grace gasped and sank back in her chair, weeping uncontrollably. "How—how can you say such things?"

"You mean you don't think a desiccated old virgin like me knows what's going on?"

The first burst of tears eased and Grace glared at her. "It's disgusting."

"What's disgusting? The words or the people?"

"What do you mean?"

"They call the women butches or bull—"

"Oh, for God's sake!" Grace jumped to her feet. "If you hoped to shock me, you did!"

Dorothy pointed to the chair. "You sit down and don't you stir until I tell you to!"

Grace sank into the chair, unaccustomed to Dorothy's anger directed fully upon herself. The old woman settled more comfortably in the bed and tried to soften her gaze. "We are talking about men and women, Grace, who are different than you and me."

"We're only talking about one that I know of, one who had the nerve to teach in a public school—"

"You certainly don't think he's the only one?"

Grace swallowed hard. "No, I imagine there are plenty more."

"You don't think they should be allowed to teach?"

"Why are you doing this to me? There is no way you can defend homosexuality. Whatever left-wing opinions you've held in the past can't possibly compare to this!"

"How dare you throw politics in my face on this issue?"

"Don't I have the right to my opinion, too? I can't believe you side with Rosemary—"

"I want to hear about this now. Get yourself a glass of water and tell me what the two of you have done to each other."

Remembering, Grace shivered. "When I heard the news that day, I drove out to find Rosemary."

"You confronted her the same day the case was made public?"

"Yes, outside her apartment."

"God Almighty, Grace."

"I told her I absolutely forbade her to defend…him."

"She probably told you it was her job."

"Hardly. She told me she'd specifically asked for the case."

Dorothy nodded.

"She turned on me," Grace continued, "and told me the case was more than—than a homosexual's right to work." She paused. "She said if she didn't defend him the door would be opened to persecute other people for other things."

"Don't you agree with her?"

"Not this time."

"Why?"

"Those…people   should stay out of the public schools."

"The gift for teaching recognizes no sexual orientation."

"It should."

Dorothy leaned back into her pillows and Grace saw tears on her eyes. "No, Grace. It should not. Homophobia destroyed—no, I destroyed—the most remarkable teacher, the finest man I ever knew."

"What do you mean? You destroyed him?"

"I killed him," Dorothy said matter-of-factly. "Oh, he was shot down over Germany in 1943 but I effectively killed him four years before."

"Oh Dorothy, really—"

The eyes that met Grace's were suddenly haunted. "It's true. Because I couldn't have him I made sure he'd never teach again. I told his secret to the superintendent of schools and that was it. All very quietly, of course, we couldn't have such a scandal for fear of ruining my career, too."

"I can't imagine you doing anything like that—"

"Why not?" Dorothy challenged. "Passion is incomprehensible, Grace. Never, never underestimate its power."

"Don't you mean love?"

"No, I mean passion."

"When did all this happen?"

"It started in 1937. Ted taught history. He was from the northeast, well educated and well traveled. He'd spent some time fighting the war in Spain the year before."

"Sounds like a real hero type."

Dorothy chuckled. "A Clark Gable type, I thought. I'd read *Gone With the Wind* earlier in the year and was sure Margaret Mitchell based Rhett on Ted. How beautiful he was! And so brilliant, too!"

"Then you were friends?"

"That's all I ever was to him. But to me…" Dorothy paused. "I was thirty-four the year I met him. I'd done nothing but teach for twelve years. There was room in my life only for school and church and his effect on me was instant, total and irrevocable. In other words it was lust, pure and simple."

Grace blushed.

Dorothy didn't seem to notice. "I planned to marry him before I even spoke to him. I never felt that way about any other man. Ever."

"Did he lead you on?"

Dorothy shook her head. "Never. Being so ignorant, I thought he was simply a confirmed bachelor. We attended faculty functions together. You see, Grace, it was an intellectual attachment, too."

"You loved him."

"Yes, and wanted him terribly. He talked me into going to Europe in the summer of '39, warning me it would probably be the last season of peace for years. How right he was!"

Grace looked away. A love affair gone wrong, she thought. It seemed so obvious now. Why else would a brilliant woman like Dorothy never have married? But she would never have gauged the intensity of those feelings, though, never in a million years!

"While I was in Paris, I bought that handbag. I made up my mind Ted and I would marry over Christmas."

"But things went wrong."

Dorothy snorted. "God, what an understatement! I arrived home early because I didn't want to spend another night in New York. It was hot, so hot. I was dying to see Ted, to tell him everything, so I dropped in at his boardinghouse. Everyone else I knew had gone to the Baptist and Methodist softball game, and I—I decided on the spur of the moment that I wanted to lose my virginity that very night. I was, after all, thirty-six and planned to marry him. Well, I sneaked up quietly to his room because I didn't want the landlady to catch me." She shuddered and looked away. "To find a man you want in the arms of another man—I couldn't have been more outraged had it been a woman—but how could it happen? The man I wanted so much sharing a love act with another man?"

Grace reached for her hand. "He was perverted—"

"He most certainly was not!" Dorothy pulled her hand away.

"What else could it have been?"

"I didn't know then, I don't know now. Fifty years have given me no peace at all with it, either!"

Grace paused while she collected herself. "That's when you told the superintendent."

"Well, I stumbled out of the boardinghouse and vomited in the rosebushes first, then spent an eternity sobbing my heart out under the front porch. When I came out of that dark hole I was determined to hurt Ted as deeply as he'd hurt me."

"You had a right to be angry and hurt—"

"Did I have the right to ruin a man's career, Grace? As I marched along those darkened streets, I knew I was destroying him. God forgive me, I was glad!"

"Did he know it was you?"

"I'm sure he did."

"He left town?"

"Yes. Then I had a nervous breakdown."

"Why?"

"Well, my dear, guilt can drive you crazy."

"You had nothing to feel guilty about. He destroyed himself, acting worse than an animal—"

"No, I don't believe that, either. I have no idea who Ted's lover was but I do remember one thing. Ted looked at him as he never looked at anyone else. He loved that man—"

"It couldn't have been love," Grace said firmly.

Dorothy narrowed her eyes. "And who are you to say so?"

"How can you, a Christian, condone such acts?"

"Well, I've struggled with it for fifty years, Grace. I've read everything I can find. This young man Rosemary is defending," she went on, "when I first heard about the case it brought the whole thing back again. Fifty years, Grace, and nothing has changed!"

"This man has AIDs!"

"Yes, poor boy!"

"He shouldn't be teaching."

"Not if he's so sick he can't. But until that time the board must honor his contract and his right to work. To discontinue his health coverage and fire him for what they shouldn't be involved in anyway is disgraceful!"

"He's a danger to society."

"Hasn't *anything* I said to you sunk in?"

"I realize you condone homosexuality and I guess it helps to know why but—"

"I simply prefer to stay out of other adults' business, Grace. It's a dangerous game, snooping around for sexual misconduct."

"Is this the way Rosemary feels?"

"I'm sure of it," Dorothy replied. She fell silent for a long time. "She's going to lose this case, Grace. Fear and ignorance will bring down that young man as bitterly as I brought down Ted. You don't have to agree with her to support her but if you don't heal this rupture soon, you'll lose her forever."

Grace's eyes widened. "Why should I—"

"Because you gave the ultimatum."

Grace remembered Rosemary's expression on that horrible day. "I don't think she'll talk to me."

"There's no need to talk. Go to court. Sit on her side. Listen to what she has to say." Dorothy smiled suddenly. "Glare at the judge."

Grace glanced out the window. "I'll have to call Harry—"

"I'll do it for you."

Grace gasped. "But you don't really like Harry—"

"Why, Grace, that's absurd. Of course I like Harry. He gets on my nerves but I like him."

Grace searched for her purse. "I've never had to do anything this hard before."

Dorothy chuckled. "Proof positive, my dear, of what a charmed life you've led."

Grace sighed again. "I know it sounds a little ridiculous but pray for me, Dorothy. You don't know how I dread this!"

*   *   *

Closing arguments were scheduled for early afternoon. The press corps as well as the curious public crowded around the municipal building and the traffic was terrible. It's already started and I'm late, Grace noted disconsolately, watching the seconds tick by on her watch. And it's rude to be late…Baptist standard time! She finally found a parking place in the lot of a fast food restaurant and gathered her courage.

She hadn't seen Rosemary in months. People said she looked tired. They said a lot about her fit of bad temper with a reporter, the contempt of court charge when she kept arguing with the judge. People said it served her right.

As she walked toward the municipal building she noted the gathering crowds were marching. Protesting! Voices were raised but she couldn't quite hear them.

People in both camps carried placards with Bible verses scrawled on them. One group reminded everyone with the appropriate verse from Leviticus about homosexuality being an abomination.

But the other group…were they serious about the Bible references they'd chosen? Some placards listed chapter and verse for acceptable slave holding. That's designed to do nothing but inflame the community, Grace thought angrily.

She flinched as she read the Exodus verse about working on the Sabbath being an abomination and commanding a death penalty. These people down here demonstrating on that Lawrence man's behalf are mocking everything I hold dear, she thought. Then she caught sight of another placard, without any reference to

Scripture, questioning how to separate an irrelevant abomination from a relevant one.

Grace stopped dead in her tracks and swallowed hard. How, indeed? In Old Testament days, abomination was abomination and there were no shades of gray.

She frowned with annoyance. Everyone knew how irrelevant those Levitical laws were to Christians. She remembered Jesus' words in the New Testament as clearly as though she was a child back in the Junior Department. *"I give you a new law to love your neighbor as yourself."*

She weakly took a step forward. But how *do* you separate them, she wondered. Because people said so? *People said...*again! Grace was as suddenly tired of the idea as she was of the words.

She forced herself to enter the municipal building. The lobby wasn't as crowded and she breathed a sigh of relief. She found the number of the courtroom on a sign and started upstairs.

Suddenly, doors on the next floor burst open, and a crowd made for the stairs. Grace froze in place as people stampeded around her, but even in her fear, she could hear snippets of conversation.

"Do you think she'll appeal?"

"It might be a test case."

"I thought Lee had it in the bag."

"But she lost."

"For now."

The last of the crowd pushed past her and Grace willed herself to move. Over now. She was too late. And Rosemary had lost.

How suddenly silent it was! All she could hear down the long corridor was the hollow click of her heels on the marble floor. She paused in front of the heavy doors to the courtroom. Clenching her teeth for strength, she pushed them open.

Rosemary sat at a table in front of the judge's bench. Two men stood near her. But there was a woman present, as well. In a split second, Grace realized it was Ross Lawrence's mother. Her heart skipped a beat.

So his own mother faced this ordeal with him, Grace thought. Funny, I assumed if he had parents, they'd make themselves scarce during this humiliation, not stand beside him.

You don't have to agree with her to support her, Dorothy had said not two hours ago. Did Ross's mother feel that way about him?

She glanced quickly at her daughter talking quietly to the two men. She's cut and permed her hair, Grace noted. I like it! But dear Lord, that awful suit! She looks like an undertaker in that drab old thing! Why doesn't she wear pretty bright colors?

Then she forced herself to look at Ross Lawrence. Why...he doesn't look at all like...like a...he's very handsome! He's too thin but he looks nice.

So caught up was Grace in staring at him that she nearly jumped out of her skin as the other man turned around and looked straight at her. She caught her breath in surprise, taking in his light brown hair pulled back into a ponytail. He seemed aware of her surprise and grinned.

God in heaven, she thought furiously, this is no more than I deserve, coming down here into this mess! That Lawrence man probably has dozens of friends like him!

She got no further in her embarrassed thoughts, however, as Rosemary suddenly and without warning, burst into furious sobbing. Before Grace could reach her, she stood and furiously kicked a metal waste can across the courtroom floor. Then she collapsed in her seat again, buried her head in the crook of her arm and wept as though her heart would break. The man with the ponytail bent over her.

Grace hurried to her. "Rosemary," she said firmly.

Rosemary cried even louder.

"Rosemary Scarlett, stop that at once!"

The hysterical sobbing ceased instantly and the curly head came up slowly, mascara staining her cheeks.

"Scarlett?" the man with the ponytail repeated, his bright blue eyes dancing with mirth. The tension broke as he exploded in laughter. Ross Lawrence, too, stifled a grin but his mother only stared at Grace.

Rosemary found a tissue and dabbed her eyes. "Why are you here, Mom?" she asked disdainfully.

The laughter stopped when the two men realized what was happening. Ross Lawrence reached for his coat. "Maybe we can get out the back way now, Rosemary. I'll talk to you later."

Rosemary nodded. "I'm so sorry, Ross—"

His mother bent over Rosemary and hugged her. "You did your best, dear. We know you did."

Grace caught her breath. Was that meant for my benefit, she wondered nervously. She forced herself to meet the other woman's eyes. What sort of woman is she to face down the wrath of the community? This trial, as bad as it was, isn't the worst thing she has to face, either. She'll see him die, her own child. That's the worst thing that can ever happen to any parent.

All homosexuals are their parents' children, she numbly realized. For every one of them who dies of AIDS, there are parents facing this nightmare. Quite suddenly, the knowledge that Rosemary was healthy assaulted Grace with such force that she gasped. There was still time to make amends.

But only if she could gain some time alone with her daughter, which wasn't going to be easy. She watched as Mrs. Lawrence and her son left the courtroom by another exit.

Then she noticed how casually but protectively, the man with the ponytail rested his hand on Rosemary's shoulder. His smile was gone and he looked at Grace defensively.

Grace took a deep breath. "I came because—because Dorothy told me—" Oh, why doesn't that man leave, she thought irritably. "She said I don't have to agree with you to support you," she finished hurriedly.

There now. It was out.

"Oh. Well then," Rosemary replied coldly.

Grace moved closer. And took in a dazzling diamond ring on Rosemary's finger. "I see a lot's happened since November."

Rosemary reached up for the hand of the man beside her. "This is Keith Marshall, Mom. He's Ross's doctor."

Not *with* that Lawrence man, not what I thought at all! But a doctor with a ponytail and blue jeans, Grace's thoughts raced in a frenzy. "You—you don't look like—" Looks, I'm falling into that damned looks trap again!

Rosemary released his hand and stood. "You'd better get going now, Mom. You're going to get caught in a lot of bad traffic as it is—"

"I came to see you, Rosie—"

"This isn't a good time."

"Yes, it is," Keith said sternly. "Listen to what she has to say."

"I want you to come home this weekend, Rosemary." She glanced at Keith. "And you, too, Dr. Marshall. Harry should meet you."

Keith smiled eagerly but Rosemary didn't seem convinced. "I have too much to do this weekend."

"Roso—"

Grace flinched at the unfamiliar nickname.

"Keith," Rosemary warned softly, "she's come here with a guilty conscience. I'm in no mood to be noble."

"Guilty—" Grace repeated blankly. Then, with her cheeks burning with embarrassment, sighed. "I want this over between us."

Rosemary turned on her, impatient and angry. "Do you think showing up today—late, of course—makes up for what you said to me last fall?"

"Roso—"

"No," Rosemary declared. "I demand nothing less than an apology and if you aren't really sorry for what you said, don't say anything now. Go on back home and forget this happened today."

Grace twisted her purse. "Apology?"

"Don't bother then. You and your other church friends got exactly what you wanted. I lost the case. Now you all can feel nice and smug because your sort of justice was done," she said bitterly.

Keith grabbed her shoulders and shook her gently. "I can't believe you said that!"

Grace fought down the lump in her throat. "No, Keith, no. She's right." She paused while he patted Rosemary's shoulder. She looked him in the eye. "I *did* want her to lose. I thought it was the only thing that would make her understand. But today—today, I finally understand why she had to defend that man."

Rosemary kept her gaze level, no longer furious but still suspicious.

Grace swallowed hard. "I don't understand what he is, Rosemary."

"I think it's very difficult for people of one sexual orientation to understand people of another, Mrs. Lee," Keith said softly.

Grace bit her lip, knowing the next move was hers. "Where I failed, Rosemary, is in compassion. For that I *do* apologize."

Rosemary looked away and Grace noticed suddenly how tired she was, bone-weary and totally defeated.

"Please come home this weekend, Rosemary. You have a lot to tell me and it seems," she paused, finding encouragement in Keith's eyes, "it seems I have a lot of listening to do."

"We'll be there," Keith replied. He grinned suddenly. "I could kick myself for not knowing you're her mother."

Grace raised one brow quizzically.

"It's the jaw," he observed. "That clenched jaw. I've always told Roso I'd not take her on in a million years when she's got her jaw clenched."

"...Jaw?" Grace repeated blankly. It's Harry's stubborn jaw...not mine, surely?

"This weekend is Easter," Rosemary remembered.

"Are you off Good Friday?" Keith asked her.

"Yes."

"Then come early if you can," Grace insisted.

"We'll be there in the late afternoon," Keith promised.

Grace stepped back, heading up the aisle. "I'm looking forward to it." She hurried out of the courtroom.

Rosemary's coming home, she thought excitedly, coming home with a fiancé! Keith Marshall...Rosemary Lee Marshall...and then, gloating, my future son-in-law is a doctor. Of course, that ponytail will take some getting used to.

But what a tidbit it was going to be to rub in at Prayer Meeting!

*   *   *

Before Grace threw herself into plans for Rosemary's visit she went to see Dorothy. The thirty minutes she thought she'd spend turned into three hours as Grace apologized for her behavior over the last four months.

"I blame myself for a great deal of the silence between us, Grace."

"It wasn't your fault—"

"In some ways it was. I've always been bad about plunging ahead and making my point regardless of other people's feelings. In this matter I didn't trust myself. I could have made things worse for both you and Rosemary, so I said nothing at all."

"I think I needed the time to make a complete jack-ass of myself."

Dorothy smiled. "And did you do that, Grace?"

"Oh yes. I've socialized with people over the last four months who make me want to be sick."

"Puke, you mean."

Grace nodded, a twitch of a smile playing on her lips. "Do you always like shocking people with a bad word here and there?"

"My mother claimed I liked the flavor of Old Dutch Cleanser and that I swore to get my mouth washed out."

Grace laughed outright. Things were back to normal with Dorothy, where they should have been all along.

20

Grace never before realized how very small her home was until Rosemary's tall Keith set foot in it. From the moment he entered the warm fragrant kitchen she felt a kindred spirit. How sweet he was! How warm and sincere!

Harry's reaction was not as immediately positive. Grace held her breath while he examined the unorthodox doctor, his eyes finally coming to rest on his thick shiny ponytail. "Well," he said drolly, ruffling up Rosemary's new curls, "I guess you two are the long and the short of it, huh?"

Keith laughed heartily. "Guess so."

"I thought that length went out of style nearly twenty years ago," Harry pressed.

"It did but I like it." Keith smiled and Grace could tell he wouldn't be pushed around.

"So do I," Rosemary put in.

"Well, kiddo," Harry conceded, "that's all that really counts."

Grace smiled triumphantly. Her future son-in-law played Harry just beautifully.

*   *   *

It was nearly midnight. Grace slipped on her bathrobe and tip-toed out of the bedroom. Suppressing a grin, she pulled shut the door to Rosemary's room, hearing Keith's soft snore. When Harry rolled over in their own bedroom the two of them would set up a symphony.

She went quietly down the stairs to the den. The fire had died down a long time ago but still sleeping on the floor in front of it was Rosemary, wrapped in a thick quilt. Grace sat down in her rocker, reaching for her own quilt, watching Rosemary all the while.

What a lovely day it had been! Keith is so full of life and so much fun, she thought. No wonder Rosemary loves him. He's like her in some ways.

Grace suffered an anxious moment when she learned he was a Catholic but a renegade one. He'd been married before but had no children. He'd grown up without a father. Grace wanted to press the issue but one look from Rosemary silenced her. In time she'd get the whole story but it wasn't right to bring up bad things on this day.

There was time enough, after all.

They planned a June wedding. How lovely and traditional—how unlike Rosemary! Grace was sad it wouldn't be a religious ceremony but weddings were for the two people involved.

They were in love and so happy. This was obviously the way Rosemary intended to feel in order to marry. What a pity Keith hadn't been in her life ten years ago, Grace thought with a sigh.

Rosemary stirred and turned over.

Grace was worried because she was so exhausted. She'd made a good effort until after dinner. After she showered, she and Harry started a fire and she stretched out just for a catnap.

That was five hours ago.

Harry nodded off at eight, went to bed and left Keith and Grace to get to know each other better.

Like any proud mother she showed him all of Rosemary's baby pictures, school awards and church mementos, telling him what she hoped were nice and funny things.

"I don't suppose she's talked much about us," Grace said to him.

"Oh, quite the contrary. We've talked a lot about you two and my mom. Childhood shapes the adult."

"I hope to meet your mother before the wedding, Keith."

"I'm sure you will. Roso's been great with Mom." He sighed. "I tell you, Grace, she's really amazing. I don't know how she coped with all the pressure of Ross's case."

"How long have you known him?"

"Three years." Keith paused and glanced at Rosemary in the next room. "I can't believe she's down for the count like that. She hasn't slept this well in—oh my God—" He stopped suddenly, blushing deeply.

Grace wanted to be outraged but there was something about his expression that was simply too comical. "You aren't very good at secrets, are you?"

"No," he confessed and brought up guilty eyes to hers. "Rosemary doesn't want to rub in her differences with you. I don't, either, but I seem to slip and she doesn't."

"I see."

He suddenly grinned again. "It won't change your mind, will it?"

"About what?"

"Letting us sleep together tonight."

Her eyes widened and her mouth flew open. As he laughed, she realized he was teasing her. "You rascal!" she cried. "No, it won't change my mind. Until you marry her, you don't sleep together. Here."

"I only want to keep you on your toes, Grace."

He'd gone up a little later and Grace finally tried to sleep, too, but to no avail.

Now, at midnight, she was still wide-awake.

Rosemary settled deeper into the quilt. It's a good sign, Grace decided. She's home and upstairs sleeps the man she'll marry. My son-in-law, the doctor, she thought again.

Another thought sneaked in, more pleasant than any other. My grandchildren will be so smart and cute, too, with her looks and his sunny temper. A boy first, just like Keith.

Then a girl. A little granddaughter. Will she be like Rosemary? Rosemary isn't like me.

The clock chimed and Grace stood and folded her lap-quilt. She glanced out the window at the starry sky. Tomorrow, Easter, would be a beautiful day!

*   *   *

Grace nursed only a faint hope that Rosemary would agree to attend Easter services and was therefore not too disappointed when she shook her head. She was totally unprepared, however, when Keith, disgustingly cheerful for so early an hour, piped up that he would be happy to go with her.

Rosemary grinned at him. "Are you sure you're ready for that?"

Keith shrugged. "How could it be worse than Easter Vigil Mass?"

During breakfast, Rosemary kept filling his coffee cup. "You're going to need the caffeine, my dear."

"Shall I wear my tie with the smiley faces, Grace?" Keith teased gently.

Grace set her coffee cup down with a thud, terrified he would. Rosemary nudged him gently. "Now behave yourself in church or you won't get any of Mom's Easter cake."

"What kind of Easter cake?"

"Angel food cake iced in yellow with dyed green coconut for grass and miniature jelly beans for Easter eggs. The jelly beans are good but the desiccated coconut is just awful—"

"Is that how she assured your good behavior?" Keith laughed.

Rosemary ruffled her tangled hair. "Bribery never entered the picture. I was an angel by nature."

Harry snorted. "Oh yeah, when was that?"

Grace laughed. "She always wore a new dress for Easter Sunday, Keith, and Harry always bought her a little rosebud corsage."

"A rosebud for a rosebud?" Keith smiled.

"I should have changed my name when I was twenty-one." Rosemary sighed.

Grace opened her mouth to speak but the ringing telephone took her by surprise. She pushed her chair back and frowned as she stood to answer it.

"Now who can that be at seven o'clock on a Sunday morning?" Harry demanded irritably.

"It might be my service," Keith replied. "I have to leave a number where I can be reached."

Grace finally managed to get to the telephone on the fourth ring. "Hello?"

"Mrs. Lee?"

"Yes?"

"This is Ms. Bradshaw at the nursing home. Miss Blackwell suffered another stroke a few hours ago and has been transferred to the hospital. She's awake and asking for you."

Grace went cold all over.

"Mrs. Lee?"

"I'm here," Grace said calmly. "I'll go as soon as I'm dressed."

"Thank you. I'll call the hospital and tell them you're coming."

Grace's hands shook as she set the receiver down and she fought back the urge to cry. Just when Dorothy seemed so much better, now this!

She returned to the kitchen, finding three pairs of anxious eyes turned up to her. "Dorothy's had another stroke and is asking for me," she said softly.

"I'm coming with you, Mom."

"Me, too," Keith added.

"What about me?" Harry demanded.

Rosemary smiled. "Well, you have some choices, Daddy. You can go back to sleep, watch Easter services on television or come with us."

Harry sighed. "I think I'll get the paper, read it from end to end and take a little nap."

Grace started clearing away the breakfast dishes until Harry gently slapped her hands.

"I'll do the dishes, too," he offered with a smile, feeling useful in the crisis.

"And subject us all to ptomaine poisoning," Rosemary said under her breath to Keith as they stood and pushed their chairs up to the table. Grace glared at her, hoping Harry didn't overhear.

God, dear God, please don't let Dorothy die by inches, she prayed as she rushed to get dressed. She herself doesn't want it and it's so hard to watch her struggling to be the way she was and will never be again. Make her better or let her die in peace!

*   *   *

Grace, Keith and Rosemary found Dorothy in the intensive care unit but because of restrictions on visiting hours they couldn't go in right away. Grace leaned against the wall of the waiting area, numbly wondering where Dorothy's nephew was.

Keith left them to go to the nurses' station. He pulled his reading glasses out of his jacket pocket and Grace realized he'd asked for Dorothy's chart.

She turned to Rosemary. "I like him so much, Rosemary. He's as sweet as he can be," she said impulsively.

Rosemary smiled with pride. "He's a great doctor, too. Dorothy adores him."

Grace chuckled in spite of her anxiety. "The pony-tail, too?"

"Well, that's another story but I can tell she's smitten with him."

Keith handed the chart back to the nurses and joined them again, taking off his glasses to reveal sober eyes.

"It's really bad, isn't it?" Rosemary whispered.

He nodded. "Afraid so. She's conscious right now and the doctors are going to let you in, Grace, but there won't be much time before she slips away."

Grace shook her head, not comprehending. "But she recovered from the last stroke—"

"She's eighty-five," Keith reminded her, "and this one has wiped her out. Everything is failing now."

"It's like she's staying alive to talk to Mom," Rosemary noted.

Keith nodded. "I think that may be the case."

Grace closed her eyes and breathed deeply. "Is she suffering?" She hoped to hear a reply in the negative but when Keith didn't answer immediately, she opened her eyes again, finding him deeply upset. "She is, isn't she?"

"She's fighting the pain-killers so she can have some last words with you," Keith explained. "She may or may not be really lucid, so even if you have no idea what she's talking about, act like you do."

The doors to the intensive care unit opened and a nurse beckoned to Grace. She took one last look at Keith and Rosemary, bit her lip for courage and went inside.

*   *   *

How could a few short days have made such a horrible difference in Dorothy? Thin and pale before, she was nothing now but a writhing skeleton in the voluminous hospital bed. Grace absently wondered how many tubes invaded the frail, dying body.

Disturbed by the sounds around her, Dorothy opened her eyes and focused on Grace. "Am I going to be too sick to go?" the cracking voice whispered hoarsely. She tossed again in the bed, heedless of the needles and tubes.

Prepared that Dorothy probably wouldn't know her, Grace weathered the surprise and reached for Dorothy's hand. How cold it was! As though the life was already gone!

"Well, that depends," she humored her, easing herself onto the chair the nurse brought for her. "You'll have to try to rest and not fight the doctors."

"But I have to go! Ted says there's a war coming and it will last for years." She gasped for breath and blinked suddenly. "Do you think there'll be a war?"

Grace nodded. "Yes, I do. It looks very bad over there."

"I wish he'd go with me," Dorothy sighed, closing her eyes. Her restlessness seemed to diminish somewhat.

"Shall I ask him?"

The brief moment of relaxation allowed the sedative to work and Dorothy drifted off to sleep; smiling, so it seemed to Grace.

Grace stroked her hand and became aware of the nurse tapping her shoulder. "I'm sorry, but your time's up," she whispered.

Grace nodded and stood, still stroking Dorothy's hand. She leaned over the sleeping old woman and kissed the thin, cold cheek. "Godspeed, Dorothy," she whispered.

She never knew if it was her imagination or not but she could have sworn the slight pressure around her own hand was Dorothy saying good-bye.

*   *   *

Three hours later it was over.

"On Easter Sunday," Rosemary said softly. "I think that's very fitting, don't you?"

Grace could only nod as she wept, glad Dorothy's suffering was at an end but grieving, as she well knew, for the void in her own life no one could ever fill.

Epilogue

Then there were the funeral and the graveside remarks leading up to the moment alone under the cemetery tent with the small flower-covered coffin. Grace brushed away her tears.

It was time to go. She stood and reached for one of the rosebuds from the spray of flowers on the coffin lid. It was a beautiful funeral after all, she thought. And a beautiful life, too, reflecting all the pain and passion of a woman who tried to make the best choices in a rapidly changing world. A life spent trying to understand and teach one of the hardest lessons of all: compassion.

Another lesson for me, Grace thought as she smiled faintly. It took Dorothy every bit of twenty years to teach me that goodness as I defined it often left no room for compassion.

Her reverie was distracted as she noticed the cool, rising spring breeze toss Keith's hair and send Rosemary rushing to catch her dress tail. The sight of her daughter's blushing face and the sound of Keith's cheerful laughter brought enough solace for her to smile.

"Is that your daughter?"

Grace turned around with a start and found Sarah smiling at her. Sarah, who was unknowingly responsible for helping her find her way back to Dorothy before it was too late and to Rosemary, too. She returned the smile. "Yes, that's my Rosemary."

"Claiming her again, are you? Your Circle friends aren't going to like it, you know."

Grace looked at her and noticed a barely repressed mocking grin. "I've really had only one friend the last twenty years."

"I think it's time you had another one, don't you?"

Grace laughed and nodded. Dorothy, she was sure, would approve.

About the Author

Jane Ford is a native of Lexington, Kentucky. She and her husband, Dr. Sridhar Adibhatla, live in Ohio. *The Nature of Grace* is her first novel.